One ~ Love

By

Lynn Ames

ONE ~ LOVE

ISBN: 978-0-9840521-2-7

This trade paperback original is published by

PHOENIX RISING PRESS
PHOENIX, ARIZONA
www.phoenixrisingpress.com

ORIGINALLY PUBLISHED AS
THE FLIP SIDE OF DESIRE
© 2006 BY LYNN AMES
ISBN: 978-1-933113-60-9

CREDITS
EXECUTIVE EDITOR: TARA YOUNG
COVER PHOTOS: JUDY FRANCESCONI, PAM LAMBROS
AUTHOR PHOTO: JUDY FRANCESCONI
COVER DESIGN BY PAM LAMBROS,
WWW.HANDSONGRAPHICDESIGN.COM

About the Author

A former press secretary to the New York state Senate minority leader, an award-winning former broadcast journalist, a former public information officer for the nation's third-largest prison system, and a former editor of a national art magazine, Lynn Ames is a nationally recognized speaker and CEO of a public relations firm with a particular expertise in image, crisis communications planning, and crisis management.

Ms. Ames's works include the best-selling novels *The Price of Fame* (which was short-listed for the Golden Crown Literary Society's inaugural award for best lesbian romance), *The Cost of Commitment*, *The Value of Valor* (winner of the 2007 Arizona Book Award), *One ~ Love* (formerly *The Flip Side of Desire;* nominated for a 2007 Goldie Award for Best Popular Fiction), *Heartsong* (a finalist for the Golden Crown Literary Society's inaugural award for best lesbian romance), and *Outsiders.*

More about the author, including contact information, other writings, news about other original upcoming works, pictures of locations mentioned in this novel, links to resources related to issues raised in this book, author and character interviews, and purchasing assistance can be found at www.lynnames.com.

Other Books in Print by Lynn Ames

Outsiders

What happens when you take five beloved, powerhouse authors, each with a unique voice and style, give them one word to work with, and put them between the sheets together, no holds barred?

Magic!!

Brisk Press presents Lynn Ames, Georgia Beers, JD Glass, Susan X. Meagher and Susan Smith, all together under the same cover with the aim to satisfy your every literary taste. This incredible combination offers something for everyone — a smorgasbord of fiction unlike anything you'll find anywhere else.

A Native American raised on the Reservation ventures outside the comfort and familiarity of her own world to help a lost soul embrace the gifts that set her apart. * A reluctantly wealthy woman uses all of her resources anonymously to help those who cannot help themselves. * Three individuals, three aspects of the self, combine to create balance and harmony at last for a popular trio of characters. * Two nomadic women from very different walks of life discover common ground — and a lot more — during a blackout in New York City. * A traditional, old school butch must confront her community and her own belief system when she falls for a much younger transman.

Five authors — five novellas. *Outsiders* — one remarkable book.

Heartsong

After three years spent mourning the death of her partner in a tragic climbing accident, Danica Warren has re-emerged in the public eye. With a best-selling memoir, a blockbuster movie about her heroic efforts to save three other climbers, and a successful career on the motivational speaking circuit, Danica has convinced herself that her life can be full without love.

When Chase Crosley walks into Danica's field of vision everything changes. Danica is suddenly faced with questions she's never pondered.

Is there really one love that transcends all concepts of space and time? One great love that joins two hearts so that they beat as one? One moment of recognition when twin flames join and burn together?

Will Danica and Chase be able to overcome the barriers standing between them and find forever? And can that love be sustained, even in the face of cruel circumstances and fate?

The Kate and Jay Trilogy

The Price of Fame

When local television news anchor Katherine Kyle is thrust into the national spotlight, it sets in motion a chain of events that will change her life forever. Jamison "Jay" Parker is an intensely career-driven Time magazine reporter. The first time she saw Kate, she fell in love. The last time she saw her, Kate was rescuing her. That was five years earlier, and she never expected to see her again. Then circumstances and an assignment bring them back together.

Kate and Jay's lives intertwine, leading them on a journey to love and happiness, until fate and fame threaten to tear them apart. What is the price of fame? For Kate, the cost just might be everything. For Jay, it could be the other half of her soul.

The Cost of Commitment

Kate and Jay want nothing more than to focus on their love. But as Kate settles into a new profession, she and Jay are caught in the middle of a deadly scheme and find themselves pawns in a larger game in which the stakes are nothing less than control of the country.

In her novel of corruption, greed, romance, and danger, Lynn Ames takes us on an unforgettable journey of harrowing conspiracy—and establishes herself as a mistress of suspense.

The Cost of Commitment—it could be everything...

The Value of Valor

Katherine Kyle is the press secretary to the president of the United States. Her lover, Jamison Parker, is a respected writer for Time magazine. Separated by unthinkable tragedy, the two must struggle to survive against impossible odds…

A powerful, shadowy organization wants to advance its own global agenda. To succeed, the president must be eliminated. Only one person knows the truth and can put a stop to the scheme.

It will take every ounce of courage and strength Kate possesses to stay alive long enough to expose the plot. Meanwhile, Jay must cheat death and race across continents to be by her lover's side…

This hair-raising thriller will grip you from the start and won't let you go until the ride is over.

The Value of Valor—it's priceless.

CHAPTER ONE

Trystan Lightfoot's heart stuttered once and stopped beating. She swallowed hard, gulping air. The green eyes that smiled at her rooted her to the spot, instantly making her mouth go dry and her palms sweat. It couldn't be. For sixteen years, she'd managed to avoid crossing paths with Jay. Now here Trystan was, standing in the middle of a bookstore, face-to-face with a life-sized cardboard standup of her. She felt lightheaded.

"Can I help you?" the woman behind the counter asked. "Do you want a wristband? Right now we're estimating the wait to have your book signed would be about an hour and a half. Don't let that stop you, though. I've read the book, it's phenomenal—her best yet, and that's saying something." The woman held out a wristband to Trystan as she prattled on, oblivious to Trystan's distress. Jamison Parker, fourteen-time *New York Times* best-selling author, was the woman who'd unwittingly shattered Trystan's heart into a billion pieces. "I can't see her again," Trystan mumbled to herself. "I just can't."

"What'd you say?" the clerk asked. "Here." She tried to give Trystan the object in her hand.

Trystan jumped back as if the proffered wristband was poisoned. She ran without looking back, not stopping until she'd gone several blocks. Bending over a garbage can, she vomited. She sank to the pavement, her body shaking uncontrollably; the shock of remembered loss was almost more than she could bear. It wasn't Jay's fault, Trystan reminded herself. She bent her head as tears flowed.

"I never should have gone back there," Trystan said, raking her fingers roughly through her thick black hair. She continued to pace around the hotel room as she talked on a cell phone. "I told you I didn't want to go."

"Get real, Trys. You and I both know you couldn't turn down a two-week gig with the Arizona Cardinals. It's what every sports physical therapist dreams of—to work with the pros."

Trystan's shoulders instantly relaxed a fraction. Becca Hamilton, her best friend, had always been the only person she could talk to about anything. "I've *been* working with the pros, Bec. The WNBA last month—do you have any idea how many lesbians play professional basketball, by the way? I mean, I knew there were some, but…"

"There's a shocker," Becca deadpanned.

"The men's tennis tour the month before that. Major League Baseball during spring training…"

"Well, aren't you just the hotshot physical therapist to the stars."

Trystan paused in her pacing. "You know what I'm saying."

"Actually, Trys? I have no idea."

"I'm saying I never should have gone to Phoenix. It's too close to home." Trystan resumed her tour of the room. "Sixteen years, Bec. For sixteen years, I've done my best to forget Jay—to forget how she looked, how it felt to be near her, how she smelled…"

"You smelled her cardboard standup? That's a little far out there, Trys, even for you." Becca laughed easily.

"Very funny. You didn't know me back then. I was an emotional wreck after Jay left."

"I know it's pointless to remind you that Jay was never really yours—that you were never physically involved with her or that she belonged to someone else at the time."

"Don't," Trystan choked out a warning. "You don't know what happened."

"I know what you've told me. I know what Jay wrote in her memoirs of the time she spent with you and your mother."

"You can't understand what I felt!" Trystan shouted.

"No, I can't," Becca answered quietly. "What I can do is point out that all that happened a long time ago. You've got to let it go." After a long pause, she added, "I just worry about you, Trys."

Trystan took a calming breath, consciously pushing her temper aside. Becca was her one anchor in the world. She hated when the two of them were at odds. "I know you do. I'm fine, really."

"Where are you, anyway?"

"Los Angeles. ESPN and Disney hired me to take care of the athletes in town for the ESPY Awards."

"What a life," Becca said.

"Tell me about it. They set me up in a private center to provide PT treatments and massages to the biggest names in sports. It's a tough job, but somebody's got to do it."

"And it might as well be you, right?"

"They've asked me to make the sacrifice, who am I to say no?" Trystan looked at her watch. "In fact, I've got an appointment in less than half an hour."

"You'd better get going. Traffic out there is horrendous."

"No kidding."

"I love you, Trys."

"Love you, too, Bec. Bye."

"Mmm. You have the most marvelous hands. But I bet all the girls tell you that." Sherinda Nathan, the fastest woman in the world, turned her head and smiled brilliantly at the astonishingly beautiful woman who was massaging her lower back at that moment.

"Not lately," Trystan said.

"I find that hard to believe," Sherinda said, seemingly intent on seducing Trystan.

Trystan backed away.

"Why are you stopping?" Sherinda pushed herself up from the table, her back muscles shifting and bunching with the effort. If she was aware of the view she was affording Trystan, she didn't seem to care.

"You're done." Trystan made no effort to look away. Instead, she raised an eyebrow.

"Baby, I'm just getting started." Sherinda beckoned with her finger. "I want you, sugar."

"I'm sorry, I never mix business with pleasure. Not only would it be unethical, but it's illegal."

"I see." Sherinda narrowed her eyes, never taking them from Trystan's mouth. "What if I met you somewhere else? I wouldn't be your client then, right?"

"True."

"Good. 2:30 this afternoon, the Beverly Hilton. Room 143. I'll be waiting for you."

Trystan considered. Her soul ached, yet her body yearned for physical contact. Sherinda was a beautiful woman. "I'll see you there."

Trystan flipped the lock on the door to the hotel room in a practiced motion.

Sherinda, standing naked in the middle of the room, merely laughed.

Trystan circled Sherinda, devouring her with her eyes, memorizing muscles and curves. Skin that glistened with sweat erupted into gooseflesh under her scrutiny. Trystan ran her index finger over the well-developed deltoid muscle, watching as her quarry twitched in anticipation and reached out for her.

"Don't move. I'm not done admiring you," Trystan cooed. But as she came around in front of Sherinda, it was Jay's face she saw. Trystan gasped, her legs weakening. She blinked hard to clear the image, standing stone still until all she could see was the flesh and blood woman shivering in anticipation just out of her reach. Trystan ran her tongue over her lips, pausing to make sure Sherinda could see nothing but desire in her eyes.

"I'm not used to waiting, you know."

"I promise to make it worth your while." Trystan circled behind Sherinda once more, this time reaching around her to cup small, firm breasts. She brushed her palms briefly over the dimpling nipples before pinching them roughly between her thumbs and forefingers. She was rewarded with a sharp intake of breath and Sherinda surging forward into her hands.

"More, baby."

"I love a woman who's willing to beg," Trystan laughed. "All in due time." Trystan smoothed her hands over straining pectoral muscles, traced sinewy trapezoids and bulging biceps. Her questing mouth blazed a path over quivering lats before feasting on a succulent neck.

Sherinda arched her back, giving Trystan easy access to her throat, an opportunity that was not squandered.

At the same time, Trystan caressed Sherinda's pelvis and thighs with her fingertips, the motion resulting in a new wave of gooseflesh. When her fingers were no more than a hair's breath away from Sherinda's center, Trystan whispered huskily, "Do you want me, baby?"

"G-God yes," Sherinda hissed out between clenched teeth. "Now, sugar. Now."

Trystan backed Sherinda up to the bed and pushed down on her shoulders until she was lying on her back. Trystan straddled her, licking along her strong jawline as she plunged her fingers into the heat, the slickness drawing her in deeper and deeper until her hand had virtually disappeared. "Is this what you want, baby?"

"Oh, yes," Sherinda cried, her hips riding Trystan's hand hard. "Just like that." Her hand closed like a vise over Trystan's, holding her in place. She arched back as if her spine was being strung like a bow, suddenly went very still, and finally let out a tremendous shriek as she came on a violent exhalation.

Trystan remained inside her as Sherinda panted, working to recover her breath.

"Good Lord, woman. Nobody's made me come that hard since…forever." Sherinda shook her head, sweat dripping into her eyes. "Woo, you are something else." She focused on the face before her, regarding Trystan shrewdly. "Your reputation is well deserved, I see."

Trystan withdrew her hand, feeling Sherinda's body shudder as she did so. "I'm glad I didn't disappoint." There was a hint of bitterness to her tone, but Sherinda didn't seem to notice.

"Hardly, baby." Sherinda grabbed Trystan's hand, trying to draw her down next to her. Trystan resisted.

"Why don't you come with me to the ESPYs tonight?" Sherinda asked impulsively. "I need an escort, and having you on my arm will make me the envy of every man and woman there."

"You sure you want that kind of attention?"

"Hell yeah."

Trystan wasn't surprised. Sherinda was known for creating controversy wherever and whenever possible.

"C'mon, sugar." Sherinda tried unsuccessfully again to pull Trystan closer. "I'm begging you here. I thought you said you liked that."

Trystan considered. "No strings. We arrive together, pose for pictures together, but for the rest of the time, I'm a free agent."

Sherinda narrowed her eyes. "As long as you're discreet and don't make me look like a fool."

"Agreed."

"I'll pick you up at six," Sherinda said to Trystan's retreating back.

Outside the Kodak Theatre, a continuous stream of limousines pulled up, disgorging famous athletes, movie stars, television sports commentators, and hangers-on. A red carpet lined the sidewalk leading to the entrance of the famed venue, best known for hosting the Oscars. On either side, behind sawhorse barricades, the paparazzi and fans surged toward the glitterati. A phalanx of police officers kept them at a distance.

Sherinda and Trystan's limo was third in line.

"You look dashing as hell in that tux, you know," Sherinda purred. "Good enough to eat."

Trystan laughed and stilled Sherinda's wandering hands. "You're the one who's going to steal the show tonight, Sherinda. You look positively radiant. Coral is definitely your color." Trystan took the opportunity to survey the sexy, low-cut dress yet again. She could feel moisture pool between her legs.

Sherinda slid closer on the seat, running her newly freed hand up Trystan's leg. "How about an encore, sugar?"

Although her body was screaming "yes," Trystan had no intention of making love to Sherinda again. Never bedding the same woman twice was one of only two ironclad rules Trystan lived by. The other was never sleeping with somebody else's wife or partner.

Trystan knew people talked about her and her supposedly prolific sex life—she heard the whispers about her character. She also knew that women wanted—no, expected—her to come on to them, perhaps even to make love to them, knowing all the while from her reputation that she would remain emotionally unavailable to them. She tried not to be bothered by the hypocrisy.

"Show time," Trystan said, as their limo arrived at the front of the line. "Ready?"

"Oh, yeah."

Trystan slid toward the door nearest the sidewalk, waiting while the driver came around and opened it. As she emerged, dozens of flashes erupted from the crowd. She leaned back into the car and extended a hand to Sherinda.

"Sure you won't reconsider, sugar?"

Trystan merely shook her head ruefully as she helped Sherinda out of the backseat. She wrapped the sprinter's hand around her elbow as they made their way through the crowd and up the carpet to the door, pausing along the route so Sherinda could wave, sign autographs, and pose for pictures.

Inside, the ballroom was beginning to fill up. Men and women dressed in formalwear milled around laughing and chatting amiably. Wine and champagne flowed freely. Trystan lifted two glasses of bubbly off a passing tray, handing one to Sherinda as they crossed the threshold. She watched as a woman dressed in a strapless pale lavender cocktail dress approached them.

"Who's the hottie in the tux, Sheri? She's yummy."

"Trystan Lightfoot, meet Kenyatta Morgan. Kenyatta is my biggest pain in the ass on the track and my best friend off it."

"It's a pleasure to meet you." Kenyatta openly surveyed Trystan. "What nationality are you? You're not a sister, although you look like you could be…"

"I'm Native American—Navajo."

Kenyatta narrowed her eyes appraisingly. "I'm thinking it ain't that simple. You don't look like any Indian I've ever seen."

Trystan returned the stare and shrugged, saying, "Will you excuse me?" She pivoted and walked toward one of the food stations set up in a corner, Kenyatta and Sherinda's voices following her.

"Doesn't like to talk about herself, does she?" Kenyatta asked after Trystan had moved away.

"Does it matter when she looks like that?" Sherinda asked, gesturing in Trystan's direction.

"I suppose not. She any good?"

"You are such a pig, Kennie."

"Well?"

"Fabulous," Sherinda sighed dreamily.

"Aren't you the lucky girl."

"It's a funny thing—even while she was inside me this afternoon, I had a feeling I'd already lost her."

"Ladies and gentlemen, please find your seats," a disembodied voice intoned over the speaker system, forestalling any further conversation.

Trystan slipped away from a rather insistent female sportscaster she'd been fighting off and was standing behind Sherinda's chair, ready to pull it out for her in a gallant gesture when she arrived at their assigned table.

Sherinda looked at her, dumbstruck. "I didn't expect to see you again."

Trystan raised an eyebrow.

"You said you'd be a free agent," Sherinda pointed out.

"I suppose you thought that meant I'd be a complete heel." Trystan shoved the chair in behind Sherinda's legs, ignoring the tender hamstring that had brought them together in the first place.

Sherinda grimaced as her legs buckled under her and she found herself sitting. "I'm…" She started to apologize.

"Don't," Trystan warned. "Leave it alone." She walked away, hands stuffed into her pockets. Within seconds, she was standing outside, hailing a cab back to her hotel.

Trystan paced around the room talking to herself. "Damn it, Trys. You set it up that way—you wanted to be a free agent—don't be mad at her for calling you on it." She flicked on the television and flipped through the channels. When she hit ESPN and the live telecast of the ESPY Awards, she threw the remote at a pillow. "Damn it all to hell." She unbuttoned her tuxedo jacket, started to take it off, then thought better of it. She snatched up her room key and headed for the lobby, intent on salvaging the evening.

The nightclub was crowded. It was a trendy West Hollywood hotspot where on any given night, one might see some of the most famous female faces. Trystan stood with her back to the bar, surveying the scene. The music was loud, the beat pulsing through her body. Everywhere she looked, there were beautiful women.

"Want to dance? You're dressed too fine to stand around brooding."

Trystan looked up into the face of a woman she recognized as a top model. She appeared to be higher than a kite. "No, thanks. I like brooding."

"Suit yourself." The woman shrugged and melted back into the crowd.

"That wasn't nice, you just broke that poor young woman's heart." The voice belonged to a lanky brunette who Trystan judged to be closer to her own age.

"She'll get over it. They recover so quickly at that age," Trystan said, knowing from her own experience how false that statement was.

"Oh, that's cold. Somebody piss in your cornflakes today, love?"

"What makes you say that?" Trystan asked.

"You've got that 'keep away' sign tattooed on your forehead." The woman tapped the body part in question.

"Didn't seem to work on you."

"I like a good challenge."

"Yeah, well, go challenge someone else. I don't feel like being psychoanalyzed tonight." Trystan turned around and put her elbows on the bar.

Several moments later, an attractive redhead with a sultry voice pressed against Trystan's side. "Can I get you something?"

"I'm all set, thanks."

"You look too dressed up for this joint, so I'm going to take a wild guess that this isn't where you expected to be."

"No, it isn't," Trystan admitted.

"Can I just tell you I'm glad you're here?" The woman reached between them, smoothing her hand over Trystan's side underneath the tuxedo jacket.

Trystan turned to face her. This is what she wanted—simple and uncomplicated. No expectations, no emotional baggage, no chance of a broken heart, nothing but pure physical satisfaction. She shifted so that her thigh pressed between the woman's legs. "I'd say the night is definitely looking up."

A palm boldly caressed Trystan's breast through the fabric of her shirt. She moaned as warmth spread through her body, igniting a burning ache.

"Mmm, responsive. I like that." The woman arched an eyebrow. She turned so that she was standing between Trystan and the rest of the room. "Let's see just how responsive, shall we?" She reached her other hand between them and ran her long fingers lightly over Trystan's crotch.

Trystan gasped.

"Oh, yeah," the woman purred, reaching for Trystan's zipper.

At the last second, Trystan's fingers closed over the woman's wrist like a vice. "I-I'm sorry. I can't," she choked, and ran from the bar.

C.J. Winslow sat in a darkened room, the only light emanating from the flickering images on the large-screen plasma television hanging on the wall. She turned up the volume.

"C.J. Winslow is clearly not up to the task of defeating Natasha Meritsa today."

"No, James, she's definitely not the great champion we've been accustomed to seeing dominate matches over the past sixteen years on tour. She's just being outclassed on the court right now."

"By a woman who wasn't even old enough to wear braces when C.J. won her first Wimbledon. I guess the question here, and I've heard others start to ask it, as well: Is C.J. done? Should she retire from tennis? Nancy, you won four grand slam titles and spent some time ranked number one in the world, what do you think?"

"I think it's something she's certainly got to consider at this point. She's thirty-four years old, she's been injured most of the season, younger players are hitting harder, moving quicker, lasting longer in matches than she is. I just don't know if she can win anymore."

C.J. hit the mute button and watched in silence as she and Meritsa shook hands at the net following her elimination from Wimbledon in the quarterfinals two weeks earlier. It was her worst finish in a grand slam tournament in fifteen years. A single tear slid down her cheek.

"I *can* win," she whispered. "I can be number one again. I know I can." She rose abruptly and began pacing. Several times, she paused by the phone and reached out as if to pick it up, only to pull her hand back. She paused on her fourth pass in front of the floor-to-ceiling picture windows, looking out at the majestic sight of the Sedona, Arizona, red rocks looming in the darkness.

This place was her haven. When everything else in the world was going wrong, C.J. would hop on a plane and come home to the splendid solitude and power of the rocks. She had designed the five million-dollar, three-bedroom, three-bathroom hideaway herself. It was tucked into the side of a mountain facing Cathedral Rock and afforded her breathtaking views on three sides. She had added a state-of-the-art gym and training facility in one wing. At Enchantment, the beautiful vacation resort nestled in the red rocks just a short distance from the house, an Olympic-sized swimming pool and tennis court were reserved for her so she could keep to the rest of her training routine.

Sedona was where she had retreated after her humiliating Wimbledon loss. Her coach and her business manager both had urged her to play the next stop on the tour—to prove she still had what it takes. But C.J. had resisted. She needed time to think, to regroup, to re-evaluate. Tennis was all she had ever known. From the time she'd been old enough to hold a racquet, it had been her life. Some, like former champion-turned-television-analyst Nancy Davidson, were saying she was finished.

If she wanted to prove them wrong, she would have to change her game. She couldn't win the way she played in England, no, but she could—and would—get back on top.

This time when she reached for the phone, she picked it up and dialed.

"Roberts."

"Grant?" C.J.'s heart pounded in her chest.

"Who is this?"

"C.J. Winslow."

"C.J.? What're you doing calling me at this hour?"

"I-I've been thinking about what you said—about changing the style of my game. I've decided you're right." She closed her eyes and swallowed hard. When Grant Roberts had intimated before Wimbledon that if she didn't update her game she was going to get left in the dust by the younger players, she'd scoffed at him. She was eating a big piece of humble pie.

"Well, I'll be. I thought you said you'd never mess with success."

"That's just it. I'm not successful anymore, am I?" she admitted.

"That was just one tournament."

"It was *Wimbledon*, Grant. If you're willing and available, I want to hire you as my new coach."

"What about Jonas? You guys have been a team for forever."

"I know. Jonas can't take me where I need to go. You can," C.J. finished quietly, hating the idea of telling her longtime coach they were through.

"You're serious?"

"Completely."

"You've got to do things my way."

"I understand that. Yes or no, Grant?"

There was a momentary pause on the line before he said, "Done."

"You're doing what?" Daniel Fitzpatrick boomed.

"I've hired Grant Roberts to be my new coach," C.J. said.

"That's insane."

"Why? Because he's younger than me? You and I both know that he would've been the best player the game's ever known if he hadn't messed up his back in that car wreck."

"We don't know any such thing. Look, C.J., I know he's young and good-looking. But we don't even know if he has what it takes to be a good coach. Jonas is a good coach."

"Dan, Jonas was a great coach—ten years ago. I need something different now. My game is floundering and you know it. As my business manager, I should think you'd be thrilled that I'm taking steps to get back to the top of my game."

"Honey, nobody wants you to succeed more than I do, but…"

"How long do you think the sponsors are going to hang around waiting for me to be a champion again, Dan? Huh? The U.S. Open is less than two months away. I've got to do something *now*."

"Have you told Jonas?" Fitzpatrick asked.

"I'm meeting him at Enchantment this afternoon."

"Do you need reinforcements?"

"No," C.J. said. "I can't ask anyone else to do this. It's my game, my decision, and I'll handle it."

"Are you really sure, honey?"

"I'm positive. I don't have that much time left, Dan. What time I do have, I intend to be at the top of the game."

"Okay, C.J. Let me know if you need anything."

"I need you to negotiate the details with Grant and get his signature on a contract today, if possible. It won't take long for word to get out. The media'll be all over this."

"Yes, they will. So will Trudy and the tour spin machine. Are you ready for that?"

C.J. thought about Trudy Skylar, president of the Women's Tennis Federation, and her blood boiled. The woman was like a vulture, feeding off C.J.'s popularity to boost the tour's image. C.J. tolerated it because she loved the game and everything it stood for and because she revered those who had come before her and made so many opportunities available to her and today's other stars. She would never turn her back on the storied history of the tour and the women's tennis movement, no matter the price.

"I'll deal with it," she said resolutely.

C.J. watched with trepidation as Jonas Svennsen walked into the player's lounge at Enchantment, a tennis bag slung over his shoulder. He looked for all the world exactly what he was, the coach of the most beloved woman on the women's tennis tour. She noted that his face registered surprise when he realized that she was in street clothes.

"Everything all right, Ceeg? Your knee bothering you again?"

C.J. smiled at Jonas, even as her heart pounded nervously in her chest. He'd been her first and only coach—the man who'd nurtured her career from the juniors right to the pinnacle of the game. Her hands shook minutely, so she clasped them together. She'd never imagined she'd be having this conversation.

Jonas's face was worn, and he looked tired, she thought. Years of traveling, training, and instructing had taken a toll on him. Perhaps he'd welcome a chance to get off the hamster wheel. She knew even as she thought it that she was just trying to make herself feel better about what she had to do. She sat up a little straighter and indicated the chair across from her.

"Sit down, Jonas. We need to talk."

"Okay," he drew the word out. "What's up?"

"Do you remember when I was just starting out? You used to tell me that if I didn't want to be the very best, I should go home and take up a hobby. 'Tennis is ten percent physical ability and ninety percent desire,' you said."

Jonas smiled. "Yep. Still feel that way."

"The game is different today, though, isn't it?"

"Yes, I suppose it is." He sat back in his chair, his shrewd eyes regarding his star pupil inquisitively.

"You taught me so much, Jonas. You taught me how to win, how to believe in myself, how to work hard, and never accept failure." Tears formed in her eyes and she paused, struggling to contain a wave of sadness. An icicle of fear tickled her spine as she wondered if she really could succeed without him.

"I can't teach you anymore, Ceeg, can I." It was a statement, not a question, and it was said without rancor. "I've given you everything I've got. It's not enough anymore." His voice was soft, wistful.

C.J. shook her head sadly, wishing for all the world that it could be enough.

"Well, that's that then."

This time when her eyes welled with tears, C.J. was powerless to stop them. "I love you, Jonas. You've been such a huge part of my life for as long as I can remember. I would never have succeeded without you."

"Aw, Ceeg, you were always destined for greatness. I just gave you a push in the right direction."

She shook her head again, and the words caught in her throat. "I'll miss you," she choked out.

He stood and gathered her in his arms, rubbing her back. "I'll miss you, too, sweetheart. If you ever need anything, you know where to find me."

"Mmm-hmm," she sobbed.

"Who's it going to be?"

"Grant Roberts."

Jonas pulled back and looked her in the eye, surprise written all over his features. "Roberts, eh?"

"Yeah," C.J. sniffed. "If I'm going to get back to number one, I'm going to have to play the game the way the new crop plays it."

"C.J., that style of play puts a tremendous amount of strain on the core muscles, not to mention wrists and ankles. The way they play out there isn't tennis—it's war."

"I know." She looked at him wild-eyed. Her pulse skyrocketed and she knew a moment of pure panic. "You don't think I can make the adjustment."

"It's not that," he said, looking away. "I'm not sure you should."

She shrugged. "I'm going to be number one again. To get there, I'm going to need to have the same weapons the other girls do."

"I'll be rooting for you."

"Thanks, my friend." C.J. watched Jonas's retreating back, knowing that for the first time, she was truly on her own. She would miss his steady guidance—his stoic, workman-like approach to the game. She would miss looking up into the stands, seeing that fire in his eyes that told her he believed in her.

She shuddered as a chill passed through her, then did her best to shake it off. The future was waiting.

CHAPTER TWO

Trystan awoke early, threw on her running gear, and headed out the door. She was in a foul mood after the debacle of the night before and was looking forward to a good, hard run to make her feel better.

She turned left out of the hotel and headed for the Hollywood Hills. The rhythmic thudding of her sneakers pounding the pavement was the only sound breaking the stillness. Her breathing was strong but not labored. Trystan worked hard to keep herself in perfect condition. She prided herself on her physique, which she imagined was the main reason women seemed to seek her company.

The buzzing of her cell phone startled her. She adjusted the wireless earpiece. "Hello?"

"How'd last night go?"

Trystan sighed. "Hi, Bec."

"Oh, that doesn't sound enthusiastic. Bad night?"

"You could say that. Two strikes in one night."

"Yikes. You losing your touch?"

"Yes and no. In the first instance, I got what I deserved."

"Okay, you're going to have to explain that one."

"One of my clients came onto me."

"You didn't…"

"Of course not. I told her I wouldn't cross that line. She fired me and suggested we take it to her hotel room. She was hot, I agreed," Trystan said.

"You are incorrigible."

"She invited me to the ESPYs as her escort. It sounded interesting, so I went."

"Don't tell me. She made the fatal mistake of wanting an encore," Becca said, laughing.

"Well, there was that," Trystan said. "Worse was when I tried to be a good escort—she threw in my face my previously stated desire to be a free agent."

"Ah. She committed a mortal sin—she wounded your pride," Becca said.

"Don't be so glib."

"Am I wrong?"

"Afterward," Trystan said, completely ignoring the question, "I went to a nightclub."

"Did you recover your form there?"

"I could have, but I turned her down."

"Do you have a temperature?" Becca asked sarcastically.

"Very funny. It just didn't feel right."

"Happens to the best of us, champ."

"Who are you kidding? It never happens to you."

"That's because I'm not as…accomplished as you."

"You're a one-woman woman."

"Don't knock it till you've tried it, Trys. When's the last time you had a girlfriend?"

"Not this again," Trystan groaned.

"Well?"

Trystan sighed heavily. "Julie, four years ago."

"Four years. And that lasted how long?"

"Two months," Trystan mumbled.

"Two whole months. Wow," Becca whistled. "It's a record. And since then, you've never slept with the same woman more than once."

"What's your point? I'm too busy to get involved. I've got a lot going on. I don't have time…"

"You don't make the time."

Trystan looked down as the phone buzzed. "I'd love to hear the rest of this lecture, but I've got another call coming in."

"Talk to you later, Trys."

"Bye, Bec."

Trystan hit the send button on the cell phone. "Trystan Lightfoot."

"Trystan? This is Trudy Skylar, president of the Women's Tennis Federation."

"How can I help you, Ms. Skylar?" Trystan came to a stop.

"The tour is in need of a new head physical therapist. Someone who can travel with us, tend to the players' injuries and give preventive care. You come very highly recommended."

"I appreciate that. Are you expecting someone who'll be on staff? Not freelance?"

"That's our thinking at the present time. Why don't you come in and meet with me? We can talk about the setup then."

Trystan considered—she'd always been a free agent. But the women's tennis tour intrigued her. "When would you like to meet?"

"How's day after tomorrow at our offices in St. Petersburg, Florida? We'll fly you down."

Trystan chewed her lower lip. "Okay. I'll be there."

"Where are you now?" Trudy asked.

"L.A."

"I'll have flight details e-mailed to you right away. E-ticket okay with you?"

"Of course. Thanks."

"See you day after tomorrow, Trystan."

C.J. wiped the sweat from her brow and took a long pull from her water bottle.

"Don't tell me I've worn you out already." Grant Roberts smiled good-naturedly.

"Not a chance," C.J. answered.

"Then get your butt back out on the court. We've got another hour of drills."

C.J. groaned but picked up her racquet and trotted to the service line. Grant had arrived in Sedona the night before and settled in at Enchantment. Since it was July in Arizona, they had started the practice session at 5:30 a.m. to avoid the heat of the day. That had been three hours earlier.

Grant, standing at the opposite service line, pounded balls at C.J. mercilessly. At a distance of roughly forty-two feet, C.J. barely had time to react. "Footwork, Ceeg, it's all about the footwork." C.J. could hear Jonas's voice in her head. She blinked, trying to clear her mind, and barely missed being beheaded by a ball.

"C.J.! Where's your head at? Pay attention, all right?" Grant, who had moved toward the net with the near miss, stalked back to the service line. "I want every ball hit at my feet, the harder, the better.

"Forget about getting your side to the net on the forehand side, damn it!" he yelled. "Forget your training. I want to see gut instinct, quick reactions, athleticism. I don't give a rat's ass about form—I want results."

C.J. summoned years of mental toughness and shut out everything except her gut instincts. "It's a new day," C.J. mumbled. "And I'm a new woman." Jaw set, eyes focused, she tuned out everything until there was only the ball and her racquet.

An hour later, she poured herself into a courtside seat, toweled off, and guzzled a bottle of Gatorade.

"How do you feel?" Grant asked.

"Like an awkward teenager," C.J. replied.

"You'll get the hang of it. You've got to unlearn before you can learn. It took you years to perfect your technique—you're not going to override that in a day."

"What, you're giving me two days?"

"I'm feeling generous," Grant answered. "I'll give you a whole week."

Before C.J. could reply, her cell phone rang. "It's Trudy," C.J. said to Grant, rolling her eyes. She debated not answering.

"You're going to have to deal with her sooner or later, right?"

"Right." C.J. sighed. "Hi, Trudy."

"Hello, C.J. I hear you've been busy this week."

"What can I do for you?"

"I see you've hired Grant Roberts as your new coach. You two make an attractive pair."

"He's my coach, not my boyfriend."

"Of course, C.J. Still, the media is very anxious to get some pictures of you two working together."

"I'm sure they are," C.J. mumbled.

"If you can make it, I've arranged a photo shoot for *Tennis* magazine here day after tomorrow. If you're willing, we can do a press conference after that."

"I'm trying to practice, Trudy."

"I understand. That's why I've got some court time set aside for you two here. The photo shoot's at 3:00 p.m."

"Fine."

"Be here by 1:00 for makeup and wardrobe."

"Sure. Bye, Trudy." C.J. disconnected the call and looked up at Grant apologetically. "Looks like we've got a road trip. Photo shoot for *Tennis*. Both of us."

"Both of us?" Grant asked.

"Yes. The WTF never misses an opportunity to market the 'femininity' of its players."

"Ah. The old princess and her new prince routine, eh?"

"Something like that," C.J. said. "There's a press conference afterward."

"That's going to mess with our training schedule."

"Trudy says she's reserved practice time for us down there."

"How very accommodating of her."

"Yeah," C.J. said unenthusiastically.

"It's the part of the game I always hated most," Grant said. "I have to admit, I didn't miss having my life under a microscope all the time."

"I bet." C.J. shrugged. "I'm not crazy about it, either, but it goes with the territory."

"And if I'm part of your team, I get sucked into that vortex, too."

"Afraid so."

"Well, the privacy was nice while it lasted."

Trystan stepped out of the taxi and looked at the sleek lines of a modern high rise. Florida in late July wasn't exactly her idea of paradise. The extreme heat wasn't a problem for her—after all, she'd grown up in Arizona. But the humidity—it enveloped her like a blanket, causing her shirt to cling to her body. She adjusted the carry-on bag she had slung over her shoulder and headed for the double glass doors.

The blast of arctic air that greeted her inside was just as shocking as the dense air outside had been. She shivered.

"Can I help you?" a uniformed man sitting behind a large console asked.

"I'm here to see Trudy Skylar."

"Is she expecting you?"

"Yes."

"Sign in here, please." He pushed a large guest register toward her and watched as she signed in. "I'll tell Ms. Skylar's assistant you're here, Ms. Lightfoot."

"Thank you." Trystan walked around the lobby admiring the artwork.

"Ms. Lightfoot?"

Trystan turned to see a perky, young brunette smiling at her. "Call me Trystan, please."

"Hi, Trystan. Nice to meet you. I'm Claire. Come this way, please?"

Claire led the way to a bank of elevators at the far end of the cavernous space. "Trudy is overseeing a photo shoot at the moment. She thought you might be interested, so we're going to meet her there."

"Okay," Trystan agreed.

The elevator stopped at the third floor, and the two women stepped out into a riot of noise and bright lights. In the center of it all stood two of the most attractive people Trystan had ever seen. The man was tall—sleekly muscled with tousled sandy blond hair, piercing blue eyes, and a strong jaw. The woman leaning against him presented the perfect contrast. Her hair was the color of burnished copper; it flowed like a waterfall down her back and spilled over her shoulders. Her face was soft, with an aquiline nose, sensual lips, high cheekbones, and bright, intelligent green eyes that reminded Trystan of fine jade. A dusting of freckles covered her lightly tanned skin.

Although the woman fit perfectly under the man's chin, Trystan got the odd sensation that there was something not quite right about the picture.

"That's C.J. Winslow," Claire whispered as her eyes followed Trystan's. "In my opinion, she's the greatest women's player who ever lived. *Tennis* magazine is doing a cover shoot of her and her new coach, Grant Roberts."

"Looks more like a model shoot than a tennis photo session," Trystan commented.

"Yeah," Claire breathed, clearly suffering a case of hero worship. "C.J. is gorgeous—the best thing to happen to the tour. She's great for our image." Claire leaned over conspiratorially. "My boss says it helps to tone down the perception that all great female athletes are lesbians, if you know what I mean."

Trystan felt the hair on the back of her neck stand up, but before she could respond, a small bird-like woman was standing in front of her, thrusting her hand out.

"You must be Trystan. I'm Trudy Skylar, nice to meet you. Sorry for the noise and distractions—I just needed to make sure everything was going okay down here." She gestured for Trystan to walk with her. "We can head up to my office now."

Trystan took one last look over her shoulder, trying to identify what it was about the look in C.J.'s eyes that was bothering her. She decided to file the mental snapshot away for later consideration.

Trystan sat in the indicated guest chair and watched as Trudy rifled through folders on her desk until she realized that the one she wanted was sitting all by itself dead center in the middle of her blotter. Trystan worked hard not to laugh.

"I swear, I'd lose my head if it weren't attached," Trudy said. "As I said on the phone, the WTF has determined that the time has come to have a full-time, dedicated physical therapist. We're looking for a consummate professional who can handle the pressures of being on the road with the girls, help them with preventive care, and obviously, deal with injuries on and off the court."

"Don't most of these ladies have their own PTs?" Trystan asked.

Trudy drew herself up straighter. "A number of them do have their own personal physical therapists, as well as a team of other treatment professionals, including orthopedists. However, as you can imagine, injuries and issues that come up on the road require immediate and ongoing attention if a player is going to continue in a tournament—it's not always possible or practical for the girls to get that from their personal practitioners."

"Even so, I'm assuming I would be expected to consult with those folks regarding diagnoses and treatment protocols." It appeared to Trystan that this aspect of the position had never occurred to Trudy. "I'm assuming the WTF would carry my liability coverage and there would be privacy issues that would need to be ironed out, as well."

"Of course," Trudy waved a bony hand in the air. "That would all be addressed."

"The players would have to sign waivers authorizing me to consult with their own health care professionals."

"I'm sure that would be fine," Trudy said.

"Further, they would indemnify me as having their permission to make treatment decisions for them without prejudice," Trystan continued.

"Naturally, our lawyers will take care of all the details," Trudy said, clearly out of her league. "Now then," she looked down at the open folder, trying to take control of the interview. "Your credentials are very impressive—I see that you're also a physician's assistant." She looked up at Trystan expectantly.

"Yes, I have dual degrees."

"That's an interesting combination—PT and PA."

"I initially trained as a PA but decided I wanted to combine my love of healing with my love of sports physiology—PT afforded me a better opportunity to do that," Trystan said, staring steadily across the desk.

"Yes, well," Trudy cleared her throat and began to read. "It seems you've been quite successful. The Connecticut Huskies women's basketball team, the Seattle Storm, the Arizona Cardinals, the U.S. Track and Field Association, the 2000 USA Olympic team, Major League Baseball. You're very accomplished."

"Thank you."

Trudy leaned forward. "One thing we insist on here at the WTF is complete confidentiality. You may hear things in the locker room or on the treatment table that…" she appeared to search for the right words, "…if made public, might not place the tour in the best light."

Trystan kept her expression inscrutable. "Confidentiality is a given in my profession."

"Of course, of course," Trudy agreed. "It's just that there are some elements out there that would like nothing better than to tar the tour with unsubstantiated accusations of rampant…improper behavior."

"I understand your concern. Perhaps it's only fair for me to tell you then that I'm a lesbian. If that's problematic for you, I won't waste any more of your time." Trystan folded her hands in her lap and waited.

Trudy seemed to consider. "My job, Trystan, is to protect our girls' images."

"Naturally," Trystan said.

"I don't have anything against lesbians." Trudy fidgeted with a pen on her desk.

Trystan merely raised an eyebrow.

"It's my job to help the WTF project a positive, family-friendly image that draws more fans to the game."

Trystan sat back in her chair, silently weighing whether she wanted any part of an organization that would publicly disavow a large segment of its base. "Let me make something clear to you, Ms. Skylar. I don't care whether a player is black or white, gay or straight. Her personal life is her business. My only interest is in helping her stay healthy and be in the best possible physical shape to go out on the court."

"Of course," Trudy said.

"Likewise, my personal life is my own."

"Naturally," Trudy said slowly. "As long as you keep a low profile and don't call attention to yourself, I'm sure your…sexuality should have no bearing on the way you do your job."

"Thanks for trusting in my professionalism." Trystan hesitated. "Are you offering me the job?"

"Did you get the fax I sent you with the terms of employment and the salary?" Trudy asked.

"I did, and my lawyer has reviewed them."

"As I said, you came very highly recommended. I like what I see, and I'm not one to waste time. So, yes, I'm offering you the job. Are you accepting?"

Trystan thought about making Trudy wait. At the very least, she knew she should have her lawyer review the additions to the contract detailing liability coverage and privacy waivers before giving an answer. "Pending my lawyer's approval of the revised contract, yes. When do I start?"

"How does now sound?"

"If all is in order, fine," Trystan said.

"I'll have a contract ready for your lawyers to review within the hour. Why don't you accompany me back downstairs in the meantime? We're about to hold a press conference for C.J. Winslow. I'll introduce you to her."

Although she was looking forward to catching another glimpse of C.J., Trystan kept her expression neutral as she rose from her chair. This job was sounding better and better.

C.J. stood behind the podium trying not to fidget. She'd held many press conferences over the course of her career, but she'd never quite gotten used to being the object of attention off the court.

The lights from the television cameras were hot and bright, and she was doing her best not to squint as questions were lobbed at her like hand grenades.

"C.J., is this your last gasp? Are you desperate at this point?"

C.J. worked hard to keep the smile on her face. "Hardly. I think I'm a student of the game, always learning, always working to improve. Jonas has been a marvelous mentor and teacher. At this point in my career, I want to expand my repertoire—get more versatile. That's what I think Grant can do for me."

"Is that *all* he's going to do for you?"

The question came from Gwen Naderson, a perennial thorn in C.J.'s side. She was a reporter for the *Miami Herald* who was more interested in tour gossip than she ever was in what happened on the court.

C.J. wanted to ignore the question but knew from experience that doing so would only make matters worse. "Before his terrible accident, Grant was one of the finest players in the game. He has a talent for coaching, and I have confidence in him to do so. We have a lot of work to do to be ready for the U.S. Open. We both intend to be very focused. Thank you all for coming." C.J. stepped away from the podium, marshalling all of her willpower to avoid storming out of the press conference. Instead, she waved and exited gracefully out a side door as the cameras and questions trailed her.

Trudy ran after C.J., calling over her shoulder for Trystan to follow.

"You did great in there," Trudy soothed as an agitated C.J. paced in an adjacent conference room.

C.J. ran impatient fingers through her hair. "Why in the world did you invite that wretched woman?"

"C.J., you know keeping Gwen out won't stop her from writing whatever she wants. At least this way there's a chance she might get it right."

"I'm tired of her sly questions and innuendo. I'm telling you, I won't do it anymore. My job is to play tennis, not answer bogus accusations. I'm no good at PR."

"You're wrong," Trystan said quietly from the corner. She'd been leaning against the wall, listening, measuring, and admiring.

"Who are you?" C.J. asked, embarrassed that a stranger had been privy to her mini-tantrum.

"C.J. Winslow, meet Trystan Lightfoot, the tour's new full-time physical therapist," Trudy said.

"Nice to meet you," Trystan said, stepping forward out of the shadows. "I meant what I said. You handled yourself admirably in what was a very difficult situation. I think I would've thrown something at her."

C.J. laughed. "Thank you. That's awfully kind of you to say."

"You'll learn that I never say anything I don't mean," Trystan said.

"When do you start?" C.J. asked.

"The contract's being drawn up as we speak," Trudy said. "In fact, I should go see if it's ready." She hesitated for a moment, looking awkward.

"It's okay to leave me here with C.J. I promise to behave." Trystan winked.

When she had left, C.J. asked, "What was that about?"

Trystan smiled, ready to unleash the charm that always came to the surface when she was alone with a beautiful woman. When she turned to face C.J., however, her instincts made her hesitate. "Nothing. It's not about anything," she answered. After a moment's silence, she said, "I know it's not my business, but I didn't get the sense you were enjoying yourself during the photo shoot."

"I can't imagine why you would think that." C.J. felt her stomach drop.

Trystan shrugged. "I don't really know why, either. It was just a feeling."

C.J. searched desperately for a way to turn the conversation away from herself. She was uncomfortable under Trystan's scrutiny for reasons she couldn't fully understand.

"Have you worked with tennis players before?" C.J. finally asked.

"The men's tour," Trystan answered, understanding that she was being deflected and accepting that for the moment.

C.J. looked at her watch. "I've got to go. I've got court time in half an hour."

"It was nice to meet you," Trystan said. "You really did hold your own in there. Don't sweat the small stuff."

"Thanks. I'll be seeing you around," C.J. said.

"Count on it," Trystan said to the empty room after the door closed behind C.J.

CHAPTER THREE

C.J. stretched out in the hot tub, her muscles aching from overuse. She leaned her head back against the natural rock into which the spa was built and closed her eyes.

For two weeks, she and Grant had been working on revamping her game. The training was difficult and required not just different physical skills, but a completely different mind-set. C.J. rolled her shoulders back, trying to ease the tension. The challenge ahead of her was daunting, the stakes high. She massaged the knots in her neck and opened her mouth to relieve the pain in her jaw from clenching her teeth—all aches that were testament to the enormous pressure she felt to succeed.

C.J. visualized herself on the court, imagined approaching the baseline to serve, watched as her toss rose unerringly straight, and served a perfect ace down the center "T."

She ducked under the water, came up, and slicked her hair back. In two days, she would be in San Diego for the Acura Classic—that would give her four events before the U.S. Open in which to test out her new game. Thinking about the impending tournament, C.J. felt butterflies flutter in her stomach; she tried to calm herself. Grant thought she was ready to be battle-tested. She wasn't sure she agreed, but she understood that there was only so much she could do on the practice court—match play would be the true test.

Water sluiced off her body as C.J. pushed herself up and out of the spa. The air was marginally cooler than the water, and she enjoyed the momentary chill before her body readjusted to the warm July night. It was monsoon season in Arizona, and she could feel the air growing heavy with the moisture that heralded an imminent thunderstorm. The suddenness of weather changes was one of the things she loved most about the desert Southwest. She glanced once again at the star-filled sky, watching in the distance as a line of clouds formed over the farthest peaks. Feeling slightly more relaxed and mellow, she threw on a terrycloth robe and padded inside, looking forward to the light show that would begin shortly.

When the lightning struck some thirty minutes later, C.J. was watching with fascination from the comfort of her living room. The force of the thunder made the floor shake and the windows rattle; for an instant, she caught her reflection in the window as she peered out. The eyes that stared back at her were filled with loneliness and longing. She turned away.

Isolation was the price she paid for her success and her image. She had told herself so on countless occasions. Still, there were moments such as this one when the ache blossomed inside her and C.J. wished it could be different. She closed her eyes, imagining what it would feel like to have strong, loving arms wrapped around her, a soul mate with whom to share the beauty of a thunderstorm and the promise of a lifetime spent loving each other. Opening her eyes to a solitary reality, she felt the sting of tears and swallowed hard.

She sat on the couch, pulling her feet up underneath her and wrapping her arms around herself. *There'll be time for all those things later, after my career is over.* It was a ploy she had often used in an effort to assuage a stab of loneliness so acute that it was a physical pain. On this night, the ruse wasn't working. She put her head down on her arm and cried.

Trystan threw her travel bag on the bed and flopped down beside it. She was bone tired. It wasn't that she was unused to being on the road—but she'd had to treat thirteen players in fourteen hours before packing her bag hastily and jumping on yet another airplane.

"What?" she asked wearily, flipping her cell phone open. "Can't I just have fifteen minutes?"

Becca's rich laughter rang in her ear. "Poor baby. Is life on the tour too much for you?"

"That's right. I surrender."

"You heard it here first, folks—the mighty Trystan Lightfoot has thrown in the towel. Seriously, hon, you sound whipped."

"I am. I don't know what I was expecting when I took this gig…"

"But you got more than you bargained for, right?" Becca finished for her.

"Exactly. First of all, you can't even begin to imagine the stress these women put their bodies through. It's inhuman. Practice six hours or more a day, strength-training, stretching, intervals. Then they sit down with their coaches and watch film—film of their own matches, scouting clips of their next opponent."

"So they're not sitting on the couch like spoiled rich kids eating bonbons?"

"Not exactly," Trystan chuckled. "But some of them do like to party. I can't figure how they have the energy for it."

"That's just because we're getting old."

"That too."

"Where in the world are you today?"

"I just arrived in San Diego this minute."

"Look on the bright side—this is a great way to see the world on someone else's dime."

"Becca, how is it that you always find the silver lining?"

"It's a gift, I admit it. You ought to try it sometime."

"If I could do it for myself, why would I need you?" Trystan asked.

"Everybody needs someone constant in their lives, Trys. Otherwise it gets too lonely," Becca said, turning serious.

"You have a point. Guess I'll keep you around for a while," Trystan joked, determined to keep the conversation light.

"Good. I was worried there for a minute that I was headed for 'ex-best friends anonymous,'" Becca quipped.

"See, you owe me. I just saved you from the dreaded ex-best friend twelve-step program."

"Hello, my name is Becca, and I'm an ex-best friend."

Trystan laughed, imagining Becca standing ramrod straight with her hands folded in front of her. "Welcome, Becca. Would you like to share with us today?"

"I had this really cool best friend, she was fun-loving, caring, intelligent, and intuitive."

"She sounds like an angel," Trystan said.

"She was, right up until the moment she fired me."

"Ouch."

"Tell me about it. There I was, with the best scam going, and poof, she just hit the eject button."

"Sounds harsh, Becca. How did that make you feel?" Trystan imitated her last therapist.

"Like road kill, naturally."

"And what did you want to do about it?"

"Get out my Trystan voodoo doll and stick pins in it."

"You keep a voodoo doll of your best friend?"

"My *ex*-best friend," Becca corrected.

Trystan laughed. "You're an evil woman, Bec. Remind me to stay on your good side."

"I knew you'd see it my way. So tell me, who's the most interesting person you've met so far?"

Trystan considered. "Define your terms. Interesting in what way?"

"Interesting as in you want to get to know her better."

Trystan chewed her lower lip. "Do I have to have treated her?"

"No."

"Does she have to have played in the last two tournaments?"

"No," Becca drew the word out. "Why?"

"I met C.J. Winslow when I was at the WTF offices in St. Pete."

"And?"

Trystan turned her head to the side and looked out the hotel room window. "She's…different."

"Different how?" Becca asked, clearly intrigued.

"I can't explain it, there was just something about her."

"You're going to have to do better than that, champ."

"She's just different, that's all." Trystan tried to keep the exasperation out of her voice. She'd found her mind drifting more than a few times to the way C.J. looked during the photo shoot and the expression in her eyes at the press conference.

"Is this one of those Navajo-spiritual feelings?"

"Something like that." Becca was the only person other than her mother to whom Trystan would talk about such things.

"Tell me what you felt. What was the energy?"

"Strong, but guarded. There was something sad and vulnerable there, too. I can't put my finger on it."

"You want to get to know her better," Becca said, wonder in her voice.

"Yeah," Trystan said quietly, "I do."

"And not in the biblical sense?"

"Don't be a pig, Bec."

"I'm not trying to be a pig. I'm just trying to see where this is going."

"What makes you think it's going anywhere?" Trystan snapped.

"Easy, tiger," Becca answered.

Trystan took a deep breath. "I'm sorry."

"I thought I saw somewhere that she fired her coach and was taking a few weeks off."

"She hired a young stud to revamp her game."

"Oh," Becca drew the word out. "She straight then?"

"I have no idea," Trystan said shortly. "I must've forgotten to ask her that at our first meeting." She knew, even as she said it, that she sounded defensive and peevish, but she couldn't help it.

"Apology accepted in advance."

Trystan accepted Becca's unspoken rebuke with equanimity, knowing that she deserved it.

"You know I love you, right?" Becca asked.

"I know. And you know I love you, too."

"Yep. I wasn't trying to push you, champ. I think the fact that this woman interests you, for whatever reason and in whatever capacity, is great."

"Bec?"

"Yeah?"

"Am I really that bad?"

"What do you mean?"

"The first question that popped into your mind when I said I was interested in C.J. was whether or not I'd slept with her."

"Trystan…"

"Yes or no?"

"Yes, the thought crossed my mind," Becca said. "But…"

"There are no buts. You thought because I found her interesting I was making time with her."

"Trys…"

"That's okay," Trystan said. "It was a fair assumption. After all, that's been my pattern, hasn't it?"

"There's nothing wrong with having a healthy libido. You're a beautiful, vibrant, single woman. Why shouldn't you have some fun?"

Trystan stood and began to pace. "I've got to go, Bec. I'll talk to you soon." She flipped the cell phone shut and threw it on the bed. She went to the window and stared out at the darkening sky, unable to shake the dark mood that was settling over her. Rummaging through her bag, she pulled out a pair of running shorts and a form-fitting tank. Maybe what she needed was a good run.

C.J. arrived at the practice court a half hour early. Putting down her bag, she walked toward the baseline, sat down, and began to stretch. She'd already put in twenty minutes on the stationary bike as a warm-up. Going through the motions of her regular pre-match routine was helping to calm her frazzled nerves. She bent her right knee behind her and to the side, stretched her left leg out straight, and leaned back until her shoulder blades were touching the court. After a count of twenty, she switched legs and repeated the process.

"You're early," Grant said, his body casting a shadow over her. "How do you feel?"

"I'm okay," C.J. said, continuing to stretch. "Nervous as hell, but otherwise fine."

"I'm not surprised you've got a few butterflies, C.J., but you're going to kick ass out there today." He crouched down beside her. "You're ready; I promise I wouldn't let you go out there if you weren't." He squeezed her shoulder, leaned in, and kissed her temple. As he did so, a camera shutter clicked.

Grant stood quickly, whirling around to see a photographer sitting on the nearby bleachers. "What do you think you're doing?" he asked, stalking toward the man.

"Hey, this is a public venue. I have every right to be here." Even as he said it, the photographer hopped down from the bleachers and backed away.

"If I find you hanging around C.J. again, I'll wrap that lens around your stinking neck. Do you hear me?"

The photographer didn't bother to answer; he simply ran.

Grant moved back to C.J.'s side. She was sitting up, staring after the fleeing form. "Don't think he'll be bugging you again," he said lightly.

C.J. hid her face in her hands. "That picture will be on the front page of every tabloid from here to Paris." Her voice shook.

Grant sat on the court next to her. "You can't think about that now. All that matters today is the match. Everything else is just a distraction and makes your job that much harder."

"Don't you care that the press is going to be all over us, Grant? I can hear it now: 'C.J., how long have you and Grant been romantically linked?' 'C.J., is the romance the reason you dumped Jonas?' The headlines… 'C.J. and Grant—the perfect love match.'" As she spoke, her voice rose in volume.

"We can't worry about things we can't control," Grant said. "The thing we can do is take care of business on the court. If they do write garbage, we'll silence them with your game."

"That sounds nice in theory, but we've just given them the story they've been dying to get their hands on for weeks."

He was quiet for a moment. "What is it that bothers you so much about being linked with me, C.J.?"

"I've spent years protecting my privacy, years ensuring that the focus was on my game. I've..." she broke off, unable to continue around the lump in her throat. *I've spent years alone and desperately lonely, sacrificing everything for my career and my image. And now none of it matters.* In one swift motion, she rose and sprinted from the court, leaving a clearly stunned Grant behind.

Trystan ducked into the training room. She wanted to be certain everything was set up for the first day of the tournament. She'd quickly discovered that it was best to be well-prepared in advance because when play began, she would be swamped.

Once inside, she stopped dead. There, sitting on a treatment table, was C.J. Winslow. She was crying, her head cradled in her hands. It was obvious she hadn't heard Trystan come in.

Trystan considered retreating, but the sight of C.J. so clearly in distress propelled her forward. "Hey," she said softly, careful not to startle the distraught woman. "Are you okay?"

C.J.'s head whipped up and she hurriedly wiped at her eyes. "Fine."

Trystan gave her a minute to compose herself. "I've heard several definitions for the word 'fine,' but none of them include crying." She kept her voice gentle.

C.J. jumped down from the table, gathering herself and lifting her chin high. "I'm fine by any standard," she said stiffly. Then, as if reconsidering, she added, "But thank you for asking."

"You're welcome. If you change your definition, I'll be here. My name's..."

"Trystan Lightfoot. I met you a couple of weeks ago, I remember." C.J. started to bolt.

Trystan stopped her with a hand on the arm, somehow loath to let her go this way. "I'm sorry if I caught you at a bad moment, I didn't mean to."

"Don't worry about it," C.J. said, hurrying out the door without looking back.

Trystan watched her go, wondering what in the world had made C.J. cry and wanting more than anything to fix whatever was wrong.

"I've been looking for you everywhere," Grant whispered desperately when C.J. appeared in the stadium tunnel before her first match.

"Sorry."

"Never mind that," he said dismissively, regarding her carefully. "How do you feel?"

"I'm fine," she said, bouncing nervously on the balls of her feet.

Grant squeezed her shoulder. "You're going to be great. Be aggressive and focus on her backhand."

"Right," C.J. shouted to be heard over the roaring of the crowd as she cleared the tunnel.

"C.J. Winslow," the stadium announcer intoned, "winner of nine Wimbledons, seven-time U.S. Open champion, five-time Australian Open winner, four-time French Open champion, and defending champion of the Acura Classic."

The crowd clapped and whistled.

C.J. sat in her seat to the right of the umpire's chair and unzipped her racquet bag. Her hands shook minutely, but she doubted anyone could see them. She tested two of her newly strung racquets, selected one, and headed for the far baseline.

Her opponent was Tandora Meisner, a fringe player ranked 126th in the world. While C.J. knew she should beat her handily, she also didn't want to take the outcome for granted, especially not with the changes she'd instituted during the past two weeks in her own game.

C.J. concentrated on her breathing in the warm-up, trying to find a nice, easy rhythm with her ground strokes, focusing on the ball while warming up at the net, and finally, timing her toss on the serve.

"Ladies, time," the chair umpire announced.

C.J. returned to the sideline, removed her warm-up jacket, took a sip of water, and glanced up at the "friends" box. Her heart lurched as realization struck—Jonas wouldn't be sitting there anymore, encouraging her with his pumped fists and warm smile. In his place was calm, cool, collected Grant, his sunglasses firmly in place, his left leg thrown casually over his right knee as if he were just another spectator. A trickle of cold, fear-induced sweat traveled down her back. *This is no time to question your decision.* Pointedly, she tore her gaze away, rose, and took her place to receive serve.

"Use this as an opportunity to test your power," C.J. mumbled to herself as she shifted her weight from side to side, bouncing on the balls of her feet in anticipation of the serve. Her first return was a torrid winner that hugged the sideline, setting the tone for the match.

At 6-love, 5-1, C.J. served for the match. She'd barely broken a sweat and her game, while not flawless, had been good thus far. The few times she'd spied Grant, he'd been in exactly the same position she'd seen him in before the match.

C.J. walked toward the back of the court and nodded for a ball. She stepped up to the baseline, bounced the ball several times, and began her service motion. As she watched her toss, a finger of fear stole through her. She arched up, extended the racquet head in the direction of the ball, and a wave of panic swamped her senses. Her fingers felt boneless on the grip, as if she didn't have the strength to hold on. Her vision tunneled as a ripple of terror swam through her. Her teeth were chattering. She let the ball drop without hitting it.

She was a young teenager again, drilling with other kids in a tennis clinic she attended once a week...

Blinking hard, C.J. fought the memory. *Not now. Not here. Oh, God.* She looked up at the spectators waiting expectantly for her to finish out the match. *You can do this.*

C.J. closed her eyes and tried to steady her breathing. It felt as though her legs would give way any second. Her head spun, leaving her momentarily disoriented. She backed away from the baseline and bounced the ball several more times, trying to stop the tremor in her arm. *Just get through it.*

She approached the baseline again, this time barely pausing before beginning her service motion. The ball sailed long. Her second serve was no better, landing in the net.

The crowd began to buzz. The sound was like a swarm of bees in C.J.'s head. She tried unsuccessfully to shut them out. *Serve out the game.* She struggled through the next three points, serving two more double faults and landing a second serve so weak that her opponent had no trouble hitting a return for a winner.

Sweat pooled at the base of her spine as C.J. walked over to her chair for the changeover. She sat down heavily and buried her face in a towel. The panic was still there, gnawing at her insides. She tried to fight back with logic, talking to herself as she rose and walked to the opposite baseline. “This woman is ranked 126th in the world, Ceeg. You’re one of the greatest champions the game has ever known. Go out there and finish her off.”

C.J. narrowed her eyes, shutting out everything except the ball and her racquet. The serve came right at her body, jamming her and forcing her to misplay her shot. Love-15.

“Win this game and you won’t have to serve again,” C.J. told herself, as she fought not to hyperventilate. She caught a glimpse of Grant in the stands. He wasn’t looking relaxed anymore. C.J. winced. *You and the ball—that’s all there is.*

She returned the next serve and followed it into the net, easily putting away a high forehand volley. At 15-all, she ripped a service return for a backhand winner. When her opponent threw up a defensive lob at 15-30, C.J. let it bounce before slamming it deep to her backhand. At double match point, C.J. felt her anxiety level rise again. She backed away, asking the umpire for time. “One more, Ceeg. Just one more point. C’mon,” she exhorted herself, slapping her hand against her thigh.

The serve took her wide, but she was able to get her racquet on it and poke it back over the net. Her opponent went for too much, sending the ball long—the match belonged to C.J.

She jogged to the net, shook Tandora’s hand and that of the umpire, and sat in her chair to gather her things. As she left the court to the cheers of the crowd, she waved, offering an automatic smile. All C.J. wanted was to get into the locker room. As she hurried down the tunnel, a commentator for the USA Network, which was televising the tournament, stopped her.

“C.J., how does it feel to be back on the court?”

“There’s no place I’d rather be,” C.J. answered, thinking at that moment she’d rather be almost anywhere else.

“Well, you had little trouble out there today—very impressive. Tell us about your new game.”

C.J. shrugged. “I’m just trying to add a little more power, a little more versatility.”

“Are you satisfied with the way you played today? It looked for a second there like you might have lost focus.”

C.J. swallowed hard but kept her voice casual. “Overall, I think I played well. Being away from match play for two weeks, I’m not surprised to have a hiccup here or there.”

“We’re looking forward to watching you during the rest of the tournament. C.J. Winslow, everybody. Let’s send it back upstairs.”

C.J. brushed past the reporter and headed for the locker room. Grant was waiting for her at the door.

"What the hell happened out there?"

"6-0, 6-2 happened."

"C.J., cut the crap. Where did you go at 5-1? Clearly, you went somewhere." Grant threw his hands up in the air.

C.J.'s stomach dropped, but she worked to keep her face neutral. "I just lost my concentration for a second, that's all."

"Good thing it was Tandora and not someone else across the net. Go get a shower. We'll get you some fruit and get back out on the practice court. We're going to work on your serve until we get it right."

C.J. slumped against the wall. Serving on the practice court, she knew, wasn't the problem, but she had no intention of confiding in Grant.

CHAPTER FOUR

Trystan opened the door to admit the room service attendant. In his hands, he held a tray laden with her breakfast and a copy of *USA Today*. She gestured for him to place it on the small table in the corner and tipped him on the way out.

She removed the items from the tray, leaving her more room to spread out the newspaper. As she did each morning, Trystan skipped the front section and went directly to the sports pages. Coverage of the Acura Classic was relegated to page three, behind Major League Baseball, golf, and preseason football.

It was the caption of the picture that caught her eye first—*Tennis beauty queen C.J. Winslow redefines the meaning of love*. Trystan struggled to swallow a mouthful of eggs. The fork clattered to the plate as she stared at the large color photo of Grant Roberts, his hand caressing C.J.'s shoulder as he kissed her on the temple.

No longer hungry, Trystan pushed the plate away. *It doesn't matter to me if C.J. and Grant are involved.* Trystan studied C.J.'s face. Her eyes seemed to be closed, and she was half smiling. *Damn it.*

Trystan shoved the newspaper away, getting up so quickly that she almost spilled the untouched orange juice. She stalked over to the nightstand and grabbed her cell phone off the charger. Impatiently, she dialed a familiar number.

"Hey, what's up?" Becca asked, her voice still rough from sleep.

"Aren't you awake yet?"

"I am now. What's with the gruffness? Something I said?"

Trystan jerked her fingers roughly through her hair. "Tell me why I should care that C.J. Winslow is having a fling with her male coach."

"Ah. Um. No reason?" Becca offered tentatively.

"Damn right there's no reason." Trystan began to pace. "I don't even know the woman."

"Right."

"She's free to do whatever she wants."

"Yes, she is," Becca agreed. "Want to tell me what this is about?"

"Go pick up a *USA Today*. There's a nice big picture of the two of them looking quite cozy."

"I see," Becca said. "You know, pictures aren't always accurate portrayals of what's really going on. Is it possible that the gesture was taken out of context?"

"How should I know?" Trystan growled.

"Just something to consider, Trys."

"Right. Anyway, I've got to go. I've got three treatments lined up this morning, and that's not including any emergencies."

"Okay. Take care."

"See ya." Trystan, still feeling out of sorts, disconnected the call.

C.J. was alone in the exercise room. She was on the stationary bike, warming up for her morning match.

"Hey, C.J. Nice picture of you in the paper this morning."

Jane Duchan was barely out of her teens and a rising star. She was also C.J.'s next opponent.

"Really? I didn't see it." C.J. understood gamesmanship better than almost anyone on the tour. From a very young age, players were taught to seek any advantage, including the psychological edge. If your opponent was easily rattled, it was your job to capitalize on that. If she could be distracted or made to lose focus, you moved in for the kill. C.J. made it a point never to engage in such tactics. She believed that if you were good enough, there was no need to stoop so low.

"He's so good-looking, what a dreamboat. Let me know if you ever get tired of him," Jane called over her shoulder as she headed for the changing room.

C.J. waited until she was sure she was alone again before dropping her head onto the handlebars and letting the tears flow freely. She'd been on edge before Jane's antics. After what had happened in the first match, she was terrified to step out on the court. She swallowed hard, shivering involuntarily as goose bumps broke out on her arms. She'd been so sure those memories were behind her.

Lack of sleep and nerves were playing havoc with her system. Her stomach was in knots and her head throbbed painfully. Not wanting to add to her stress level, she had specifically avoided looking at the papers before leaving the hotel. Thanks to Jane, her efforts were for naught.

Trystan stood some fifteen feet away, watching C.J.'s body shake with sobs. She'd been about to round the corner into the room when Jane had entered from the opposite direction. Her eyes narrowed. *Bitch.* Her hands balled into fists.

Trystan's first instinct was to offer comfort. Then she remembered how C.J. had reacted the last time she had caught her by surprise. She pursed her lips. C.J. looked miserable—certainly not like someone who was giddily in love. Trystan tapped her finger against her lips thoughtfully. Maybe Becca had been right—perception wasn't always reality.

Roberta Ries-Mantonia lay stretched out on the treatment table as Trystan massaged her lower back. Her head was turned to the side, and she was talking to Cynthia Quick, who was warming down on a bike after her match.

"What do you think? Has the ice princess finally melted?"

Cynthia laughed. "I'd have bet any money that she was asexual." She sighed. "C.J. the frigid proves she's human after all."

"Let's not get carried away," Roberta said, and both women laughed.

Trystan worked hard not to growl out loud. She shrugged her shoulders to loosen the tension there, careful to keep her touch light, despite a rather unprofessional desire to throttle Roberta. Of the three treatments she had given that morning, this was the third time C.J. had been the topic of conversation. The tenor of the gossip had been similar each time.

It was obvious to Trystan that the other players were jealous of C.J. It was the level of cattiness that surprised her. She wondered how much of the nastiness ever reached C.J. and if that was why she'd been crying earlier. Maybe it wasn't the picture, but her peers' reaction to it that had upset her. Frown lines etched their way between Trystan's brows.

"Hey, why are you stopping?" Roberta asked when Trystan's hands stilled on her back.

"You're finished."

"No, I'm not. My back still feels tight."

"I've been massaging it for half an hour. If that didn't loosen it up, we'll need to look at some different stretches for you." Trystan hadn't felt any tightness in Roberta's muscles for at least five minutes.

Roberta glanced furtively at Cynthia. "I think I prefer the personal touch." She winked.

"If so," Trystan said testily, "you'll have to find someone else to touch you. I have another appointment coming in shortly. I'll grab you a sheet that outlines the stretches. Twice a day, morning and night."

"Where's the fun in that?" she called after Trystan, who was already walking away.

Trystan needed some time to cool off. In reality, she didn't have another patient scheduled for at least the next two hours. She craved a good, hard run; unfortunately, since play was still in progress on several courts, she couldn't leave the grounds. She found herself walking in the direction of the stadium court where the featured match, Winslow v. Duchan, was under way.

C.J. sat in her chair on the changeover, her legs bouncing in a nervous rhythm as she toweled off. She'd just lost her serve for the seventh time and was down 1-4 in the second set, having barely eked out the first set 6-4. So far, she'd held her serve only once—the first game of the match.

She chanced a quick glance up at the stands and saw the unmistakable look of concern on Grant's face. Her skin prickled with shame. *I owe him an explanation, I should tell him the truth.* The very thought made her limbs turn to ice.

She turned her head to the side discreetly and eyed her opponent. Jane Duchan was smiling and blotting at her face. A muscle in C.J.'s jaw bunched and her nostrils flared. *Smug little witch.*

C.J. rose from the chair abruptly and threw the towel at it. She squared her shoulders as she passed Jane on their way to opposite ends of the court. *Let me show you what it means to be a champion, little girl.*

She ripped the first service return down the line and past a clearly stunned Duchan. On the next serve, she charged the net, putting away a crisp backhand volley. C.J. felt a surge of confidence flow through her. She was all business, shutting down her brain and letting her instincts take over. "I can do anything," she told herself. And she did.

Over the course of the following five games, C.J. slipped into what she called "the zone." She moved briskly from one side of the baseline to the other between points, barely taking any time at all between her own serves. Within thirty minutes, she had won the set and the match, jogging to the net to shake hands with a shell-shocked Jane Duchan.

Grant was waiting for her in the tunnel, just as he had been after the previous match. He wore a bemused expression.

"I don't get it." He shook his head. "It's like you were two completely different players out there. What happened?"

C.J. turned her head from side to side, easing the tension in her neck. She closed her eyes, breathed deeply, and let go of the anger that had fueled her performance.

"You okay?" Grant asked, as he watched her closely.

"Fine, thanks," C.J. said. "What happened? I got mad." She shrugged.

"Well, you ought to get mad more often then." Grant massaged her shoulders, but C.J. pulled away. His hands fell to his sides. "Why don't you get a shower and we'll go somewhere we can talk."

C.J.'s eyes widened in trepidation, but she headed toward the locker room.

Trystan heard a loud commotion outside the exit leading from the locker room to the VIP parking lot. She dropped the towel she'd been folding and ran, shoving open the double doors and emerging into the bright sunlight. Shielding her eyes, she caught sight of C.J. standing stock-still in the middle of a massive mob of reporters. There were television cameras, microphones, and notepads being thrust at her from all directions. Questions were shouted without pause for answers. C.J. looked so trapped and vulnerable it broke Trystan's heart.

Without thought, she pushed forward, tossing bodies out of her path until she reached C.J.'s side. She placed one hand under C.J.'s elbow, wrapping the other arm around her waist protectively. "Come on," she whispered harshly. "Let's get you out of here."

C.J. didn't seem to hear her but offered no resistance. The crowd continued to press in.

"C.J., are you and Grant getting married?"

"How long have you been together?"

"Have you talked to Jonas? He must be feeling pretty used."

At that remark, Trystan felt C.J. stiffen. Trystan put gentle pressure on her back to propel her along. "Don't answer them," she said in C.J.'s nearby ear. "Don't let them bother you or goad you into anything."

Trystan put her head down and used her shoulder to push through the throng. She dug the keys to her rental car out of her pocket and steered C.J. to the passenger side.

"I can't…" C.J. began weakly.

"Easy. I'm just going to drive you around the block until they clear out. I'll bring you right back, I promise." Trystan tried unsuccessfully to force eye contact, wanting C.J. to see in her eyes that she was safe.

Once in the passenger seat, C.J. sat with her hands folded in her lap, staring blankly out the side window.

"Why don't you have security protecting you?" Trystan asked, trying to clamp down on her annoyance as she started the ignition.

"I never had a problem like that before." C.J.'s voice was hollow.

"You do now. Is there someone I can call for you?"

"No. I'll be fine." C.J. finally turned from the window and looked at Trystan. "Thank you for intervening like that. I couldn't seem to get away from them."

"You're welcome. I've always had a bit of a 'knight in shining armor' complex." Trystan winked and returned her eyes to the road as she circled around back into the parking lot.

"You make a great knight." C.J. said.

Satisfied that the media hounds had gone, Trystan stopped the car in front of the locker room entrance. She noticed Grant Roberts nearby leaning against a sports car. "Isn't that your coach?"

"Oh, yes. I was supposed to be meeting him when I got waylaid by the mob."

Trystan felt a sudden flush of heat rise in her chest. "I hope I didn't delay you too much," she said curtly. She waited for C.J. to get out and join Grant before peeling out of the lot.

"Where were you?" Grant asked. "And who was that you were with?"

"That's Trystan Lightfoot, the tour's new physical therapist. She rescued me from the press. They ambushed me on my way out here from the locker room."

"Ah. That was nice of her."

"Yes, it was," C.J. answered, watching Trystan's car fade into the distance.

"Okay, well, let's go," Grant said, stepping aside and opening the car door.

"Where are we going?"

"I've never done the coaching thing before," Grant said apologetically, "but it seems to me like I've skipped a critical step."

"You have?" C.J. asked uncertainly.

"Uh-huh." He glanced at her as he pulled out of the parking lot. "We've spent weeks together working on your technique. Hours in each other's company watching film and analyzing strategy. What we haven't done is get to know each other personally." Grant reached out and touched C.J.'s hand briefly, pulling back when she flinched.

C.J.'s heart jumped. She clutched at the door handle. "Grant, I…"

"Relax. I just want us to kick back, have some fun…and I want to introduce you to someone."

"Who?" C.J. asked, a knot forming in the pit of her stomach.

"You'll see."

Several minutes later, C.J.'s mouth dropped open in surprise when Grant pulled the car into the parking lot at Sea World San Diego. She turned to him, her eyes shining brightly. "How did you know?"

"That you like the sea critters?"

"Yeah."

"I talked to Dan Fitzpatrick."

C.J. turned fully in the seat to face Grant. "You called my business manager?"

"Actually," Grant said, shifting somewhat uncomfortably in the driver's seat, "yeah." He held up his hands to forestall any comment. "Look, I could see that you were uptight and on edge. I wanted to help, and you don't really seem to have anyone close to you, so I turned to the one person I thought might know what you enjoy doing in your downtime."

"Why didn't you just ask me?"

"You haven't exactly been forthcoming with personal information."

C.J. sighed. Although she hated to admit it, Grant was right. She felt a stab of guilt for shutting him out so completely. After all, they were a team. She relaxed her posture slightly. "I'm sorry about that—old habits." She smiled wryly.

"No problem." Grant gestured outside. "I think we'll be safe from the press here." As an afterthought, he asked, "You do like the sea critters, right?"

C.J. laughed, feeling lighter than she had in days. "I love them. Thanks for bringing me here."

"Okay then," Grant smiled. "Shamu awaits." He looked at his watch apologetically. "We'll only have time for a quick visit, though."

"That's okay. It's more than I expected." C.J. grinned, her eyes lighting up like a child's.

As they approached the front entrance, Grant stopped C.J. with a hand on her arm. "Remember when I told you I had someone I wanted you to meet?"

"Yes."

"You're about to run into him. Before you do, there's something you should know." Grant shifted from foot to foot nervously and licked his lips as a blush covered his cheeks.

C.J. watched him expectantly. She'd never seen him look bashful before.

"He's my partner. I'm gay." The words came out as little more than a whisper.

The wave of relief that rolled through C.J. left her weak in the knees. There would be no unwanted advances—no sexual tension. She smiled.

"Is…is that okay?" Grant asked. "If it's not, now is the time to find out. I just thought…"

"Stop," C.J. said, gently placing her hand on his arm. "Stop, Grant. It's fine. More than fine, really."

"Yeah?" Grant smiled, too. "Mitch is a really cool guy. We've been together since we were kids."

C.J. could tell by the look on Grant's face that he was very much in love. For a brief moment, envy burned hot inside her chest. *Someday. Someday you'll be able to have that, too.*

Grant was motioning to someone in the crowd. "Here he comes. We've never told anyone, but I wanted you to know... I thought it might ease your mind if you understood..." He threw up his hands, exasperated at his inability to say what he meant.

"That was very sweet," C.J. said, leaning up and kissing him on the cheek.

Grant blushed as Mitch reached them, his eyebrow raised in question as C.J. pulled back from the embrace.

"So this is the other woman," Mitch said, a twinkle in his eye.

"Um, Mitch Burke, this is C.J. Winslow. C.J., this is Mitch."

Mitch reached out his hand to shake C.J.'s. His face registered shock when she bypassed his hand and hugged him tightly instead. "I bet this is how you greet all the guys," he managed.

"Only the gay ones," C.J. answered, winking.

Mitch looked at Grant. "This is not the reclusive, sullen woman you described."

C.J. pivoted to face her coach, who visibly shrank back in embarrassment. She opened her mouth to speak, then shut it, shoving her hands in her pockets instead. *That's how people see you, C.J.—it's all you give them.* After they'd walked a short distance, she said, "Sullen, eh? I guess that's fair." They walked several more paces. "Can we just say that I'm a very driven, private person without much time for a social life?"

"Will it make you feel better?" Mitch asked.

"Yes."

"Okay. You're a person with an incredible ability to focus on a single goal."

C.J. laughed and nodded. "I can live with that."

"I'm sorry, C.J., I didn't mean to..."

"It's okay, Grant," C.J. said quietly. "I haven't given you any reason to think anything else." She shrugged, not knowing what else to say.

The uncomfortable silence hung over them like a cloud for several minutes as they navigated their way through the crowd on the way to see the Dolphin Encounter show.

C.J. chewed her lower lip. She knew the awkwardness was her fault. "I love old movies, classic novels, and breakfast is my favorite meal," she said in a rush.

The two men looked at each other, then at C.J. "All righty then. It's a start," Grant said, laughing.

"Favorite movie," Mitch said.

"*Casablanca*," C.J. answered without hesitation. "Here's lookin' at you, schweetheart."

Grant laughed so hard he staggered sideways. "Favorite musical."

"Broadway or movie?"

"Both." The two men answered in unison.

C.J. scrunched her face up in thought. "I saw *Fiddler on the Roof* on Broadway once. It was magical." Her eyes lit up at the memory. "My parents took me as a birthday present."

"Sounds divine," Mitch said.

"In the movies, it would have to be *Grease*. I love the songs, and Olivia..." Embarrassed, C.J. turned bright pink.

"It's okay, honey," Mitch said. "For the longest time, I wanted to *be* Olivia."

Grant and C.J. laughed.

"What?" Mitch asked.

"Just keep moving," Grant said, urging him forward as they climbed the bleachers in the dolphin stadium.

The three of them sat transfixed during the show as several sets of trainers guided six different dolphins through a series of phenomenal stunts.

"Did you see that?" C.J. grabbed Grant's arm as they descended the bleachers after the show ended. "Those dolphins must've been thirty feet in the air."

"Twenty-five, tops," Grant countered.

C.J. glared at him. "We could always ask the trainers. Twenty bucks says it was thirty feet."

"You're on." Turning to his right, Grant said, "Honey, go ask the trainer for us, will you?"

"Me? Why me?" Mitch protested.

"Because you're impartial."

"He's not impartial. He's got to live with you. I'll go ask," C.J. said, rising from her seat.

"How do I know you'll tell the truth?" Grant asked.

"Come with me." She pulled him by the ear.

"Well?" Mitch asked when they met him at the exit.

"He was wrong," C.J. announced proudly.

"So were you, and I was at least closer to the truth," Grant countered.

"What was the answer?" Mitch asked.

"Sixteen feet," C.J. and Grant said together.

"You owe me the twenty because I was closest."

"This isn't golf. We never said 'closest to the pin.' Forget it." C.J. shook her head.

"You're cheating," Grant said.

"Am not."

"Children." Mitch took one of each of their arms. "Nobody wins. There, is that better?"

"Scrooge," C.J. said.

"Spoilsport," Grant chimed in. He checked his watch. "As much as I hate to say this, we've got to get going. You need to get a good night's sleep. Quarterfinals tomorrow."

"Don't remind me," C.J. groaned.

"I've been watching," Mitch said. "You've been playing great."

"Have you been sneaking him in?" C.J. looked at Grant. "I haven't noticed him in the 'friends' box."

"First of all, you're not supposed to be watching the box. Second of all, no, Mitch bought tickets for the week to watch you play."

C.J. looked aghast. "You let him *buy* tickets? Mitch, that's crazy. You're more than welcome in the box."

"Thank you, C.J. You're very sweet. But I didn't want to be the cause of speculation. The paid seats are fine, really."

Grant shrugged. "He did it for years when I was playing. We've never been out."

C.J. squeezed both of their hands. "Your secret is safe with me." She turned to Grant. "Thank you so much for today. I can't remember when I've had so much fun."

"You're welcome, C.J. It was really, really nice to see you smile. You ought to do it more often—it's beautiful."

"I'll work on it. *After* my career is over." She kissed Mitch goodbye as he left them to find his car.

"He's great," C.J. said, as she and Grant walked to his sports coupe.

"Yeah, he's a pretty fantastic guy. I'm lucky."

"You sure are," C.J. said wistfully.

CHAPTER FIVE

C.J. was up 5-3 in the second set and serving for the match. Everything had been going exactly according to the game plan she and Grant had established at practice that morning. She was hammering away at her opponent's forehand, jumping on weak second serves, and taking huge swings from both sides of the ball.

As she handed a towel to the ball boy, C.J. looked up, making eye contact with Mitch, who was sitting in the stands almost directly behind the baseline. He gave her a thumbs-up—she winked at him in return.

Don't lose focus, Ceeg. Still, her skin tingled with the warm glow of budding friendship, a completely foreign, but not unpleasant, sensation. She bounced the ball several times to regain her concentration. *Down the middle*, she decided, starting into her service motion.

The serve caught the tape directly down the center of the court—ace. She kicked the next two serves wide, forcing her opponent to make desperate and unsuccessful stabs at the ball. It was triple match point. C.J. lost the next point on a brilliant service return.

Okay, Ceeg. Time to close this out. How about something unexpected? She arched high into the toss, sending the serve deep into the service box and directly at her opponent's body. Before the ball had even landed, she was streaking toward the net. The service return came at her face, knocking C.J. off balance. She twisted out of the way, barely getting her racquet on the ball. C.J. felt a brief, sharp twinge in her lower back. The ball skidded off the sideline for a winner, giving her the match.

I can't afford to get hurt now. Experimentally, C.J. bent over, as if to tie her shoe. *Not too bad.* She straightened up, shook her opponent's hand, gathered her things, acknowledged the crowd, and headed for the locker room.

"What happened at the end out there?" Grant asked in the tunnel.

"I won?"

"Very funny, C.J. I swear I saw you grimace. Did you get hurt? What is it?"

"It's no big deal. I just felt a little pull in my back on that last shot."

"How does it feel now?"

"Fine. I'm fine, I promise."

"Still, I don't like it. Let's have the physical therapist check you over."

"It's perfectly okay, Grant."

"Humor me. If you're a good girl, Mitch will take us out to dinner."

C.J. let out a long-suffering sigh. "If it will make you happy and it means a free meal, I'll do it."

"I knew you'd see things my way." They stopped at the locker room door. "I'll see you in an hour or so."

C.J. stuck her head into Trystan's temporary office. "Hey."

Trystan, who had been absorbed in a report she was writing, jumped at the sound of C.J.'s voice so close by.

"Sorry, I didn't mean to scare you."

"No problem." Trystan closed the folder, her heart racing. "Something I can do for you?"

"I'm sure it's nothing, but Grant wants you to check my back."

"I see. What is it that Grant thinks is wrong?" An undercurrent of annoyance seeped into her voice, and Trystan hated herself for it.

"Maybe this isn't a good time," C.J. offered, seemingly uncomfortable.

Trystan took a deep, calming breath and stepped out from behind the desk. She consciously softened her tone. "No, now is fine." *Get your head out of your ass, Trys.* "You just finished your match, right?"

"Yes."

"Congratulations. I saw the first set—slam dunk. I imagine the rest of the match was more of the same."

"Pretty much," C.J. said, blushing. "I didn't realize I was being watched."

Trystan laughed. "Only by me and a few million others."

C.J. shuffled her feet. "That didn't come out right."

"I knew what you meant. I was just being a smartass. So what happened?"

"I was serving and volleying—thought I'd finish with a flourish, you know?"

"Nobody likes a showoff," Trystan said jokingly.

"Now you tell me. Where were you when I needed you?"

Trystan's heart stuttered, surprising her. *I was right here, waiting for you.* "Um, come on over here, hop up on the table, and let's have a look." She turned her back to C.J., leading the way into the treatment area—using the time to recover. *You're a professional, Trys, she's a patient, and she likely belongs to Grant.* "Which motion was it that hurt, and what did it feel like?"

"It was on the volley—I had to twist to get out of the way. It felt like a…I don't know…like someone poked me in the back right here." C.J. pointed to a spot barely above her buttocks.

"PSIS," Trystan said, nodding. "Were you still moving forward when you hit the ball?"

"Yes. Is that bad?"

"Hard to say. It depends on the angle. Stand up for a second and put your legs about shoulder-width apart. Yeah, like that." Trystan moved around behind C.J. and reached for the waistband of her shorts. Trystan was mortified to see that her hands were shaking. She wiped them against her thighs. "I need to see what's going on, so I need to pull these down a little, okay? And can you hold your top up a bit?"

"Okay."

Trystan stood directly behind C.J., staring at her lower back, her eyes narrowed in concentration. She stepped in a little closer, breathing in C.J.'s scent. "Is this the spot?" Her fingers prodded gently at an area slightly off-center and to the right.

C.J. flinched.

"I'll take that as a yes," Trystan said. "On a scale of one to ten, how bad is the pain?"

"Not more than a three," C.J. said, looking back at Trystan over her shoulder.

"Head straight forward, please," Trystan said, hesitantly reaching under C.J.'s hair and turning her neck to a neutral position. *Your skin's so soft.* "A normal person's three or a stubborn tennis player's three?"

C.J. laughed. "My three."

"That's a big help. I'm going to poke around a little more. I'll try not to hurt you—too much."

"No pain, no gain, right?"

"Not a popular saying in my line of work, I'm afraid."

"I could see that," C.J. said.

Trystan closed her eyes as she palpated the area around C.J.'s injury with her fingers. "I'm just trying to determine if you're out of alignment." After several moments, she opened her eyes again, readjusted C.J.'s shorts, and backed away. She ignored the tingle in her fingers.

"What do you think?"

"Not too bad." Trystan came around to face C.J. "You're not really out of alignment, but I'd like to do a little work on you to be sure we keep you in good shape. It'll take me about an hour. You're not in a rush, are you?"

C.J. considered. "No, let me just tell Grant I won't be joining him for dinner."

"By all means." Trystan turned away, busying herself with preparations for C.J.'s treatment. When she heard the door close, she rested her forehead against a cabinet, too aware of C.J.'s lingering scent and wondering at the lump in her throat. *Get a grip, Trys. You're a mess. She's just another patient—and it's nothing to you that she's got a boyfriend. Get over it.*

"Hi," C.J. said, breezing back into the room.

Trystan pushed off the cabinet and spread two towels on the treatment table. "Everything okay?"

"Yep. All set."

"I'm going to need you to lie facedown, lift your top up so it's even with your bra, and roll your waistband so it's below the injury."

C.J. complied with Trystan's instructions.

"Do you care if your shorts and underwear get a little wet? I'll try to prevent that, but there are no guarantees. For now it'll just be water."

"No problem."

"First, I'm going to ice the area. Since the injury just happened, I want to reduce any swelling right away. After that, I'll switch to heat, electronic stimulation, and massage."

"That'll be tough to take," C.J. joked.

"Just remember you've got to get through the first course to get to the rest."

"No skipping ahead, huh?"

"Not if you want to prevent further injury."

"Killjoy."

"That's me. Or as some patients refer to me, 'the doyenne of pain.'"

"Now I'm very afraid."

"You should be." Trystan laughed evilly as she tucked a towel into the back of C.J.'s shorts. "Do you like music?"

"Love it."

"Any requests? You're going to be facedown for a while."

"You pick," C.J. said, turning her head to the side to watch as Trystan moved around the room.

"Eyes forward. The idea is to keep your spine in a neutral position."

"Sorry."

Trystan selected some soft jazz. "Feel free to take a nap. I'll be back in about fifteen minutes. If you need me, yell. I'll be in my office. You'd never believe how much paperwork goes along with this job."

"I don't get it, Bec," Trystan said quietly into her cell phone. "C.J.'s straight, but there's something about the way she watches me."

"Back up. What makes you so positive she's straight? That picture in the paper? I told you before—that could've been innocent."

"It's not just that." Trystan fiddled with her pen. "She drove off with him yesterday after I beat the press off her with a stick."

"Okay. Maybe he was taking her back to her hotel."

Trystan felt her stomach drop. "Great."

"Get your mind out of the gutter."

"Just now, when I told her the treatment would take an hour, she had to go cancel a dinner date with him."

"I'll admit," Becca said, "that's a bit more incriminating. Still, you don't have any real hard evidence."

"You're not helping me here," Trystan snapped.

"What do you want to hear, Trys? I thought you didn't care about this woman. Isn't that what you told me yesterday?"

"I asked you why I should care that she was straight, as I recall."

"Trys, what's going on? You can't sleep with her anyway—she's a patient."

"Now whose mind is in the gutter? Nothing's going on. Never mind. I've got to go."

"I think the problem is that you don't want to sleep with her, and that's what scares you. I've never heard you this wound up about a woman in all the years I've known you."

Trystan grunted. "You've got an active imagination, Bec, I'll give you that. I've got a patient to treat. Bye." Trystan hung up the phone and tapped it against her chin. *She's nuts.*

"How do you..." Trystan trailed off when she saw that C.J.'s eyes were closed and she appeared to be asleep. For a moment, she stood there watching her. Strands of silky hair formed a curtain around the lightly tanned face. A dusting of light freckles covered high cheekbones.

As Trystan studied her, C.J.'s face transformed—her eyes began to move rapidly under the lids and her face became tense. She twitched and twisted, as if trying to get away from something. Trystan hurried forward to soothe her.

At the same moment, C.J. screamed, "No!" As Trystan's hands touched her shoulders, C.J. surged up, shoving hard at the restraint.

Trystan, caught off-guard, stumbled backward. Her head and shoulder hit the wall and she bounced off, landing on the floor.

C.J. sat up wild-eyed, breathing heavily and trying to get her bearings. "Oh, my God!" she cried when she realized what she'd done. She scrambled off the table, sending the ice pack flying. "Oh, my God. Are you okay?" Her whole body was shaking as she reached Trystan.

"I'm fine," Trystan said, picking herself up off the floor.

Without thought, C.J. pulled her into a hug. "I'm sorry. I'm so, so sorry." Tears streamed down her face. "I didn't mean..."

"Shh, it's okay." Trystan's head throbbed and her shoulder ached. She knew she'd feel like hell later. But at the moment, she was far more concerned about C.J.

Trystan stroked C.J.'s back, rubbing in soothing circles. "You're shaking."

"I'm just worried I hurt you."

Trystan pulled back, still holding C.J. loosely in the circle of her arms. "You're crying." There was something so vulnerable in those eyes.

"It's nothing." C.J. tried to draw away.

"Wait. I want to know what happened. What were you dreaming about?" Trystan searched C.J.'s face, noting the faint black smudges under her eyes and the haunted look that dwelled within.

"I-I don't know."

Trystan reached out and captured a tear on her fingertip. "You're not a very good liar—and I mean that as a compliment."

C.J. squirmed uncomfortably.

"But I have no right to pry, so I'll let it go."

C.J. smiled weakly. She reached up tentatively and felt the back of Trystan's head. "You've got a bump."

Trystan's scalp tingled from C.J.'s touch. "I've got a hard head. It's fine."

C.J. looked down, as if realizing for the first time that she was standing practically half-naked in another woman's arms. She stepped back, breaking the embrace. "I've got some ice if you need it," she joked, covering her embarrassment.

"Thanks, I'll keep it in mind." Trystan let C.J. go, despite a fervent wish to pull her closer. "Let's see if you did any more damage to the back. Usually, folks don't leave here in worse shape than they arrived." Trystan winked. "It's bad for business."

"I bet." C.J. lay back down on the table. As Trystan worked on her back, C.J. said, "You've got great hands."

"Thanks. I picked them out special."

"You're too funny. Listen, I feel terrible for what happened."

"No need. I'll just remember that you're more dangerous asleep than awake from now on."

"That's a heck of a reputation to live down. Can I buy you dinner?"

Trystan's hands stopped dead and her heart skipped a beat.

"I mean, I want to make it up to you," C.J. said.

"You don't owe me anything." Trystan scowled.

"It's not that. I really want to."

"What will Grant say?" The words were out before Trystan could call them back.

"Why would he care? I'll be ready to play tomorrow," C.J. said, perplexed. "I will, won't I?"

Trystan had no idea what to make of that—it wasn't the response she'd been expecting. C.J. confounded her at every turn. "Your back seems to be fine. What happened was your body's way of warning you. Pay attention—stretch before you go out there and try not to push it."

"Sure, I'll just play half speed in the semis and finals." C.J. laughed.

The sound wrapped around Trystan's heart. "If hypothetically, I let you buy me dinner, where would we go?"

"Well, hypothetically speaking, there's a great Italian restaurant not too far from here."

"Sounds good."

"Was that a hypothetical acceptance?" C.J. asked.

"Actually, that was a real yes," Trystan said, surprised at herself.

They sat at a corner table tucked away in the back of the restaurant. The owner had seated them himself; apparently, he was a big C.J. Winslow fan.

"I'm sorry for the interruptions," C.J. said, blushing as yet another diner asked for her autograph. "I didn't think it would be like this." She put down her dessert fork.

"You're the best female tennis player in the world, and there's a tournament in town—you didn't think people would know who you were? Besides, you're the most beautiful woman in the room. I imagine folks would be ogling you even if they didn't know you were C.J. Winslow."

C.J.'s blush deepened to a bright red glow. She averted her eyes. "I'm sure I don't agree with you on either count."

Trystan watched her carefully. "Please don't tell me you don't know how very attractive you are," she said, captivated by C.J.'s eyes sparkling in the light from the candle on the table. *You'll scare her. Stop now.* Trystan played with her fork, resisting the urge to reach over and take C.J.'s hands in hers.

"I guess I don't see myself that way." C.J. shrugged. Her mouth was dry, and she wasn't sure why looking at Trystan made her heart beat a little faster.

"You said you disagreed on both counts. Do you doubt that you're the best? Don't all players think they're the best?"

C.J. laughed. "In public, that's what they'd have you believe, and you'll never hear me say what I just did in front of the media or anyone else for that matter."

"But you don't really think you're at the top of the game?"

"Not right now." There was a fire in C.J.'s piercing gaze as she leaned forward. "But I will be again—and soon."

Trystan was mesmerized by the transformation. C.J. was no longer vulnerable and unsure of herself. She was a tiger. "I believe you." It was all Trystan could think to say.

"Thanks."

"I saw parts of your last two matches."

"I'm not there yet," C.J. cut in.

"I was going to say, I thought you were fantastic. Strong, fast, and agile. But the thing about your game that has always impressed me most is your ability to anticipate what your opponent is going to do and to outthink her with effortless ease."

"I don't know about the effortless part—but thank you. That's awfully nice of you to say. I didn't realize you were watching."

"I'm allowed out of my cage every now and again." Trystan winked.

"I'm glad. Will you be there tomorrow?" C.J. didn't know why, but suddenly, the answer seemed critically important.

"Unless some emergency comes up, wild horses couldn't keep me away."

"Good. Speaking of wild horses, do you mind if I ask where you're from? I thought I heard someone say you were Native American." All the blood rushed to C.J.'s brain as the reality of what she'd said hit her. "Oh, my God." She covered her mouth in horror. "That came out all wrong. I'm sorry. I-I didn't mean that to be offensive. God, I'm an insensitive moron."

Trystan couldn't help herself this time—she reached across the table and placed her hands over C.J.'s. "Stop. Please, stop beating yourself up. It was an obvious segue. I know you didn't mean anything by it." *And I'd do anything to make that frown go away.*

Trystan hurried on, intent on helping C.J. get past her embarrassment. "Where I come from, there are still a few wild mustangs in the canyon. They're beautiful—such noble creatures and so powerful. I used to just sit and watch them for hours."

"I wish I could see them."

"If you really mean that and you have the time at some point, I could take you there," Trystan offered, holding her breath. *Please, say yes.*

C.J.'s face lit up with child-like glee. "I'd love that. Just where is 'there,' anyway?"

"Oh, I'm sorry. I thought I'd said. Chinle, Arizona."

"I have a house in Sedona," C.J. said. "I can't believe I've never been up that way."

"Well, it is considerably north and east of Sedona. I don't imagine you have much time for sightseeing when you're home."

"Perhaps we could rectify that," C.J. said, meeting Trystan's gaze shyly.

"Count on it."

"Is your family from Chinle?" C.J. asked.

Trystan shifted uncomfortably in her chair. She was unused to talking about herself. "I'm an only child. My mother raised me on the reservation by herself. I never knew who my father was—she never said."

"Is that hard for you—not knowing who your dad is?"

"Not really, but if I at least knew his nationality, it would answer some questions."

"What do you mean?"

"My mother is Navajo, but I don't look like any Navajo I've ever seen, including her."

"You're striking," C.J. said.

"Thank you." Trystan's heart tripped in her chest.

"What's your mom like? If she raised you by herself, she must be a very strong woman."

Trystan smiled. "Growing up, she was my best friend, although she could be plenty tough when she wanted to be. She's a medical doctor, but she's also a healer—in our culture, that means she's got great power and standing."

C.J. was fascinated. "Is that why you went into medicine yourself? Why you became a physical therapist?"

Trystan played with a napkin ring and stared at her water glass. It had been a long time since she'd shared this much of herself with anyone. "Actually, I became a physician's assistant first, but there wasn't much call for many of those. I went back to the reservation for a little while to find myself."

"When was that?"

"1989. I didn't stay long." *It hurt too much.* Trystan willed her hands not to shake. "I decided going back to school would be the best thing for me, so, um, I left again and got my bachelor's and master's degrees in PT."

It was obvious to C.J. that Trystan was anxious. It was almost as if she was on the verge of fleeing. "Wow. That sounds like a lot of hard work and discipline," C.J. said, searching for something neutral to say.

"I suppose it was. I've been working ever since—I did some practical rotations with college and semi-pro teams. You know how it goes—a connection here, a connection there. And here I am." Trystan visibly relaxed as the conversation shifted away from her and toward her career.

"Are you enjoying working with the WTF?"

"In general, I am," Trystan said. "The traveling is murder, and I'm not even playing. I don't know how you guys do this all year round."

C.J. shrugged. "It's all I've known for most of my life. You get used to it." C.J. seemed surprised when she looked around the restaurant to find that they were among the last patrons in the place. She picked up the bill.

"No, let me get that." Trystan gestured to the check.

"Absolutely not. As I recall, I'm the one who asked you to dinner."

"In that case, we'll have to do it again, and I'll buy."

"It's a date."

C.J.'s smile lit up the room, and Trystan found herself smiling in return. A date. She liked the sound of that.

CHAPTER SIX

C.J. was going through her pre-match stretches. She was whistling tunelessly to herself—something she never did. As she visualized the match, running through scenarios and strategies, her mind wandered briefly to Trystan. *Careful, Ceeg, you might have made your third friend in two days. What will people think?* She chuckled, trying to remember the last time her heart had felt so light.

"Ms. Winslow? It's time."

C.J. thanked the tournament steward who had been sent to accompany her to the court, collected her tennis bag, and headed for the stadium. When she arrived in the tunnel, Monica Duschene was already there. Monica, ranked number two in the world, was one of three players standing between C.J. and the number one ranking.

At 6'2", Monica had the wingspan of a 747, with enough speed and agility to make it next to impossible to get the ball by her. She was also twelve years younger than C.J.

Monica had won their last three meetings and led the overall series six matches to two. C.J. was well aware that most commentators and newspaper reporters had picked Monica to beat her again this day. *Like hell.* Aware of the eyes upon her, C.J. turned to acknowledge her opponent, unsurprised to see a smug sneer on her face. *Arrogant punk.*

They walked onto the court together, C.J. waving to the cheering crowd, Monica with her eyes fixed on a point directly in front of her.

During the warm-ups, C.J. focused on taking fluid, easy swings, trying to loosen up her back. She was grateful that so far she wasn't feeling any residual soreness or stiffness. *Thank you, Trystan.* As the thought crossed her mind, she looked up in the stands, trying to spot her.

"Two minutes," the chair umpire intoned.

C.J. dragged her eyes from the stands, surprised at the stab of disappointment at not being able to find Trystan. She accepted the balls from the ball girl and began practicing serves—half speed at first, then with increasing velocity as her shoulder loosened.

"Time."

C.J. served one last ball and returned to her seat at the sideline. *Stick to the game plan, and the match will be yours.* She could hear Grant's voice in her head. She smiled. *I'm going to kick her ass.*

C.J. won the toss and elected to serve first. In less than the time it had taken Monica to saunter from her chair to the baseline, the score was 30-love. A stinging backhand return and a lucky stab evened the score. Up 40-30 after an easy put-away volley, C.J. went into her service motion. With the toss hanging in mid-air, she heard a lone fan yell, "You're the best, C.J."

The toss fell to the court untouched—C.J. seemingly frozen in mid-motion.

"You can do it, C.J., you're the best. Someday, you're going to be number one in the world."

A wave of nausea washed over C.J. For a brief second, panic rose as she thought she might vomit on the court. She dropped the racquet to her side as the ball rolled away. She looked up, half expecting to see him standing there, even as her adult mind knew that was ridiculous.

"Quiet, please," the umpire warned.

Legs trembling, C.J. turned to accept another ball from the ball girl. *Deep breath—he can't hurt you anymore. One serve at a time.* She bounced the ball several times. *Focus on the here and now.* Despite knowing she was completely safe, C.J. felt the familiar fear. A cold sweat trickled down her back. She squared her shoulders. The toss was too far left, the serve some six inches long. *C'mon, Ceeg. He's not here. You're fine.* The second toss was too far behind her, but C.J. adjusted by arching back. She managed to place a weak spin serve deep in the corner. Monica, expecting something with more pace, sailed her return long. Game to C.J.

When she reached the sideline for the changeover, C.J. stood over the chair and buried her face in a towel. *Pull yourself together. You don't have to serve again right now. Win this next game and you'll be up a break.*

Trystan watched C.J.'s movements and facial expressions from her vantage point in the tunnel—something was wrong. She clenched her fists, chafing at having to stand idly by when she wanted to help. The problem didn't appear to be physical—C.J. wasn't favoring her back or anything else.

Trystan pushed forward to the edge of the tunnel until she was standing less than ten feet away when C.J. passed by on her way to the near baseline. Trystan could see that her face was pale and drawn.

Trystan willed C.J. to look up—nearly calling out to her. The only thing that kept her from doing so was not wanting to disrupt C.J.'s concentration.

C.J. bounced on the balls of her feet, shifting from side to side, working at loosening up muscles gone tight with fear. She exhaled forcefully. *This is your game. Just get this one.*

Monica's serve was hard and at C.J.'s body. C.J. hit a defensive backhand that barely made it beyond the service line. Monica, already at the net, slammed the ball deep into the forehand corner.

It's only the first point—her first serve is inconsistent. Stay aggressive—wait for a second serve and go for it. C.J. paced at the baseline in the ad court, waiting for Monica to serve. Monica's torturously slow play was one of the things C.J. resented most—it was a deliberate tactic designed to wreak havoc on an opponent's concentration. *Stay within the game plan.*

C.J. breathed a sigh of relief when Monica netted her first serve at 15-love. C.J. took the second serve on the rise and belted it directly at Monica, causing her to hit the ball off the frame. The ball flew high in the air, just clearing C.J.'s side of the net. C.J. knocked it away for an easy winner. The crowd cheered wildly.

An ace made the score 30-15. Two more service winners and Monica had evened the match at 1-all.

As C.J. watched the balls being sent down to her end of the court, she felt the fear return. She cocked her head from side to side, trying to relieve the tension knot at the base of her neck. If she wasn't careful, it would soon morph into a horrific headache. *One point at a time. Nothing to it, Ceeg.* She closed her eyes momentarily, visualizing her first serve.

When she opened them and looked for the ball boy, she noticed Trystan standing just inside the tunnel. She smiled broadly, despite her inner turmoil. When Trystan returned the smile with a thumbs-up, the ball of anxiety in C.J.'s stomach eased slightly.

This time, she didn't hesitate—she launched into her serve—a bullet that caught the back of the service line and nearly hit Monica in the gut. She risked a peek at Trystan and saw her grinning from ear-to-ear. C.J. winked.

Fueled by Trystan's tacit support, C.J. reeled off three of the next four points for a two-games-to-one lead. *That's two holds, Ceeg. You can win a set with that—it just takes one break. This is your game.*

C.J. took less than the allotted time, which left her pacing at her end once again as Monica used every second available to her. C.J. took advantage of the opportunity to glance around. She had no trouble locating Mitch, having pinpointed his seat location the day before. Grant was sitting in his customary "I couldn't care less" pose in the "friends" box, and Trystan was in the tunnel, though out of sight from her present vantage point. All in all, the day was looking up.

Monica's first serve pulled C.J. wide to her forehand side. She punched it back, forcing Monica to run to her left. With two strides remaining before she could reach the ball, Monica launched into a slide. As she made contact, her left knee hyperextended, and she fell to the court with a shriek of pain.

Trystan was out of the tunnel and at Monica's side within seconds. "Relax. Shh, relax and stay still."

Monica was writhing on the court. "Oh, my God. It's killing me."

"I promise you it won't." Trystan hoped a little humor might help calm Monica down. "Let me see. That's it—lie back and let me have a look." Trystan evaluated the injury with a critical eye, noting the almost-instant swelling. "I need to test it, to see what's going on. You tell me when it hurts."

C.J., who had come around the net and stood watching, said, "What can I do?"

"Hold her shoulders so she doesn't move too much," Trystan answered, giving C.J. a tight smile.

"Got it." C.J. squatted down and put a hand on either of Monica's shoulders.

Trystan placed her right hand on Monica's calf and her left hand just above the knee joint. When Trystan rotated the lower leg inward, Monica's reaction was a yelp.

"Where does that hurt—on the outside of the knee?"

"Yes. Oh, damn, yes," Monica cried.

Trystan looked up at the approaching paramedic. "Lateral collateral. Could be just a sprain, but you probably should transport her for x-rays and a possible MRI."

C.J. squeezed Monica's shoulders sympathetically.

The umpire, who had come down from her chair, leaned over Monica. "Do you wish to continue?"

Monica fixed her with a murderous glare. "I can't," she said, through gritted teeth.

"Very well then." The umpire returned to the chair and announced to the crowd, "Match to Ms. Winslow, 2-1, retired."

Trystan helped the paramedic immobilize Monica's leg as a gurney was wheeled over.

"You'll be good as new in no time," C.J. told Monica.

"You're lucky—I'd have wiped the court with you."

The venomous words clearly caught C.J. off-guard. Her hands trembled—she removed them from Monica's shoulders.

"You ought to learn some manners, little girl," Trystan growled. "I don't care how badly hurt you are. C.J. didn't have to come over here to help."

"She shouldn't have—I wouldn't have if it had been her."

"That's the difference between you and her—class," Trystan hissed, nodding at the ambulance attendants to take her away. "You could stand to learn a lesson or two from her."

Turning to C.J. after Monica had been wheeled away, Trystan asked, "Are you okay?"

The knot in C.J.'s stomach eased. Trystan had stood up for her. For a brief second, someone had protected her. "You shouldn't have said anything. You could get in trouble."

Trystan jammed her hands in her pockets. "I don't care—she's an arrogant little pissant and there are a lot more things I would've said to her if you hadn't been standing here."

C.J. laughed, pushing away the last vestiges of Monica's outburst and feeling her good humor return. "That means you owe me for saving your bacon. I'll put it on your tab."

"You do that. Everything all right? You looked a little out of sorts in that first game."

C.J. felt pinpricks of anxiety claw at her throat. *It must've been obvious to everybody.* "I'm fine," C.J. cut her off. "I've got to get my stuff." *Oh, my God. Everybody knows.*

"C.J…" Trystan could only stare after her as C.J. hurried away. "What's that about?" Trystan asked herself, wondering if she'd ever get the answer.

C.J. stood rooted to the spot. Her hair was still damp from the shower and her eyes brimmed with unshed tears. The commentators for the USA Network were scrambling to fill airtime as a result of the brevity of the match.

"There's no way C.J. wins that match if Monica doesn't get hurt," Nancy Davidson said. "I'm sorry. I like C.J. personally, I think she's been great for the game, but I think Monica sweeps the court with her if she stays healthy."

"Jonas Svennsen, you're C.J.'s former coach, what do you think?"

"I'm not sure, James. C.J. is a great champion—she's very smart and crafty. I think we'll never know who would've won. I noticed something odd in that first game that I've never seen before, though, and I think if the match had continued, it might have been a problem for C.J."

"What was that?"

"It was something in her service motion—something was not quite right. I think it's safe to say that C.J. is no longer the unbeatable player she used to be."

Jonas saw it, Trystan saw it. Everybody saw it.

Trystan, who had walked into the players' lounge seconds earlier, saw the telecast, heard the words, and watched as C.J. covered her face with her hands and cried. Trystan closed her eyes momentarily at the rawness of C.J.'s pain.

Trystan stepped forward as if to go to her. *She ran from you less than twenty minutes ago—leave it alone.* She turned in the opposite direction, to head toward her office, but stopped after only a few steps and looked back over her shoulder. *She needs a friend.*

Sighing heavily and bracing for rejection, Trystan approached C.J. from behind and put a supportive hand on her shoulder. "He's wrong, you know," she said softly in C.J.'s ear.

C.J. stiffened, relaxing only minutely when she realized it was Trystan. "About what?"

"You can beat anyone out there."

"I wish I was as sure as you," C.J. said quietly, not turning around.

"You're smarter, more determined, and you've got game. You just have to believe it."

"You make it sound so simple—but it's not."

"You make it look so simple—but I know it can't be," Trystan countered.

"Jonas knows my game better than anyone, and he doesn't think I can do it."

"First of all, he didn't say that. Second, he doesn't know your game—or your heart—better than you do. Where's that determined woman I saw in the restaurant last night? Trust yourself, C.J."

"You're so kind," C.J. said, finally turning to face Trystan, whose hand still rested on her shoulder. "So very gentle. I've done nothing to deserve that from you."

"You're under a lot of pressure—I understand. I want to be your friend, if you'll let me."

C.J. said nothing, but wordlessly stepped closer to Trystan and enveloped her in a hug. "I could use a friend like you," she murmured.

Trystan closed her eyes and savored the feel of C.J. in her arms, even if it was only a friendly hug. She inhaled deeply, memorizing C.J.'s scent. "I'll be here if you need me."

"Okay," C.J. said, pulling back and wiping her eyes. "I've got to get going. Because the match was so short, Grant's going to put me through a long practice."

"Make sure you stretch first," Trystan called as C.J. headed for the door.

"Amá? I need some advice," Trystan began.

"Is that what it takes to get my only child to call her mother?" Terri Lightfoot asked.

"I'm sorry. I know I've been scarce, but we've been on the road so much…"

"You know you don't owe me any explanations, Acheehen. How can I help you?"

Trystan sighed, wondering where to begin. "There's a woman—I've come to care about her very much."

"I see," Terri said.

"It's not like that," Trystan snapped.

"Like what, my child? I merely said, 'I see.'"

"You were reading something into it."

There was a momentary silence on the line.

"I'm sorry, Amá, I shouldn't have snapped at you. It's just…"

"You're feeling things you haven't felt in a very long time, and your heart is fighting your head."

Trystan exhaled forcefully. "How is it you always know what's going on with me even when I don't?"

"First, you're my child, my blood. That is the strongest bond. Second, unlike you, I use my gifts. As a healer, I must. Now what is it that has you struggling so?" Terri asked.

"Her name is C.J. Winslow—she's one of the greatest tennis players to ever play the game."

"I've seen her play."

"You have?" Trystan asked, nonplussed.

"Yes, Acheehen. I take an interest in my daughter's life. If she's working with professional tennis players, then I shall watch tennis so that I might hold an intelligent conversation about her work."

"Have I told you lately how much I love you?"

"A mother never tires of hearing it."

"She's—special. I can't explain it, but there's something about her that's different from anyone else I've ever met."

"Different, how?"

"She's strong—so very strong, and yet there's something fragile about her—a vulnerability."

"You want to know why you feel that—if there's something specific behind it."

"Yes."

"Have you tried to focus on the energy?"

"Every time I ask her about it, she shuts down and practically runs away. She won't talk about it."

"You didn't answer my question. Have you tried to focus on the energy—not on her words, but on her energy?"

"What?"

"Trystan, if you want to understand what she's not telling you, you need to use your gift. You have as much intuitive and empathic power as I do."

"I'm not a healer, Amá," Trystan said quietly.

"You're my daughter, and you have a spirituality that guides you when you let it. What's in her eyes?"

"Something hidden."

"Something that needs healing," Terri said.

"Yes—that's exactly how it feels. I've seen glimpses of it, but I can't identify it."

"You're frustrated."

"I want to help her, but she won't let me in."

"Patience is a virtue. Whatever it is that's inside her, she may not be ready to face it yet herself."

"What if she never is?" Trystan asked, a note of desperation creeping into her voice.

"Tell me how it's been manifesting itself."

"I was treating her for a minor back injury yesterday. She fell asleep on the treatment table and was obviously having a nightmare. When I asked her about it, she said she didn't remember what she was dreaming."

"But you think she knew."

"I know she did."

"Okay, what else?"

"Today, during her match, something happened. I don't know what it was, but it scared her. She wasn't the same player afterward. Again, when I questioned her about it, she cut me off and ran away."

"I see," Terri said.

"What does that mean—'I see?'"

"I'm no psychologist, but it sounds to me like whatever is bothering her is getting closer to the surface. The episodes you describe indicate that she's having trouble blocking this thing from her consciousness."

"And?"

"And I don't think you need to worry about her never being ready—I'm guessing her mind is very near to laying her issue bare, whatever it is."

"What should I do?"

"You obviously care about C.J. a great deal. Be there when she needs you—let her know she's safe with you, no matter what. Don't push her—let her come to you."

"You're saying I should be on standby."

"Essentially, yes."

Trystan blew out an impatient breath. "Is that all I can do?"

"It's all you can do if you don't want to scare her away. Her actions are telling you she needs time, Acheehen. She's not rejecting your friendship, is she?"

"No, she doesn't seem to be."

"Then be patient. I think you'll be rewarded in the end."

"And in the meantime, I just have to sit around and watch her suffer."

"She is suffering, yes, but she is also healing."

"Easy for you to say."

"Yes, it is. Acheehen? She's lucky to have you in her life."

"Thanks, Amá. I promise to talk to you again soon."

"That's good—I'm not getting any younger, you know."

"You'll always be young to me."

"You know what they say—youth is wasted on the young."

"Goodbye, Amá. I love you."

"I love you, too, Acheehen."

"That's it—strong finish on that swing. Pretend it's Monica's face."

"Grant, you're bad," Mitch said from where he sat on the nearby bleachers.

"I'm just trying to bring out C.J.'s killer instinct."

"You're just being catty," Mitch rejoined.

"Whatever. Okay, let's switch over to the three drill—backhand, followed by forehand, followed by swinging volley. Got it?"

"Got it, boss." C.J. returned to the baseline for the start of the drill. They'd been at it for more than an hour. She was feeling loose and relaxed—drilling was her favorite part of the game. There was no pressure, no overthinking—just technique, power, and skill.

The first ball came screaming over the net and C.J. ripped a backhand down the line. She barely had a chance to get back to the ready position before the next ball came hurtling toward her. She whacked a forehand crosscourt, moving into the net as soon as the ball left her strings. Before she had time to think, the next ball was careening at her body with frightening speed. Instinct drove her to twist out of the way, blocking the ball with her racquet.

Blind agony drove C.J. to the ground. A white-hot searing pain shot through her lower back, radiating up and down her spine. From someplace far away, she heard a scream, then realized it was her own voice.

Grant vaulted the net, dropping his racquet. He cradled C.J.'s head. "What is it? C.J.? What happened?"

C.J. tried to speak, but the words wouldn't come.

"Lie still," Grant instructed, panic causing his voice to shake. He looked up at Mitch, who was running onto the court.

C.J. closed her eyes for a second, then opened them. Through a haze of pain, she saw Grant and Mitch, their faces pale with worry, leaning over her. "Get Trystan," she managed to choke out through gritted teeth.

"Who?" Mitch asked, looking from C.J. to Grant and back to C.J.

"Trystan," C.J. ground out again.

"The physical therapist," Grant said, name recognition finally dawning. "Good thinking. Mitch, she's probably in the area of the women's locker room. There's a treatment facility inside."

"I can't go in the women's locker room."

"Knock on the door, for heaven's sake. Almost everybody's gone for the day anyway. Hurry!" Grant's hands were shaking. "You're going to be all right, C.J. I promise you. Hang in there. Mitch is getting help."

C.J. swallowed hard. It hurt even to breathe. She closed her eyes tightly, her heart hammering in her chest. *Hurry, Trystan, please. It hurts so much.*

Trystan was tidying the papers on her desk when there was an urgent pounding on the door to the locker room. It was late afternoon, and almost everyone had left the complex. She frowned, unsure whether she should answer it.

When the knock sounded again, accompanied by cries for help, she ran to the door and threw it open.

"Are you Trystan?"

"Yes. Who are you?"

"My name is Mitch Burke." He doubled over, wheezing and holding his stomach. "Grant Roberts sent me."

Trystan's heart stopped. "What is it?"

He gasped for breath. There was panic in his eyes.

"Is it C.J.?"

Mitch nodded. "She… She's in so much pain."

Without another word, Trystan sprinted out the door. Belatedly, she called over her shoulder, "Where is she?"

"Practice court number one," Mitch yelled, trying to get his legs moving again to follow. "Please, hurry."

Trystan barely heard him as she streaked across the complex toward the practice courts. *Please, God, let her be okay. Just let her be okay.*

CHAPTER SEVEN

As the practice courts came into sight, Trystan's heart leapt out of her chest. Grant was kneeling over C.J.'s supine body, his head bent close to her ear.

"What happened?" Trystan asked as she skidded to a halt next to C.J.

"It's all my fault," Grant said, his voice still shaking. "We were drilling, and I hit a shot too close to her body. She twisted to get out of the way and…"

"Back," C.J. said, looking up at Trystan, a plea in her eyes.

With a start, Trystan realized she had no defense against this woman. The door she had shut tightly so many years before flew open. She put her hand over her chest. Helplessly, she stood by as her heart opened to let C.J. all the way inside. She fought the urge to gather C.J. in her arms. *Focus on the injury, Trys—that's how you can help her.* "Same spot as before?"

C.J. nodded shortly. "Yes, only a million times worse."

"What did it feel like?"

"A sort of pop, then pure agony."

"On a scale of one to ten, ten being the most painful, how does it feel now?" Trystan asked, squatting down next to C.J., unable to resist patting her thigh reassuringly.

"Nine and a half."

Trystan struggled to remain dispassionate. "Okay. We need to get you back to the locker room so I can evaluate you properly." She looked to Grant and Mitch, who had arrived back on the scene. "I'm going to need help getting her there."

"What do you need?" Grant asked, tension marring his handsome features.

"For starters, I need one of you to get behind C.J. and lift her like this." Trystan turned Mitch around, wrapped her arms around him from behind and pulled from underneath his armpits.

"Is it safe?" Mitch asked.

"You won't injure her further, if that's what you're asking. C.J.?" Trystan put a hand gently on her shoulder. "We'll do this as carefully as we can, okay? Just hang in there and let yourself go limp. You don't have to help except to get your feet under you."

Grant moved behind C.J.

"Make sure you bend your knees, Grant. I don't want to have to treat you, too," Trystan warned. She moved in front of C.J. to help stabilize her hips. "Ready?"

Grant nodded.

"One, two, three."

Grant lifted and Trystan used her hands to help take the pressure off C.J.'s back.

C.J. yelped but managed to get her feet under her.

Trystan squeezed C.J.'s hip comfortingly. "Easy, just stand there for a second," Trystan said. "Grant, get under her right elbow. Mitch, you want to take the other one?"

"Right."

"Catch your breath, C.J. That was the hardest part." Trystan winked.

"Easy for you to say," C.J. smiled tightly.

Nothing is easy about watching you in pain. "Okay, guys, let's take it nice and slow."

With Grant and Mitch supporting her weight and Trystan walking alongside, C.J. made her way back to the locker room. Every step was jarring, and she felt like she might throw up.

"Guess I'm not going dancing tonight, huh?"

"Signs point to no," Trystan said, laughing.

"And it was so high on my list of activities."

After a brief silence, Grant asked, "Will she be able to play tomorrow?"

It was a question that had been hanging in the air from the moment C.J. had gone down on the court.

"It's too early to tell," Trystan said. "I need to get a look at her back and find out what's going on. Even then, we may have to wait and see. Once I've evaluated the situation, we can talk about all that. Right now I think we should focus on C.J.'s health and reducing the pain, don't you?"

"Of course," Grant said.

They paused awkwardly at the locker room door.

"I'll take it from here, guys," Trystan said.

"I'll call you later," C.J. told Grant as she walked gingerly through the doorway.

"No, we'll wait out here," Grant answered.

"I'm going to need to get a good look at your lower back," Trystan said as she guided C.J. toward the treatment table. Emotions long dormant swirled thick and deep inside her, and she took a breath to steady herself. *I can't care this much about you. I can't. I won't.* But her pulse betrayed her, quickening at the mere idea of being alone with C.J., regardless of the circumstances.

"I don't know if I can get my shirt over my head," C.J. said, pain blurring her vision.

"I'll help you. Can you hold your arms away from your sides a little?"

With effort, C.J. lifted her arms so that they were slightly out and away from her body. The resulting pain was so sharp it brought tears to her eyes.

"I'm sorry, baby," Trystan murmured, the term of endearment slipping out of its own accord. "I'll be as gentle as I can." *And as professional as I would be with anyone else.* She worked quickly, grabbing the hem of the T-shirt and pulling it up so that it cleared first her left arm, then C.J.'s head, and finally her right arm. "Okay, you can put your arms down now."

C.J. stood trembling in her sports bra and gym shorts.

Trystan kept her eyes level with C.J.'s, careful not to stare at the lithe, athletic, mostly naked body just inches in front of her. "I'm guessing the pain just went off the charts, eh?"

"Yeah," C.J. said shortly, her breath coming in shallow pants.

"I'm going to make it better, C.J., I promise you." Trystan held C.J.'s gaze, trying to keep her expression neutral.

"I know you will. I trust you," C.J. said, losing herself in intense brown eyes that shone bright with concern and caring.

"I'm going to have to lower your shorts so I can get a good look at your PSIS, okay?"

"Okay. Do you need me to take them off?"

"No," Trystan said a little too quickly. She walked behind C.J., put her fingers underneath the waistband of her shorts and panties, and inched them down until they were midway down her buttocks. She stood back, staring at C.J.'s lower back and narrowing her focus to the injured area. "Your right side is elevated."

"What does that mean?"

"The PSIS is the joint that connects the sacrum to the iliac crests—the bones that form your pelvis. Your right PSIS is out of alignment—that's what's causing the shooting pains."

"Can you fix it?"

"Eventually, yes."

"Not in time for tomorrow?" C.J. asked, disappointment coloring her tone.

"I'll do everything I can to try to get you out on that court, C.J., but I can't make any guarantees." *I'd give anything to give you what you want.*

"I'm sorry, I know you'll do your best. It's just that…"

"I know. One step at a time, okay?"

"Deal."

"Because it just happened, there's a chance we can do a muscle energy and pop it back in place right away. We'll try that first." Trystan guided C.J. onto the treatment table so that she was on her back with her knees bent. Trystan placed her hand just above C.J.'s right knee. "I want you to push gently up against my hand now."

"What will that do?" C.J. asked.

"In theory, it will make your muscle contract and hopefully pull your PSIS back into alignment."

"And in practice?"

"I don't know if it will work—your back is very inflamed at the moment. We may have to wait for tomorrow." Trystan watched as C.J. hesitantly flexed upward to create pressure. The look of intense concentration, combined with obvious pain, nearly left Trystan undone. She looked away, afraid her emotions were too apparent.

After several minutes of pushing, C.J. shook her head. "I don't think it worked."

Again Trystan resisted the urge to take C.J. in her arms. "Let's ice it and take another look." She helped C.J. lift up enough to slide an ice bag wrapped in a towel against her lower back, just above her butt. "I'd tell you to take a nap, but that could be hazardous to my health."

C.J. blushed. "I'm sorry about that."

"I'm just joking, really."

"Be honest with me, Trystan. What are my chances of playing tomorrow?"

"Honestly, I don't know. After we're done icing you, we'll get you dressed, and you, Grant, and I can discuss it together."

"It sucks to get old," C.J. mumbled.

"You're not old. It has much more to do with body position and weight distribution at the point of contact than it does with age." This time, Trystan allowed her eyes to roam over C.J.'s body. "You're in great shape. Believe me, I've been looking at bodies all week, and yours is by far the best I've seen." *Smooth, Trys. Very smooth. Quit while you're behind.*

"Good to know I pass the comparison test," C.J. said, smiling.

"I'm sorry. I didn't mean that the way it came out." *I always seem to be tongue-tied around you.*

"You're fine, Trystan. I understood what you meant. It's like studying thoroughbred horses—which one is built best for the race distance."

"Please note—the comparison to four-legged behemoths was yours, not mine." Humor allowed Trystan to regain her equilibrium.

"So noted."

"I don't suppose you have a button-down shirt in your bag, do you?" Trystan asked.

"Nothing but T-shirts and tank tops. Why?"

"I don't want you to have to struggle with getting a shirt over your head. You and I might be close to the same shirt size. Let me see if I've got something handy."

"If not, I've got a zippered warm-up jacket."

Trystan returned carrying C.J.'s bag several minutes later. "I'm afraid a warm-up will have to do for now." In stages, she helped C.J. to a sitting, and finally a standing, position. "Let's have another look at you," she said, removing the ice pack.

As she had before, Trystan stood back and evaluated. "Does it feel any better?"

"Not much."

"I'm not surprised, you're still elevated on the right." She helped C.J. into the warm-up jacket and readjusted her shorts and panties. "Ready?"

"I guess."

"I'll support your weight, let me do most of the work." Trystan positioned herself on C.J.'s right side and secured her elbow and forearm.

Grant and Mitch were waiting outside when C.J. and Trystan exited the locker room.

"How do you feel?" Grant asked C.J. before the door had even closed behind her.

"Ready to run a marathon."

"Very funny." He looked at Trystan. "How is she?"

"Her right PSIS is out of alignment, which is causing her significant discomfort. At the moment, it's too inflamed to do much with—tomorrow will be a better barometer."

"There's no way she can play tomorrow in this condition," Mitch said.

Grant glared at him. "What do you think, C.J.?"

"I don't want to pull out. I need this championship."

"Trystan?" Grant asked.

"I think it's too early to make any determination. A good night's rest combined with a full treatment in the morning will tell us more. What time is the match?"

"1:00 p.m."

"That'll give us some time in the morning to work on it. How close to match time can you forfeit?"

"Any time, really," Grant answered.

"If I do decide not to play, I want to give the tournament officials enough time to come up with a plan B for the fans," C.J. said.

Grant looked as though he might object, but he kept his mouth closed.

Trystan focused her attention on C.J. "What's your timeframe then?"

"11:00 a.m."

"Okay. You'll need to be in the treatment room at 8:30."

"I'll be there."

"If you do play tomorrow, you won't be able to practice ahead of time. I don't want to take a chance on you aggravating it before the match."

C.J. looked at Grant.

"Okay. No practice," he agreed. "Whatever Trystan says goes."

"You shouldn't stay alone tonight. It's going to be a tough night for you," Trystan said.

"You can stay with us, C.J." The words were out of Mitch's mouth before he realized their impact.

Grant blushed scarlet.

Trystan kept her face neutral. *They're partners.* Suddenly, Mitch's presence made sense; she felt her mood lighten.

"I don't want to trouble you, Mitch, but thank you for the offer," C.J. said.

"Why don't I stay with you, C.J.?" Trystan asked, her heart hammering in her chest. "That way, if you run into problems, I can be there to help and keep an eye on you."

"I'm sure you have better things to do than baby-sit me."

"I'm happy to assist you, I'm professionally trained, and I want to give you every chance to be well enough to play tomorrow. You really shouldn't be alone tonight—you're going to need help." *I won't sleep knowing you're in pain and I'm not there.*

"When you put it that way, it's hard to say no."

"That's settled then."

"What time should we meet tomorrow?" Grant asked.

"We won't know anything until I'm done treating her," Trystan said. "That'll take about two hours. So we should be able to make a determination by 10:30 a.m."

"We'll meet then," Grant said. "Take care of yourself tonight, C.J."

"I'm in good hands," she answered, winking at Trystan.

Trystan smiled in return. *Yes, you are.*

Trystan busied herself putting together an ice pack in the mini-kitchen of C.J.'s hotel suite. The familiar activity helped to settle her nerves. At the moment, C.J. was lying flat on one of the beds with her knees bent.

"What do you usually take for pain?" Trystan called.

"Ibuprofen," C.J's voice floated to her from the other room.

"Do you have some here?"

"In my toilet kit."

"Good," Trystan said, as she approached the bed. "You've got choices. I can either prop you up with pillows right now and put the pack on your back or you can stay flat as you are for a few more seconds and I'll slide it under you. What's your pleasure?"

"Neither." C.J. attempted a smile.

"That wasn't an option."

"I know. I can't imagine changing positions, so I guess I'll go for option B for as long as I can get it."

"Let me get a towel to put under you."

"I feel awful that you have to wait on me like this," C.J. said to Trystan's retreating back.

"Don't—I wouldn't have offered if I didn't want to be here. Honest," Trystan said, returning with a towel, a glass of water, and a bottle of ibuprofen. *The thought of my empty hotel room was unbearable.*

"I know you don't want to hear this, but now you've got to sit up. I'm going to put the towel under you on the bed and the ice pack inside your shorts so it'll stay put. Plus, you need to take these." Trystan held out her hand with four pills in it.

"I think I hate you."

"Yeah, but in a really good way, right?"

"Right." C.J. rose up on her elbows. "Agh!"

"Hey, wait a minute. What the hell…" Trystan wrapped her arms around C.J.'s torso, relieving the pressure on her back. "You were supposed to wait for help."

"Now you tell me."

"Easy. Swing your legs over the side of the bed. That's it." While C.J. took the pills, Trystan slipped behind her and spread a towel out over the bottom sheet. "As long as you're sitting up, let's do as many things as we can. I don't suppose you have a button-down pajama top?"

C.J. blushed. "Ah, I usually don't, um…wear anything to sleep in."

"Oh," Trystan said, surprised that she could get out any intelligible sound. *I so didn't need that visual right now.* "Um, I've got one you can wear. I'll swap you for a T-shirt."

"Deal."

Trystan fished in her bag, coming out with a powder-blue satin pajama top. "I think this'll fit you. If you stay still this time, I'll do all the work. Okay?"

"Okay." C.J. sat ramrod straight on the edge of the bed as Trystan straddled her legs.

Trystan ignored the pounding of her pulse and the pooling of moisture between her legs as she brought shaking fingers to C.J.'s zipper. As the warm-up jacket cleared perfectly proportioned shoulders, Trystan concentrated on steadying her breathing. "Is this okay? I'm not hurting you?"

"No, you're very gentle," C.J. said, an unfamiliar flush staining her cheeks.

"I'm assuming you want the bra off?"

"Yes, please." C.J.'s voice was little more than a whisper.

"Can I?"

"Yes."

Trystan ran her fingers under the bottom edge of the sports bra. "I need you to bend your left elbow and hold it out a little...Good." Trystan noted the flicker of pain cross otherwise faultless features. "I'm sorry. I'll get this over with just as quickly as I can."

"I'm okay. Don't worry."

Trystan slid the bra up over C.J.'s breasts, careful to keep her eyes on C.J.'s face. She peered down only for a second to ease C.J.'s arm through the arm hole. *Oh, my. You're glorious.* "Okay, almost there." *You're a professional, Trys, and she's a patient. Period. Act like it.*

"Now keep your arm just like that." Trystan worked the satin top over C.J.'s right arm, around her back, and helped her left arm through. Normally sure fingers fumbled with the buttons as Trystan tried to avert her eyes from erect nipples as they strained against the satin. "That wasn't too awful, was it?"

"No," C.J. answered, her voice huskier than normal.

The timbre of C.J.'s voice sent a chill down Trystan's spine. She swallowed hard. "Let's get you lying back down," Trystan said, wrapping an arm around C.J.'s waist and sliding the other arm under her knees. Carefully, she lowered C.J. back to the mattress, positioning her over the towel.

C.J. winced. "Tell me the truth," she said, meeting Trystan's gaze. "Is there really a chance I'll be able to play tomorrow?"

"There's always a chance, C.J. Is the match that critical to you?"

"Yes. With Monica out, I can move up in the rankings with a win tomorrow against Randi. Every tournament victory helps me solidify a better seed for the Open. A better seed means the potential for a better draw."

"Okay. You know I'll do everything in my power to help you compete."

"I know you will."

Trystan decided to give voice to a question that had been niggling at her for hours. "By the way, how did Mitch know to come get me?"

"I sent him. You were the first person I thought of when I went down," C.J. said matter-of-factly.

"Oh." Trystan didn't know what to say to that.

"I won't do more damage if I play tomorrow, will I?"

"More damage? No, probably not. But you might prolong the time it takes for you to recover fully."

"I understand," C.J. said, her lips pursed in a determined line.

Trystan reached underneath C.J. and positioned the ice pack inside the waistband of her shorts.

"Damn, that's cold."

"It's ice—it's supposed to be cold."

"Very funny."

"Are you hungry? We're a little late for dinner, but I don't want you to go to bed on an empty stomach—it's bad enough I let you take the ibuprofen that way."

"Actually, I'm still a little nauseated."

"Okay," Trystan said. "In that case, let's just ice you for half an hour and put you to bed."

"What are you going to do?" C.J. asked.

Trystan caught another glimmer of vulnerability in C.J.'s eyes, then it was gone. "I'll be right here with you," she said softly, indicating the second double bed. "Nice of you to have a spot ready for me."

C.J. visibly relaxed. "A girl never knows when a sleepover might break out."

"Too true," Trystan answered. "T-shirt?"

"Bottom drawer."

"Which shirt? There are about twenty in here." Trystan called as she looked through the stacks of neatly folded shirts.

"Pick one you like." C.J. yawned, her eyelids starting to close.

Trystan selected the shirt that read: "Anything worth doing is worth doing well."

"How about this one?" she asked, turning around. C.J. was already asleep.

It was dark and the wind was whistling through giant maple and oak trees. The parking lot was deserted, save for piles of dead leaves. The olive-green Impala loomed like a living being, beckoning to her. The passenger door swung wide and the opening yawned before her like a black hole. A disembodied face, distorted, laughed at her. An arm appeared out of nowhere and shoved her inside...

"No! No! I won't...you can't. No!"

C.J. shot bolt upright—a silent scream on her lips. Pain ripped through her. She wasn't sure if it was the stab in her back or the nightmare that had her gasping for air. Sweat rolled down her back and between her breasts, and she clutched at the drenched sheets.

"C.J.?" A voice, rough with sleep, came out of the darkness. "Are you okay?"

She couldn't answer—no words would come. The terror lingered.

"Hey? Can I sit here?"

The voice was closer—gentle, kind. She knew that voice. *It's Trystan; it's not him—you're safe.* She nodded, before realizing that Trystan couldn't see her. "Yes," C.J. choked out. She felt the bed give a little and a warm hand take her own.

"You're safe here, C.J. Nothing can hurt you, I promise."

Without understanding why, the kind words unlocked something deep inside C.J. A small piece of her stoic reserve cracked. She leaned forward into the comforting touch, not caring about the agony the motion caused. Hot tears flowed down her face and onto the pajama top.

Strong arms wrapped around her, slowly lowering her body back to the mattress—C.J. didn't resist. Tender fingers stroked the matted hair from her forehead and she closed her eyes. A steady, compassionate heart beat against her ear. She felt her pulse slow and her eyelids droop and she surrendered to sleep once more.

CHAPTER EIGHT

Trystan knew she should probably go back to her own bed or go running. Instead, she continued to stroke C.J.'s hair as she slept. She wondered who was more comforted by the motion—she or C.J. Helplessness, cold and foreign, made her muscles contract. *I can't shield you from harm if you won't let me in.*

She looked tenderly at the woman lying in her arms. Her eyes adjusted to the darkness, and she could see the smooth contours of C.J.'s face finally relaxed in sleep. *I want to protect you like this for the rest of your life.* Her head buzzed slightly as she took in the significance of the moment.

Holy mother.

For the first time in what seemed like forever, Trystan didn't want to run. Nothing could have surprised or terrified her more. She decided to focus on something else.

Her mother had said to intuit what C.J. wasn't saying. Butterflies fluttered in Trystan's stomach. It had been a long time since she'd used her ability to tune into another person's energy. Trystan closed her eyes and breathed deeply, concentrating on the moment when C.J. had fallen into her arms, broken and scared. There was something child-like about the vulnerability—as if she had no defense against whatever haunted her.

Trystan heard again the words C.J. uttered just before awakening—strained, terrified. Trystan's heart constricted. *She's frightened to death.* She tightened her arms around C.J.'s shoulders.

She had looked into C.J.'s eyes. Even in the darkness, she had seen shame and humiliation. Anger burned hot beneath Trystan's skin. *I can't just stand idly by—I need to do something. Damn it all to hell.*

Her mother was right, Trystan knew—whatever was troubling C.J. had a great deal of power—to confront her about it would only scare her more. Waiting for C.J. to come to her was the only way. She settled back against the pillows and closed her eyes, attempting to rest. *I'll go running in a little while.*

Trystan lay very still, savoring the moment. C.J. was tucked securely in her embrace and sleeping soundly. Because she could, Trystan ran her fingers once more through the silky copper strands. She loved the way the hair was splayed over her arm and chest—as if it belonged there.

C.J. looked like an angel to her, soft and serene. Trystan closed her eyes, memorizing the scents, the sound of C.J.'s even breathing, the feel of her body. *I could stay like this forever.*

C.J. felt so cozy and safe, she wondered if she was still dreaming. Her back throbbed painfully, but she had an overall feeling of contentedness she couldn't ever remember feeling before. As her mind came increasingly awake, she determined the source of the warmth. *I'm lying here in Trystan's arms.* An unfamiliar heat burned in the pit of her stomach and spread throughout her body. *Oh, my God. I'm lying here in Trystan's arms.* The reason for her position—the nightmare and its aftermath came screaming back at her, and her face turned red with shame. Her eyes popped open.

"Good morning. I didn't mean to wake you." Trystan smiled down at C.J.

"You didn't," C.J. said, forcing herself not to bolt.

"How're you feeling this morning?"

C.J. wasn't sure how to take the question. She wondered if Trystan had left it intentionally open-ended. She decided to stay on comfortable ground. "Sore. My back is throbbing."

C.J. wouldn't meet her eyes, and her body was vibrating with tension. "Okay, well. Let's ice it again before you try to get up. You can watch some morning TV while I shower."

C.J. considered how easily Trystan was handling the situation—as if nothing out of the ordinary had happened. *She's being gracious. You kept her up half the night and made her sleep with you. You should tell her.* The very thought made her feel a little woozy.

"I need to go over the tapes," C.J. blurted.

If Trystan noticed how uncomfortable C.J. was, she ignored it. "What tapes?"

"Randi's last two matches. I need to study them."

Trystan disentangled herself and walked over to the large entertainment center across from the bed. "Well, there's a VCR here. How are we going to get the tapes?"

"I've got them—they're in my bag."

Trystan retrieved C.J.'s bag, found the tapes, and popped one into the VCR. "Let me get you squared away and you can study to your heart's content."

Several minutes later, Trystan was back with a fresh ice pack, which she placed behind C.J. after propping her up on some pillows and handing her the television remote.

"If you need anything, yell."

C.J. looked up and smiled. "You've been great—thanks. I think I've got everything I need."

When Trystan had departed for the shower, C.J. hit the play button. She watched as Randi Pace systematically demolished her opponent. She tried to focus on weaknesses in strategy or strokes, but her mind kept wandering back to Trystan.

Trystan must think I'm crazy. C.J. knew what the dream was—it was always that awful, dreadful night. Although she tried to block it out of her memory, it kept coming back. C.J. closed her eyes and rubbed her temples.

She heard the familiar voice. *"If you tell, no one will believe you. Everyone will think you're crazy."*

"No," C.J. said out loud. "You can't think about that now. You've got to focus. This match is all that matters."

"Everything okay?" Trystan asked, towel-drying her hair as she walked back into the room. "Were you calling me?"

"No," C.J. fumbled. "Just talking to myself. You know, pre-match pep talk and all that."

"Okay. How's it going?" Trystan asked, pointing to the TV screen.

"The woman has virtually no weaknesses. But here, watch this…" C.J. paused the tape and beckoned to Trystan to join her. "See how she tips off her forehand?" She started the tape again. "Right there." She pointed. "Do you see how you could tell she was going to go down the line with it?"

"No," Trystan said, laughing.

"Look again." C.J. rewound the tape. "Watch. See how she steps across more with her left foot? Now look at a crosscourt forehand." C.J. fast-forwarded to another segment. "See the difference? Here her stance is more open. She doesn't step the same way."

"You're going to be able to see that on the court?"

"Now that I know it's there, I will."

"Wow. That's amazing."

"Not really. I'm sure she's analyzing me the same way. God knows there's plenty for her to find."

"Hey, you've been playing great." Trystan squeezed her shoulder. "Listen, we've got to get you up and moving. Are you ready?"

"And if I'm not?"

"We've still got to get you up."

"Glad to know I had a choice in the matter."

"Tough to play a match from your hotel room."

"You've got a point." C.J. started to move, then stopped as a searing pain lanced through her torso. She fought to catch her breath.

"Don't." Trystan was instantly by her side. "C.J., you're not just going to be able to get up and start moving at full speed. We've got a lot of work to do before you'll feel like you can even put one foot in front of the other. I've got you, don't push yourself."

"If I can't even get out of bed by myself, how in the world am I going to beat Randi?" Tears formed on C.J.'s lashes.

"Shh. It's way too early to worry about that." Trystan smiled down at her. "I haven't worked my magic yet."

"That better be some powerful magic."

"The most powerful there is." Trystan winked. "First things first. Let's get you standing."

After several minutes and much effort, C.J. was standing in front of the bathroom mirror. She could see the dark smudges under her eyes. She knew Trystan had seen them, too. *You have to say* something. *It's not like you can pretend last night didn't happen.* Her stomach flipped. "I'm not ready," she mumbled. "Everybody has nightmares. It doesn't have to mean anything."

"You need help in there?" Trystan called from the other room.

"No, I'm okay. Thanks." C.J. brushed her teeth.

Trystan appeared behind C.J. in the mirror, startling her. "I'm sorry. I just wanted to tell you not to bother with the shower right now. It's going to be very painful for you, and I'm going to be putting you in a whirlpool, anyway. Why don't you wait and take one after the treatment when we see where you are?"

"Okay, that makes sense."

"I ordered breakfast. Bacon and eggs, some oatmeal, a fruit plate, and some toast. I didn't know what your routine or food intake was before a match." Trystan blushed.

"I'd say you covered the bases quite nicely. Thanks again for taking such good care of me." *She's something else.*

"I'm happy to help you, C.J. That's what friends are for, right?"

C.J. met soft brown eyes in the mirror. "Yeah, they are. I haven't had much practice, I have to admit—having friends, I mean."

"You live in a tough world. Most of the people around you want to be you or to eat you for breakfast. I imagine it's hard to find genuine friends."

"That's true. I'm glad I met you, Trystan."

"Me too. Hurry up, your breakfast is getting cold."

By 8:30 a.m., C.J. was semi-reclining on the treatment table.

"If you go out there, you're going to want to keep as much weight off your right leg as possible," Trystan said, as she prepared a moist heat treatment for C.J.

"Oh?"

"Every time you step or put weight on that right leg, you're going to feel it in the injured area. Unfortunately, there isn't really any way around it." Trystan sighed. "Just do the best you can." Trystan placed the heating pad behind C.J.'s back.

"Mmm, that feels great," C.J. said, as the heat penetrated her aching joints.

"Let me know if that gets too hot for you."

Trystan bustled around the treatment area, giving C.J. some downtime. C.J. hadn't mentioned anything about the night before, yet at times Trystan could've sworn she'd wanted to. *Don't push her, let her come to you. If you push her, she'll disappear.*

"Trystan?" C.J. called.

"Yes? Are you okay? Too hot?"

"No, it's fine. I-I'm glad you stayed with me last night. You were a big help. Thank you."

Trystan watched C.J.'s eyes look everywhere but at her. "You need to stop thanking me. A girl's liable to get a swelled head." Trystan touched C.J. on the arm. "You would've done the same for me, right?"

"Of course."

"So you see, it's like I said before—that's what friends do—they help each other when they're in trouble."

"I swear to God, if you start breaking out into a Beatles tune…"

Trystan laughed. "You obviously have never heard me sing. It rates somewhere between a wounded duck and a pregnant cow."

"You make it sound so appealing," C.J. said.

"There's a reason they never wanted me joining the chantways on the reservation. Are you ready for phase two?"

"I was enjoying the heat."

"I bet you were. How do you feel about massage?"

"Oh, now you're talking."

Trystan guided C.J. over onto her stomach and placed a pillow underneath her hips, noting C.J.'s grimace of pain. She spent a moment spellbound, just staring at the muscular back. *Get a grip, Trys. You're a professional. Act like it.* Trystan recognized that the words were quickly becoming a refrain where C.J. was concerned. She occupied herself by heating the lotion for the massage.

"You really do have wonderful hands," C.J. mumbled.

"So you've said before."

"Must be the truth then. Careful, you're going to spoil me."

You should be spoiled. And loved. And protected. "Yeah, next thing I know, you'll be in here every day looking for a massage." Trystan continued to work for several minutes in silence. "Am I hurting you?"

"No, it really does feel great."

"That's because I haven't gotten to your lower back yet."

"It felt good when you gave me a massage the other day."

"That's because the PSIS wasn't out of alignment. Today's a different story, believe me."

"Torture to follow?"

"Afraid so." Trystan moved her hands lower, to the junction of back and buttocks. Her hands trembled slightly and she felt her pulse quicken, despite her best efforts to remain detached.

"Argh. I was liking it better a few seconds ago. Let me guess—this is where the torture comes in."

"Very perceptive."

"Hmm. I think you secretly enjoy inflicting pain."

"As I recall, I warned you about that the other day."

"Yes, you did. I didn't believe it then, but I'm starting to see an evil streak in you now."

"Ah, my darkest secrets revealed. There goes my reputation."

"This will make me better, right?"

"If it doesn't kill you, it'll make you stronger," Trystan said.

"Well, the jury's out on the killing issue."

"Almost done with this part—hang in there."

"I can't wait to see what's next."

"Trust me, you won't like it."

"Great. What, you're going to hang me upside down and stretch my spine?"

"Oh, there's an idea I hadn't considered."

"Me and my big mouth."

"Actually, I'm going to do a joint mobilization on you."

"A what?"

"I'm going to try to pop your PSIS back into place, at least temporarily."

"I thought you tried that yesterday."

"I did, but you were very inflamed then. I'm hoping we can at least move it a little today to ease the discomfort, if only for a few hours."

"Long enough to get me through the match."

"Exactly."

"What happens after that?"

"How about if we worry about one thing at a time, hmm? Okay, are you ready?"

"Will I ever be?"

"Probably not. This is going to hurt, C.J. There's no way around it, so I'll apologize in advance." Trystan placed her hands on the center of C.J.'s sacrum and pushed gently. She heard C.J.'s stifled cry, and her heart bled. "Almost done."

"Wow," C.J. said several seconds later. "That feels much better."

"It does?"

"Yes. How did you do that?"

"You're not just saying that to get me to stop, are you?"

"No."

"Good. Congratulations."

"For what?"

"You get to skip the next two steps."

"Lucky me. What were they, or don't I want to know?"

"You don't want to know."

"So what's next?"

"Ultrasound, then whirlpool."

"That doesn't sound so bad."

"No, I'm done torturing you—for now."

"I'm not sure I like the way that sounds."

By the time C.J. lowered herself into the whirlpool, she was feeling much more relaxed. Her back ached, but the sharp, shooting, debilitating pain was gone.

Trystan had retreated to her office to finish up the week's reports, promising to come back and check on C.J. in twenty minutes.

C.J. thought about Trystan—she'd been fantastic—professional, attentive, and kind. *I'll have to find a way to thank her properly.* A warm sense of well-being washed over her as she contemplated their budding friendship. She was just about to drift off when she heard the locker room door open on the other side of the wall.

"I really appreciate your staying behind to hit with me."

C.J. recognized Randi's voice.

"Are you kidding? I figured if I was here at the end of the week when it's quieter, I might get a shot at that hot new physical therapist."

It sounded to C.J. like the second voice belonged to Margaret Wycross, who'd been knocked out of the tournament in the quarterfinals.

"What's her name? It starts with a 'T,' doesn't it?" C.J. heard Randi ask.

"Trystan. Even her name is hot."

"You've got it bad, Maggie. What makes you think she plays for our team?"

"You know Sherinda Nathan?"

"The sprinter?"

"Yeah. She's a friend of mine. Says she and the lovely Miss Trystan enjoyed a little afternoon delight just before the ESPYs."

C.J.'s nostrils flared.

"Even if that's true, what makes you think you'd stand a chance with her?"

"Sherinda says it's common knowledge that Trystan gets around."

C.J.'s hands balled into fists and a muscle in her jaw bunched. *Liar!*

"Did Sherinda say if she was any good?"

C.J. nearly rose out of the whirlpool in her indignation.

"Said she was fabulous, but really cold, you know? Like impersonal."

"And you want a piece of that, why? Sounds like she's a waste of time."

"It's a challenge—to see if I can melt the icicle."

"You're sick, Mag, you know that?"

"Yeah, what of it?"

"Let me know if she's any good."

C.J. focused on controlling her breathing. As the voices faded away, she tried to relax again. The idea that Randi and Maggie could cavalierly gossip about Trystan and sully her reputation made C.J. furious. They were spreading malicious untruths; Trystan was as fine a person as C.J. had ever met—honorable and professional.

"You're wondering if what they said was true."

C.J. jumped as she looked around to see Trystan leaning against the doorjamb.

"I didn't…I wasn't…I'm not wondering any such thing."

"It's okay, C.J."

"It's not okay. They're spreading vicious lies and innuendo about you."

"Not really," Trystan said, her voice betraying a weary acceptance of the facts. "I probably was all those things."

"I don't believe it." C.J. searched Trystan's eyes, looking for a hint of denial or fire. What she saw there, remarkably, might have been regret.

"I'm grateful for your faith in me—honestly, I am—but you should save that for someone who's earned it. You can get out of the whirlpool now. Come see me when you're done showering."

C.J. watched Trystan walk away, her shoulders slumped, head bent low.

Trystan sat in her office chair, her head in her hands. She had never questioned the choices she'd made—the way she'd lived her life—until C.J. had walked into her world. When she'd stood in the doorway and seen the look of confusion and outrage on C.J.'s face, for the first time she could remember, Trystan was ashamed of herself.

I can't take back who I've been. I can't pretend they weren't telling the truth because they were. Maybe that's all I'll ever be.

"Trystan?" C.J. asked uncertainly.

Trystan glanced up to see C.J. standing on the threshold to her office, her hair still damp from the shower. Trystan thought she looked like an angel. *What must you think of me now, C.J.?* She felt a lump form in her throat as regret threatened to choke her. "All set? How does your back feel?"

"Much better, thank you."

"Let's go see Grant."

There was an uncomfortable silence as they exited the locker room. Grant was pacing outside.

"How do you feel? You look like you're walking much better."

"Trystan's a miracle worker. I'm not ready to scale Mount Everest, but I feel a thousand times better than I did a few hours ago."

"Are you up to playing?" Grant asked.

"Yes."

They both looked to Trystan.

"Can she play without injuring herself further? Should she?" Grant asked.

"What I was able to do was to pop her PSIS back into alignment. I can't guarantee it'll stay there, but it might. I don't think she's in danger of doing any permanent damage if she plays, other than popping it back out. The choice whether to play or not belongs to you two."

"Is there anything specifically she can do to avoid popping it back out?"

"No." Trystan turned her attention to C.J. "Play your game and try to forget about it. If you're guarding—trying to protect the injury—it'll only increase the chances of your hurting something else."

"Okay."

"I want you back here a half hour before match time—I want to put more heat on it to loosen it up before you go out there. Otherwise, no practicing and just some light stretching."

"Okay." C.J. looked like she wanted to say something more but changed her mind.

"I'll see you in an hour and a half." Trystan turned on her heel and retreated inside.

C.J. had her headphones on and her eyes shut. The moist heat felt like a soothing balm on her back. Trystan had barely spoken to her when she returned for the pre-match treatment. Worse still, she wouldn't look C.J. in the eye.

Focus on the match, Ceeg. Focus on Randi. C.J. visualized the court, the ball, her racquet, and her opponent. She recalled what she'd seen on the videotape and pictured how she wanted to set up points.

"Are you sleeping?" Trystan asked, standing several feet from the treatment table.

"No, I'm awake." C.J. opened her eyes. "Just running through the match in my head."

"It's almost time."

"Okay. Trystan?" C.J. asked, as Trystan reached behind her to remove the heated pads.

"Yes?"

Trystan still wasn't looking at her, so C.J. laid a hand on her arm. "Will you be out there today? Will you be watching?" C.J. knew the vulnerability she felt must be obvious in her eyes, but she didn't care. She suddenly realized just how important it was to her to have Trystan by her side.

Trystan seemed momentarily stunned. "It-it's my job to be there in case you need me, C.J."

"No," C.J. said, still holding on to Trystan. "Will you be there as my friend?" C.J. felt Trystan try to draw away but held on tight. "I want you there."

Trystan hesitated a long time before answering. "I'll be there for you, C.J."

"In that case, I can't lose," C.J. said, giving Trystan's arm one last squeeze before letting go. She winked. "Show time."

CHAPTER NINE

C.J. glanced back one last time as she exited the tunnel. As promised, Trystan was standing in the background. C.J. thought she looked sad and profoundly uncomfortable. She smiled at her before making her way onto the court and sitting in her chair.

Randi sat in the chair on the opposite sideline lacing her sneaker. C.J. watched her as she scanned the crowd, her eyes stopping when she spied Trystan, who was moving forward to the edge of the tunnel. A sly smile crossed her lips.

C.J. narrowed her eyes. She rose abruptly and headed to the baseline to warm up. It was all she could do to rein in her temper. *You.* She smacked a forehand. *Will.* She hit another. *Not.* She ripped a backhand. *Touch.* She sent an overhead screaming in Randi's general direction. *Trystan.*

When C.J. sat down again before the start of the match, her nostrils were still flaring and she was breathing fire. She barely gave her back a thought as she accepted the balls to start serving. The first set was a blur. The crowd was stunned and so was Randi.

"I'm just getting started," C.J. mumbled as she walked to the baseline to start the second set. Every time C.J. felt her anger waning, she had only to look across the net at Randi and remember the way she'd looked at Trystan.

At the changeover, with the score 3-2, C.J. glanced into the tunnel and saw Maggie standing by Trystan's side. Her heart dropped like a stone and an unexpected wave of nausea washed over her. *Keep your head in the match. Trystan's not going anywhere, with anybody.* She rose from her chair and walked determinedly to the opposite baseline. *First things first.* She readied herself to receive Randi's serve. Despite her best efforts to block it out, C.J. couldn't erase the vision of Maggie standing so close to Trystan.

She failed to return Randi's first two serves and netted the third serve for Love-40. Angry with herself for her lapse in concentration, C.J. vowed to attack the next serve. She shifted back and forth, bouncing on the balls of her feet. When the serve came wide to her forehand, she slid several steps to her left to get it, sending the ball deep to Randi's backhand. Without waiting to see where the shot landed, C.J. rushed the net intent on attacking. Randi's next shot forced her to reach wide. She extended her racquet as far as she was able, barely catching the ball on her strings, and depositing it neatly just over the net for a winner.

The roar of the crowd was lost on C.J. as she dropped to the court in agony, her own scream drowning out the cheers. For a brief moment, the world around her went silent. She blinked hard and could have sworn she glimpsed Trystan running in her direction. She closed her eyes tightly against the pain.

Gentle hands caressed her shoulders and a familiar voice crooned in her ear, "Stay still. Don't move. I've got you."

Trystan felt a cry rise up in her throat as she stood by helplessly watching C.J. stretch wide. Instinctively, she knew that the motion would cause great pain. She was halfway out of the tunnel before C.J. hit the ground.

Trystan kept her hands on C.J.'s shoulders for an extra beat, pausing to gain her professional equilibrium. Her heart wanted simply to cradle C.J. and to take the pain away. She looked up briefly at the "friends" box and saw Grant on his feet. It helped to ground her and remind her of what she was there to do. Leaning close to C.J.'s ear, she whispered, "It's out again, isn't it?"

C.J. simply gasped, the look in her eyes bespeaking her pain more eloquently than any words.

Trystan repeated, "I've got you. Focus on me." Briefly, her grip turned into a caress.

C.J. whispered hoarsely, "Help me."

Trystan felt tears prick her lashes. "I will—I promise."

The chair umpire leaned over C.J.'s other side. "Ms. Winslow, will you be able to continue?"

Trystan shot the umpire a withering glare. "I haven't finished my evaluation yet. Please give us a few moments."

"Of course," the umpire replied, flustered. She backed away, leaving Trystan and C.J. alone.

C.J. looked at Trystan, myriad emotions swirling in her eyes. "Can I?" she whispered. "Can I finish the match?"

"Let me try a few things and we'll know better," Trystan answered, her voice conveying more certitude than she felt. Gently, she rolled C.J. onto her stomach, placing several towels underneath her hips. As she'd done that morning in the treatment room, Trystan placed her hands gently on C.J.'s sacrum, trying to pop her PSIS back into place without success.

Trystan waited several moments and tried the joint mobilization a second time.

Leaning over, she whispered in C.J.'s ear, "Any change?"

"Not much," C.J. said grimly.

"Don't worry," Trystan said, "I haven't run out of tricks yet." She winked at C.J. and rolled her carefully onto her back. "You remember how to do the muscle energy?" Trystan asked her, bending C.J.'s knees so that her feet were flat on the court. "Push up against my hand," Trystan said, placing her hand just above C.J.'s right knee. "Gently—not too hard, not too fast." C.J. did as she was told, pressing her leg against Trystan's hand.

"Any relief yet?" Trystan asked.

"Only a little," C.J. answered, capturing Trystan's gaze. "I want to finish this match," she said bravely. "Can I do it?"

Oh, baby, it's going to hurt so much. Trystan forced herself to smile. "Better keep it to two sets," she joked, earning a small smile from C.J.

"I'll see what I can do."

Trystan left her hand on C.J.'s leg for a few seconds longer than she should have, well aware that there were millions of eyes watching. She bent low again next to C.J.'s ear, "You can do this, C.J. You can take her."

C.J., her mind clouded by the pain, managed to say, "Stay away from Maggie, she's not good enough for you." She laughed briefly at the shocked expression on Trystan's face, and the two of them shared a fleeting smile.

"What are you, my mother?"

"Hardly," C.J. answered, her heart obviously feeling lighter than it had seconds earlier. She stifled a cry as Trystan helped her get up.

Trystan squeezed her hand. "You can get through this. Just a little longer, then I promise we'll make it better."

As C.J. stood, the chair umpire approached, an expectant look on her face.

"I'm going to play," C.J. said, squaring her shoulders. With one last look at Trystan, she took her racquet and returned to the baseline.

"Ms. Winslow has elected to continue," the umpire announced, once she had returned to her chair. The crowd, which had been eerily quiet, erupted into cheers.

C.J. acknowledged them with a half-wave. She thought she saw Randi send a disgusted look in her coach's direction, and it strengthened her resolve even more. *You can do this, Ceeg. Let's make it short and sweet.*

Randi wasted no time testing C.J. She moved her side to side mercilessly, trying to take advantage of the weakness.

Her back screaming, C.J. refused to cede any point. Repeatedly, she brought Randi into the net where she knew Randi felt least comfortable. The strategy paid off—Randi committed several unforced errors, allowing C.J. to take the game.

When it was her turn to serve, C.J. tossed the ball experimentally in the air, testing the amount of discomfort the movement would cause. White hot lances of pain shot through her lower back, down her legs, and up her spine as she mimicked her service motion. "This ought to be fun," she mumbled to herself. Taking a deep breath and holding her back ramrod straight, she stepped to the baseline and prepared to serve in earnest.

Cutting back on her motion, C.J. spun a weak serve into Randi's body, forcing her to fight the ball off and allowing C.J. to put away an easy forehand. "That's it, Ceeg. Use your head. You're smarter than she is. Use what you know."

A high-kicking serve at 15-love pulled Randi out of the court and forced a weak return. As a result, C.J. was able to knock away a crosscourt winner. C.J. noted the look of utter frustration on Randi's face, which prompted her to smile inwardly. Two more strategic points and she was up 5-2.

As C.J. returned to the sideline, she looked to Trystan in the tunnel, a question in her eyes. She pointed to the chair. Trystan shook her head no. C.J. nodded, instead standing next to the chair and toweling off. She sent Trystan a silent thank you.

When the break ended, C.J. walked to the far baseline. "5-2, Ceeg. Break her one more time and you won't have to serve again." She knew she couldn't get away with the same tricks she had used her previous service game. "You're going to have to put the game away here and now, Ceeg."

Randi seemed intent on exploiting C.J.'s injury. On successive points, she hit the ball low and short, then long and wide. In each instance, C.J. felt as if arrows were being shot through her legs and back. Still, she persevered, despite losing both points.

At 30-love, C.J. looked first to the tunnel, where she was comforted by Trystan's reassuring presence, then to the stands, where Grant was leaning forward in his chair. It was as if they were willing her to succeed. She readied for Randi's next serve, determined to prove them right. Although the serve was one that C.J. normally would have returned with her forehand, she adjusted, moving around the ball to take it with her backhand. She slashed it crosscourt. The move was so unexpected that Randi had no defense for it. 30-15.

C.J. gritted her teeth, walking slowly toward the ad court. "Three more," she told herself. "Just three more points." After Randi missed the first serve, C.J. took three steps into the court, challenging Randi to overpower her. As she anticipated, Randi went for a big serve—it was too much. The double fault evened the score.

C.J. continued her monologue as she prepared for the next point. "You know it'll be down the middle, Ceeg. It's the serve she always goes for when she's uptight or in trouble." C.J. waited until Randi was mid-motion, then slid two steps to her left, allowing her to hit a service return winner. Match point.

"Make her beat you, Ceeg. Put the burden on her." C.J. rocked from side to side, feinting first left, then right, doing her best to intimidate Randi. The first serve missed the sideline by six inches.

"Okay, Ceeg. This is it, one more serve. Make her bring what she's got." C.J. moved in several steps, waited until the ball was tossed, then shifted back and to her right, toward the center of the court. It left her in perfect position to rip a backhand down the line, which she did. Game, set, and match.

C.J. had nothing left to give. Emotionally exhausted, physically destroyed, she simply dropped her racquet and stood there trying to absorb the moment. Eventually, and with great difficulty, she made her way to the net for the traditional handshake. The crowd rose to its feet as one, saluting her with a standing ovation. She had never felt such adulation, not even at Wimbledon.

C.J. tried to acknowledge them, raising her hand in a weak gesture of thanks. Even that small effort sent shockwaves of pain through her torso. She gasped and swayed slightly, surprised to find Trystan and Grant by her side to catch her. Together, one at each elbow, they led her off the court. A tournament official came running toward them.

"Where are you going? There's a trophy presentation."

Trystan's growl was practically audible. C.J. was the one who stopped short, saying softly, "I need to do this. I owe it to the fans—it's expected."

A protest died on Trystan's lips when she saw the warning look in C.J.'s eyes. By silent agreement, Trystan and Grant helped C.J. shift directions until she was standing in the center of the court where the podium had been hastily erected. Trystan took one look at the stairs and said to the nearest official, "She can't do that."

Hearing the finality in her tone, he scurried off to make new arrangements. C.J. shooed Trystan and Grant away and stood patiently awaiting the ceremony.

Nancy Davidson, the USA Network commentator, appeared at C.J.'s side. She leaned toward C.J. "Great match. This'll be live in the stadium, as well as on television. I'll keep it short, I promise."

"Okay," C.J. answered. She wanted to call Nancy to task for her less-than-flattering remarks on air but refrained, keeping a smile on her face.

Into the microphone, Nancy said, "How about that, folks, was that not the most courageous performance you've seen?" The crowd roared its approval. "C.J., tell us what was going through your mind during the last half of that second set."

"Randi is tough on a good day. I was just hoping to be able to stay in the match and compete."

"Well, I'd say she did a little bit more than that, didn't she, folks?" The crowd went wild a second time. "How bad is your injury and do you think you'll be able to play next week?"

"Back injuries, as you know, can be difficult. We'll evaluate this one and make appropriate decisions. Fortunately, I have next week off and I'm sure that will help."

"The U.S. Open is looming large on the schedule. How do you feel about your chances?"

"I don't know, Nancy, I think it's too early to tell. That's nearly a month away—so much can happen between now and then. But I promise you that I'll be there to compete."

"C.J. Winslow, ladies and gentlemen." Again, the crowd whistled and stomped.

The trophy and check presentation was mercifully brief. C.J. thanked the fans, the tournament officials, the sponsors, Grant, and, spontaneously, Trystan, for giving her the ability to finish the match. When it was over, Grant and Trystan assisted C.J. off the court.

"Let's get her into the treatment room," Trystan said.

They moved toward the locker room door, where Grant hesitated.

"I don't care who's in there," Trystan said, understanding his reticence. "C.J's not walking in there on her own, and I need some help."

Without saying a word, Grant pulled open the door and walked inside with both women, C.J. leaning heavily on his arm.

When they reached the treatment area, Trystan thanked and dismissed Grant.

He seemed reluctant to leave. He looked first at C.J. whose features were marred by pain, then at Trystan. "Is she going to be okay?"

"Eventually," Trystan said. "The fact that she has next week off is a huge bonus because she would have had to take it off anyway. I'll treat her now, but she's going to need continuous physical therapy over the next few weeks, wherever she's going. She certainly won't be able to practice this week. Her back has got to be rested. After that, you can re-evaluate the situation and make decisions about the next few tournaments."

"We're running up to the U.S. Open," Grant said. "We've got to get her out there."

Sparks flared in Trystan's eyes. "We've got to get her healthy or getting her out on the court means nothing."

C.J. put a hand on both of their arms. "I love that you talk about me like I'm not here," she said, forcing a smile. "I'll take this week off, do everything Trystan tells me to do, and we'll talk again on Saturday."

"Can she travel?" Grant asked Trystan.

Trystan considered. "It won't be comfortable for her, but she can travel." She looked at C.J. "Where are you headed?"

"Sedona, I guess," C.J. said. "Home."

"It's a pretty short flight to Phoenix from here," Trystan reasoned, "so I don't think that'll be too much of a problem. How were you planning on getting from Phoenix to Sedona?" she asked C.J. "Were you driving or flying?"

"I was going to drive," C.J. said.

Trystan shook her head. "I think you'll be better on a plane. It'll be faster and less jarring."

"Okay," C.J. said. "I'll fly."

Grant said, "You were great out there today, C.J. I'm really proud of the way you hung in there."

"Thanks."

"I'll check in with you tomorrow to see how you're feeling," Grant added, heading toward the door.

When he was gone, Trystan began preparing an ice treatment. With her back to C.J., she said, "You were very courageous out there—Grant's right. That was incredibly smart tennis at the end. You never cease to amaze me."

C.J. blushed. "I just did what I had to do to win."

"A lot of women would have quit—you didn't. You've got great heart, C.J. That's what makes you a champion."

C.J. didn't know what to say to that, so she simply remained silent.

"Ready?" Trystan asked, turning around.

"If I have to be."

Trystan placed the step stool in front of the treatment table and took the bulk of C.J.'s weight as she settled on the plinth, the ice pack resting against the small of her back.

"Where will you be next week?" C.J. asked quietly. It still seemed to her that Trystan was uncomfortable. She wished she could go back in time to erase Randi and Maggie's conversation—it seemed to have changed something fundamental in Trystan.

"I don't know yet," Trystan said, moving around the room.

"You're not with the tour next week then?" C.J. asked.

"No. It's a pretty minor tournament, so they gave me the week off. They're going to use locals to cover."

"Oh," C.J. said, biting her lower lip. She wanted to invite Trystan to join her in Sedona but couldn't bring herself to ask.

"I'll be right back," Trystan said, excusing herself. Being with C.J. felt suddenly awkward, and it pained her. She went to her office and sat at her desk. She fiddled with her pen, pushed some papers around on her desk dejectedly, and tried to decide where in fact she would go on her week off, wondering if a spot existed that was far enough away for her to forget C.J. Her heart lurched.

She didn't want to get away—she wanted to go to Sedona and take care of C.J. *Face it, Trys, whatever chance you might have had went out the window when she overheard Randi and Maggie.* Suddenly, Trystan didn't want to sit still. Something had been bothering her ever since C.J.'s first injury.

Trystan exited the locker room, hoping to find Grant before he left. After checking in several places, she found him just as he was preparing to get into his rental car. "Can I talk to you for a minute?" she asked.

"Where's C.J.?"

"Icing," Trystan answered shortly.

"What do you need?" Grant asked.

"I want to talk about C.J.'s training."

"What about it?"

"Tell me what you're doing to promote core stability."

"C.J.'s doing the same routine she's been doing," Grant answered.

"And what does that entail?" Trystan pushed.

"Weight training, cardio, court time," Grant ticked the items off on his fingers.

Trystan took a slow breath, trying to keep a lid on her temper. "I'll ask you one more time. What are you doing," she said the words slowly, "for core stability—for her trunk muscles?"

"You want to know what weights she's using?" Grant asked, clearly at sea.

"No," Trystan said, expending her last ounce of patience. "Are you using anything like a therapy ball or a Katamibar?"

"No," Grant said, his confusion obvious.

"It's no wonder she injured her back," Trystan spat.

"What are you saying?"

"I'm saying her training is all wrong."

"She's been doing that training for years," Grant answered defensively.

"And that's exactly the problem," Trystan said, getting in his face. "Didn't it occur to you that when you changed her game, you needed to change her training, too? The game you have her playing is much more wide open. Her whole torso is involved in a completely different way. Having her train the same way as she was before you changed her game is irresponsible."

Grant looked as if he were about to explode. "I would never do anything to hurt C.J."

"Not intentionally, no," Trystan said. "But she *is* hurt and it's a direct result of the wrong training program. When she's able to work again, you'd better have a more appropriate program in place." Afraid she would say something more she would regret, Trystan turned on her heel and walked away.

She returned to her office, where she sat for several minutes trying to calm herself. "Moron," she said to herself, thinking about Grant. She ran her fingers impatiently through her hair. "Jeopardizing her career, her health, her well-being... He should have known better," she said, slamming a stapler on the desk. "Damn it all!"

Get yourself together, Trys. You have a patient out there. She got up and paced around the room several times, paying attention to her breathing to get her emotions under control.

When she finally felt she was able, she went back to check on C.J. "How do you feel?"

"Like an ice cube," C.J. answered.

"How's the pain?"

"It's about a twelve."

"I'm not surprised," Trystan answered. "You stressed it pretty good today. I'm going to give you a couple of instant ice packs for the flights. Use one every twenty minutes. When you get to Sedona, make sure you start the physical therapy right away." Her eyes looked everywhere but at C.J. "You do have a physical therapist, don't you?"

"I'm sure there's one at Enchantment," C.J. said, her voice lacking any enthusiasm.

"Okay," Trystan said, a stab of envy and protectiveness twisting her gut at the idea of someone else treating C.J. "How are you getting to the airport?"

"There's a car waiting to take me."

"I'll help you to the car then," Trystan offered, removing the ice pack from C.J.'s back. She gave her a hand down from the plinth. "Do you need a shower first?"

"It would be nice."

Trystan blushed. "It'll be hard for you. Keep your arms low." To offer assistance with such an intimate detail after what had happened earlier was impossible, she knew. The idea of C.J. rejecting her that way was more than Trystan could bear. She jammed her hands in her pockets.

C.J. returned from the shower dressed in a warm-up suit.

"Ready?" Trystan asked.

"I guess," C.J. said. She walked slowly and deliberately, her pain exacerbated with every step. Fortunately, her ride was parked just a short distance away.

The driver opened the back door for C.J. and took the bag from Trystan. C.J. searched Trystan's face. Her expression was unfathomable. "I-I can't tell you what all your help has meant to me this week."

Trystan shrugged. "It's my job."

"It was more than that and you know it," C.J. said.

"I suppose it was," Trystan answered, her eyes fixed on some distant point. "Anyway, have a safe flight. Make sure you see that PT tomorrow. And use more ice tonight when you get home."

There was so much more C.J. wanted to say. Instead, she accepted Trystan's help getting into the car, able to do no more than watch as the distance grew between them.

With a last glance at the disappearing taillights, Trystan dug for her keys in her pocket and trudged to her rental car. She had no idea where she was headed.

CHAPTER TEN

C.J. stared moodily out the floor-to-ceiling window. It had been three days since she'd left San Diego—three days since she'd seen Trystan. For the millionth time, she found herself wondering how Trystan was, what she was doing, and where in the world she'd gone.

A familiar emptiness echoed in C.J.'s heart. Their parting had left her unsettled. It was almost as if Trystan was anxious to send her on her way. *What changed so quickly?*

She recalled the look on Trystan's face as she stood in the doorway listening to the conversation between Randi and Maggie. It was almost as if she was embarrassed or ashamed, C.J. thought.

Before that conversation, Trystan had been tender, caring, and friendly. Afterward... *She's afraid of what I must think of her. She's afraid I don't want her around. Oh, Trystan.*

C.J. turned slowly from the window. Her back was still very painful, despite two days of treatments. C.J. frowned. She'd been less than patient with the PT at Enchantment. *No, you've been downright surly, simply because he's not Trystan...*

C.J. sighed. She'd thought perhaps Trystan would call her—just to see how she was feeling. *She's not going to call you, Ceeg. Get over yourself.* She picked up a novel from the coffee table, hoping a good book would distract her.

Trystan redoubled her pace. The run along the creek where she grew up usually settled her spirit. It wasn't working at the moment. *Damn it all to hell.* She'd thought almost constantly about C.J.—how she was feeling, whether she'd gotten any relief from the PT, and if she was having nightmares. It disturbed Trystan that there was no one to comfort her—to soothe away the fears. *She doesn't need you, Trys. She knows how you really are now.*

Trystan stopped abruptly in the middle of the trail, bent over, and put her hands on her knees. "Damn it all to hell," she repeated out loud.

She sat on a nearby rock to catch her breath. She couldn't blame Randi and Maggie for talking about her—after all, she'd certainly done enough to earn that reputation. Still, she wanted to blame them. It would be easier than facing herself.

Trystan buried her face in her hands and cried. She cried for the life she'd wanted and for the life she'd lived. But most especially, she cried for the life she knew she'd never have.

She had no idea how much time had passed as she sat staring vacantly at the brook burbling before her. She noticed that the sun, so high in the sky when she'd started out, had begun to set. Wiping her eyes with the heels of her hands, she rose wearily, stretched, and began to jog back up the path.

Half an hour later, Trystan was seated at her mother's kitchen table.

Terri was bustling around the stove. She could feel Trystan's distress but knew her daughter well enough to know it was prudent to wait until she was ready to talk.

It didn't take long.

"Amá?" Trystan asked. "Do you think we're ever allowed to outgrow our past?"

Terri didn't turn around but paused as she was removing a plate from the cupboard. She answered carefully, "I believe that we have many lives, some of which we live in the same lifetime. So, yes, I suppose we can always start another lifetime within this one."

"But, Amá," Trystan said, clearly troubled, "What happens when our past follows us into our present?"

"Then we must reconcile our past, face our mistakes if we've made any, beg forgiveness if necessary, and start anew."

"Can it really be that simple?" Trystan asked.

"There's nothing simple about facing one's fears," Terri answered. "When we examine our past with an eye toward changing our future, it's not simple. In fact, it can be very, very hard at times."

"Is that what happened to you?" Trystan asked hesitantly.

Terri stiffened. "I don't know what you mean."

"You never talk about my father. Obviously, that was another lifetime for you. Yet here you are, all these years later—still alone. Did you not face your fears? Have you not faced them yet?"

Terri hesitated. *Perhaps it is time she knew.* "Sometimes we think we've made the right choices, only to discover later that we were mistaken." In a quiet voice, Terri continued, "I was a young woman—vulnerable and impressionable. I'd never been in love. Jarrod was dashing, handsome, and seemed to hold the world in his hands. He was a very charismatic person. It wasn't just his looks, either—it was his dreams, his passion for life, his vitality that drew me to him. I believed his stories, I thought he could do anything…be anything. I wanted to be part of that.

"He wanted me to give myself to him. I wanted to wait for marriage, for surely that was where we were headed." A note of self-contempt crept into Terri's voice. "Still, I was afraid I would lose him if I didn't give in—that he wouldn't want me as a wife. How foolish I was." She shook her head sadly and steadied herself on the sink. She did not turn around.

"So I slept with him. Once. That was the night you were conceived. When I told Jarrod I was pregnant, he blamed me for not being careful. We had a terrible fight. I never saw him again after that."

Terri finally pivoted to face her daughter, terrified of what she'd find in her eyes. She looked directly at Trystan's face, ready to live with whatever she might see.

What she found there surprised her—it was not the disgust she feared, but a mixture of shock, empathy, and compassion. She sat opposite Trystan.

"Anyway… For a while, I felt that I could hardly trust my judgment. Then I had you to raise." Terri smiled at her daughter. "That was quite a job." She shrugged. "I guess it was easier to throw myself into my work where I felt confident than it was to face my personal failures." Terri's expression was sad. She captured her daughter's gaze, touching her on the hand.

"Don't make the same mistake I did, Acheehen. Don't lock yourself away, hiding behind your professional competence. Live your life. Existence simply isn't an adequate substitute."

Terri stood again, uncomfortable at having bared so much of her soul. Before she could move, however, she was enveloped in a warm embrace.

"Thank you, Amá, for sharing that piece of your life. Why did you keep it from me for so long? Did you think I would love you any less? Never," Trystan said with feeling. "Did you think I would judge you harshly? You who raised me single-handedly while working long shifts in the hospital, then coming home to tend your own people?" Trystan held Terri even tighter.

"You are the most amazing woman I've ever known—a shining example of what I could be. I only hope I can be half the woman you are, Amá."

Terri pulled back enough to bring them face-to-face. "What did I ever do to deserve you, Acheehen?"

"It's simple—you were you. And that was more than enough. I love you, Amá."

"And I, you, Trystan. And I, you."

C.J. couldn't stand it anymore. She picked up the phone.

"Hello, Trudy?"

"C.J.? How lovely to hear from you. How are you feeling?"

"I'm not making much progress, unfortunately. That's why I'm calling you."

"Me? What can I do for you?"

Moment of truth, Ceeg. "Do you have a phone number for Trystan?"

"For who? Oh, Trystan Lightfoot, the physical therapist."

"Yes."

"Well, I keep every employee's contact information on file. Let me just see here... Yes, I have a cell phone number for her. Why?"

"She did such a wonderful job helping me during the tournament, I thought perhaps she could be of some assistance now."

"Oh," Trudy said, a note of uncertainty in her voice. "You want her to consult with your specialists. Of course."

I want her...here. "Can you give it to me?"

"Just a minute... Yes, here it is..."

After thanking Trudy, C.J. hung up and sat thoughtfully with the phone pressed against her chin. She wanted to dial, but she was afraid. *What if Trystan doesn't want to talk to me? What if she's busy? She probably has lots of friends...and girlfriends.* C.J. frowned, putting the phone down next to her on the couch.

Just as quickly, she snatched it back up, punching in the numbers before she could lose her nerve. A wave of queasiness washed over her.

"Trystan Lightfoot."

C.J. felt her heart rate quicken.

"Hello?" Trystan said again.

"H-hello, Trystan. It's C.J."

There was a second's hesitation on the line, and C.J. wondered if Trystan had hung up on her.

"Hi," Trystan said softly. "Are you okay?"

The concern in Trystan's voice gave C.J. more confidence. "I'm fine. Well, I'm mostly fine." *I just miss you.*

"How's your back feeling? Have you been getting regular PT? What are they doing for you?"

"Slow down," C.J. said, laughing. "My back is feeling only marginally better than it did. And yes, I've seen the PT every day."

"Back injuries take time, C.J. It isn't going to heal overnight."

"I know."

There was another pause on the line.

"Do you want me to talk to your PT for you?"

"Actually," C.J.'s palms began to sweat. "I know it's a lot to ask, but I was wondering if you'd consider coming out here. I'd pay you," she rushed on.

"I see," Trystan said. "I don't need or want your money, C.J."

"Wait, Trystan. That came out all wrong. Please don't be angry or offended. I wasn't trying to buy you." The silence on the line scared C.J. "I miss you, and I've spent days wishing you were the one treating me. Eric is probably doing a fine job—but he's not you."

"So you want me to come treat your back?"

"Yes," C.J. said softly. *I want you here with me.*

"I don't have the equipment I'd need, C.J. The folks at your therapy place might not take kindly to me just waltzing in and using their facilities to treat you."

"I'll take care of the arrangements. Will you do it?" C.J. held her breath.

"Okay," Trystan said quietly. "If you clear the way, I'll call them and tell them what I need."

"I'll call you right back. When can you be here?" C.J. knew her excitement was showing. She didn't care.

Trystan laughed. "Tonight if everything works out. I'll get myself a hotel."

"No," C.J. said quickly. "I've got plenty of room. I won't hear of you staying in a hotel in my hometown."

"Okay. I'll wait for your call."

C.J. hung up the phone. Trystan was coming. She breathed a huge sigh of relief as her world seemed to right itself. She refused to think about what that meant.

Trystan got out of the car. She still wasn't sure coming was the right thing to do. The offer of payment for her PT services really irked her. She didn't like feeling as if she was a servant who could be bought—or worse. If not for the fact that she hadn't been able to think of anything but C.J. since she'd left San Diego, she would've turned her down cold. *She needs you if she's going to have any chance of winning the Open.*

"Hi. I've been waiting for you." C.J. stood in the doorway in form-fitting jeans and a T-shirt.

"Sorry I'm late. I forget sometimes that these roads aren't the best."

You're here, and that's all that matters. "You're fine. Please, come in." C.J. led the way into the living room. "Are you hungry? Thirsty? I could order us something."

"No, thanks. I'm fine." Trystan sat in a leather chair. "I spoke with Eric."

"And?"

"And it sounds to me as though he's doing everything I would've done for you."

C.J. blushed. "I'm not saying he's not good at what he does. I'm just saying he's not you."

"You don't like him personally?"

"No," C.J. said, exasperated. "It's not that. He's a very nice guy."

"I don't understand," Trystan said, "what's the problem then?"

C.J. began to pace agitatedly, emotions swimming too close to the surface. "It's not only the way you treated my injury, Trystan. It's you."

"Me?"

"Well, it *was* you, before..." C.J. stopped herself. She hadn't meant to go down this road with Trystan.

"Before what?" Trystan narrowed her eyes.

Aw, hell. "Before Randi and Maggie's conversation."

"Oh," Trystan said flatly. "Why am I here, C.J.? I thought we discussed that at the time." Trystan rose from the chair as if to go.

C.J. rushed to her and put a hand on her arm. Everything was turning out wrong. "Don't. Please, don't go. I-I shouldn't have said anything. I don't want to be without you."

Trystan's eyes opened wider. "You don't know what you're saying."

C.J. spoke from her heart, without thinking. "I'm saying I've been miserable since San Diego. I'm saying I've been thinking about you non-stop. I'm saying I missed you. I'm saying...oh, God."

C.J. stepped forward and claimed Trystan's lips. Her mouth was hungry, questing. She tasted, explored, pillaged. She felt herself melting into a soft, sensuous haze, her whole body thrumming. She could feel Trystan's heart pounding against her chest.

Trystan placed her hands on C.J.'s shoulders and pushed her gently away. "C.J., what are you doing?"

C.J. opened her eyes, confused, her mind trying to catch up with her body. "I-I'm sorry. I shouldn't have...I just..."

Trystan's expression morphed from confused to angry. She was breathing hard. "Yes, you shouldn't have. Don't worry about it. I'm a lot more honorable than Randi and Maggie gave me credit for. I'll just see myself out."

"No," C.J. said, trying to regain her balance. "Where are you going?"

"It was a mistake for me to come."

"Trystan, I'm sorry. That was my fault—I don't know what came over me. I've never done anything like that before."

Humiliation mixed with anger for Trystan. "What—you figured I'd be a good person to practice on?"

"No! You're getting this all wrong." C.J. trembled as she felt her world slipping away.

"I'm getting it all wrong? I'll see you, C.J." This time, Trystan didn't give her an opportunity to object.

The sound of the front door slamming reverberated throughout the house.

C.J. crumpled to the floor, ignoring the shooting pain down her spine. Tears flowed down her face. She was suddenly cold—so very cold. She couldn't make any sense of the emotions raging inside her. She had no idea what she wanted. She'd never kissed a woman before. She'd never allowed herself to feel anything for anyone before. It was as if Trystan had unleashed something buried deep inside her. *What have you done, Ceeg?*

She got to her feet and ran to the door. There was no sign of Trystan. *How am I going to fix this? Was I experimenting with her? Is she right?* C.J. rubbed her tear-stained eyes and thought about the prospect that Trystan had just walked out of her life forever. Her heart constricted painfully. *No, Ceeg—this is real.* She collapsed on the floor.

C.J. had no idea how long she stayed in a heap on the area rug. Eventually, she pulled a fleece throw off the couch, covered herself, and surrendered to a fitful sleep.

Trystan drove aimlessly. Her body was alive with sensation. No matter how she tried to erase the memory of C.J.'s lips on hers, their bodies pressed tightly together, she failed. *Damn you, C.J.* She pulled over at the base of Cathedral Rock, staring at its hulking form in the darkness. Her hands were trembling on the wheel.

Why did you have to do that? Trystan was completely befuddled. Unless she had totally misjudged C.J., she didn't seem the type to use someone sexually. Yet she had deliberately brought up the Randi–Maggie conversation. Trystan closed her eyes and relived the moment C.J. kissed her. She'd seemed as confused as Trystan had been. *Were you, C.J., or is it wishful thinking on my part?*

Trystan struggled to remember what C.J. had started to say before she'd lost her temper. It was something about how she was before the Randi–Maggie thing… *You cut her off before she could finish, Trys. Nice going.* Trystan thought about her behavior of late—there was no question she'd stepped back from C.J. after the overheard conversation. *Is that where you were headed, C.J.? Were you contrasting my behavior before and after?* Trystan thought about her mother's words. *Reconcile the past, face your mistakes, and start anew.*

"No time like the present, Trys."

The house was dark when Trystan pulled into the drive. She hesitated before knocking, not wanting to wake C.J. with the doorbell if she'd already gone to bed. There was no answer. She knocked again. She was about to leave when she heard a scream from inside.

Trystan put her shoulder against the door and twisted the knob, not expecting it to give. She stumbled as it swung open, then regained her balance. She burst inside, prepared for battle, only to find C.J., alone and huddled on the floor, deeply asleep, her face contorted with fear.

A second scream had Trystan kneeling on the floor at C.J.'s side. She began talking before she touched her, trying to ensure C.J. knew she was safe.

"I've got you, sweetheart. It's me—Trystan. You're safe, baby. I won't let anybody hurt you. Let it go." Trystan reached out carefully, pulling C.J. tightly into her arms. *Oh, C.J. You should never have to do this alone.*

C.J. twitched and struggled briefly before settling down. She fell against Trystan's chest, still seemingly asleep.

Trystan noted C.J.'s position—her back had to be killing her. "Honey? C.J.? C'mon, baby, wake up. We've got to get you to bed."

Slowly, groggily, C.J. opened her eyes and focused. "Trystan?"

"Mmm-hmm." Trystan ached at the sight of C.J.'s tear-streaked face and swollen eyes. *Did I do that? Or was it the nightmare?*

"Did you come back? Am I dreaming?"

Trystan swallowed hard. "No, baby. I'm right here. Let me help you up and put you to bed."

"Okay." C.J. allowed herself to be lifted to her feet. "Trystan, it hurts so much."

"I know. That was an awkward position. We'll get you comfortable, I promise. Which way is the bedroom?"

C.J. directed Trystan to one end of the house. "Will you stay with me?" C.J. asked, as Trystan sat her on the edge of the bed.

Trystan's heart stuttered because of the child-like vulnerability in C.J.'s voice and her own need to hold C.J. close. "Yes. Yes, I'll stay with you."

Trystan didn't bother undressing them—she simply pulled down the covers, arranged the pillows for C.J.'s maximum comfort, and helped her climb under.

"Where are you going?" C.J. asked, a note of panic in her voice, as Trystan walked away.

"I don't think I shut the front door. I'll be right back."

When Trystan returned, C.J. was half-asleep. She crawled under the covers, only half-surprised when C.J. snuggled against her shoulder. Warmth and contentment flowed through her. She wrapped her arms protectively around C.J. and closed her eyes.

C.J. woke to that same feeling of extraordinary well-being that she'd experienced with Trystan in the San Diego hotel room, only this time, she didn't feel embarrassed. If it hadn't been for the debilitating pain in her back, in fact, she might have enjoyed staying like that forever. She shifted slightly.

"Are you okay?" Trystan asked sleepily.

"Mmm. I'm fine. Go back to sleep."

"Your back hurt?"

"Yes."

"I'll go get you some ibuprofen and a heating pad."

"No," C.J. said, putting a hand on Trystan's arm. "Not yet. I'm not ready to let go of you." She blushed scarlet.

Trystan pushed up so that she could see C.J.'s face. "I'm right here."

"What made you come back?"

"It was something my mother said to me."

"Remind me to thank your mother if I ever get to meet her."

Trystan laughed. "You'd like her a lot, I think."

"What did she say?"

"Something about reconciling my past and facing my mistakes. C.J.?"

"Mmm-hmm?"

"Why did you bring up the Randi and Maggie conversation last night?"

C.J. tensed. *Be honest, Ceeg. This is no time to chicken out.* "Before that conversation, I felt like we were really getting to be friends—like you cared about me and wanted to be around me. Afterward… Well, it was like you were a different person—like you were only helping me because you had to. I was just trying to tell you I liked the earlier version of you better, and I want her in my life."

Trystan mulled that over. "What about what you heard?"

"What about it?"

"They didn't paint a very flattering picture of me."

"I don't care about that." C.J. pushed herself up so that she, too, was propped against the headboard. She ignored the shooting pain. "Do you think I give a damn about what those idiots were gossiping about?"

"You may not care for them or the fact that they were gossiping, but, C.J., the bulk of what they said was true. I was that person they described."

C.J. forced eye contact. "The Trystan I know is warm, friendly, honorable… I don't care if what they said was true or not. It doesn't matter to me."

"How can it not matter to you?" Trystan asked incredulously.

C.J. shrugged. "It just doesn't. Trystan, nobody's perfect. We've all done things we're not proud of. But that doesn't change who you are to me or how I feel about you."

Trystan shook her head. "I don't understand you."

"Maybe it's just that you underestimate yourself and how people would feel about you if you really let them know you."

A self-derogatory retort died on Trystan's lips. *Reconcile the past, start anew.*

"Why did you kiss me?" Trystan asked softly.

C.J.'s face flushed scarlet again. "I didn't plan that. It just happened. I'm sorry…"

"You are?"

C.J. hurried on. "I'm sorry you felt like I was taking advantage of you. That was never my intention. I'm *not* sorry I kissed you, although I still don't fully understand it myself."

"Are you a lesbian, C.J.?"

C.J. laughed shortly. "I have no idea. I've never felt for anyone, male or female, what I feel when I'm around you." She smiled grimly at Trystan's bemused expression. "I know, hard to believe I'm thirty-four years old and I've never been in love, right? Not even in lust."

"I think it's incredible," Trystan said honestly.

C.J. squirmed. "All my life, it's been about my career. I've always been focused—single-minded, I guess." She shrugged. "I told myself I could worry about love after I retired." A tear slid down her cheek.

Trystan wiped it away. "You must have been very lonely."

"I didn't realize how lonely I was until you walked into my life." The words fell out before C.J. could censor them. Strangely, she found that she didn't want to take them back.

"I've got you now, C.J. You don't need to be lonely anymore." Trystan pulled C.J. into her arms and rested her cheek on top of C.J.'s head. They stayed like that for a long time—each wondering if perhaps she'd finally found the place where she belonged.

CHAPTER ELEVEN

Trystan adjusted her wireless earpiece and answered her cell phone. She was just cresting Submarine Rock at a full run. "Hello?"

"So you're alive. I'll be damned."

Trystan laughed. "Hey, Bec. What's happening?"

"I think I should be asking you that question. Where've you been? Last time we spoke, you had your panties in a twist about C.J. Winslow having a fling with her coach. Next thing I know, I'm watching you kneel over her on national television with your hand on her knee."

"I was treating an injury. What's your point?" For the first time Trystan could remember, she didn't want to share her personal life with her best friend.

"What do you want me to do, beg? Normally, I hear from you every day. All of a sudden, you disappear, and I've got to wonder—what the hell's going on? Are you sleeping with the girl? Is she straight? Isn't she? Or have you stopped obsessing about her?"

"Pick a different topic," Trystan warned.

"Uh-oh. That sounds serious."

"Let it go, Bec."

"Are you okay?"

"Yes."

"Where are you?"

"I'm in Sedona."

"Sedona? The tour plays in Sedona?"

"No. I have the week off."

"I thought you were going to come see me on your next week off," Becca said, obviously miffed.

Trystan mentally slapped herself. "I had to go home to see my mother."

"Last time I checked, your mother was in Canyon de Chelly, which by my map isn't exactly next door to Sedona."

"I'm sorry, Bec."

"Never mind. Let me know when you're ready to have a real conversation. See you, Trys."

"Bye," Trystan said to dead air.

C.J. looked at the readout on her cell phone and smiled. "Hi, Grant."

"Hey, C.J. How're you feeling? How's the back?"

"Not much better."

"Damn. Are you sure they're doing everything they can?"

"Funny you should ask that. I've got great news."

"Yeah? What?"

"Trystan's here. I called her yesterday and asked her to come over. She'll be doing my treatments from now on—at least until she has to go back to the tour."

"Fantastic."

There was a pause on the line.

"Why do I feel like there's something you're not telling me?" C.J. asked.

"It's nothing—I don't think I'm Trystan's favorite person at the moment."

"Why would you say a thing like that?"

"Let's just say she wasn't very happy with me at the Acura."

"Because?" C.J. drew out the word.

"She went up one side of me and down the other about your training program and how it lacked certain essential elements given your style of play."

"When did that happen?"

"The last day—after you won. I think you were getting iced down at the time."

"I'm sorry, Grant. I didn't know. She did such a great job with my back, I thought…"

"You were right to call her, C.J. She really knows her stuff. I looked into her recommendations—they were on target."

"Maybe you two should talk then," C.J. suggested.

"How about if I come out tomorrow? I'd love to be able to pick her brain some more on the new training regimen—maybe even let her help design it."

"That sounds like a great idea. I'll ask her about it later."

"Grant told me about the tongue-lashing you gave him in San Diego," C.J. said. She and Trystan were sitting on C.J.'s deck, enjoying the view after C.J.'s PT session.

"I shouldn't have," Trystan said. "I overstepped my boundaries."

"Stop." C.J. reached out and put a hand on Trystan's arm. "After he got over the initial shock, Grant was impressed. Since you talked to him, he's been doing some research into different training techniques. He says you were right."

Trystan shrugged.

C.J. turned to face Trystan fully, her expression intense. "Don't downplay what you did, Trystan. I can't afford to be injured. If you hadn't stepped in, I might not have any chance at the Open. I would've been training exactly the same way I have been, with a high probability of re-injuring myself."

"In that case, I'm glad I said something."

"Grant will be here tomorrow. We've discussed it, and we both want to know if you'd consider helping us design a program that will work for me—one that will make me stronger, less injury-prone, and better able to compete." C.J. was about to offer to compensate Trystan for her time, but she managed to swallow the words. She remembered only too well Trystan's reaction to her last offer of payment for her expertise.

C.J. shifted anxiously from foot to foot, waiting for Trystan's reaction. She realized she was holding her breath.

"Are you asking me in my professional capacity?" Trystan asked after a moment's silence.

"Does it make a difference?" C.J. searched Trystan's face for a hint of her feelings. *Please say it doesn't matter. I need you.*

"I'm paid by the tour. It's ethically inappropriate for me to appear to be giving preferential treatment to any one player."

C.J.'s shoulders slumped. "I hadn't thought about it that way," she said, trying without success to keep the disappointment out of her voice.

Trystan chewed her bottom lip. "On the other hand, if I were simply doing for you what I would do for any player who asked, I don't see why it would be a problem."

C.J. jumped into Trystan's arms, nearly knocking her over.

"Whoa! You shouldn't be doing that—I just spent two hours trying to fix that back. You're going to make my job tougher."

"Thank you," C.J. said excitedly. "Thank you," she repeated, in a completely different tone of voice. Her pulse quickened at the feel of Trystan's body pressed against hers, and C.J. lost herself in the sensation.

She inclined her head and captured Trystan's mouth. *Your lips are so soft.* C.J. could feel Trystan's power just beneath the surface. *You're holding yourself back.*

"Please don't run," C.J. breathed against Trystan's mouth several long moments later.

"I'm not going anywhere," Trystan assured C.J. as her heart pounded wildly. "You do realize, if I offer you this service," she indicated their intimate position, "I have to offer it to all the players."

"What!" C.J. exclaimed, taking a step backward.

"I'm kidding," Trystan said, chuckling. "Although I can't say you're making it ethically easy for me."

"What do you mean?"

"I shouldn't be intimately involved with a patient, C.J."

"Oh," C.J. commented, nonplussed. Her heart stood still for a moment before resuming its rhythm.

"Do you know what you want?"

"What do you mean?" C.J.'s head pounded.

"Have you given this any thought?" Trystan again indicated the two of them.

C.J.'s stomach flipped and she took a deep breath. *What* do *I want?* "I've never done anything like this before. I-I don't know anything other than I can't seem to control myself around you." She looked at Trystan defiantly. "And I don't want to."

Trystan shook her head. "I can't be the person Randi and Maggie were talking about, C.J.—not with you. I won't take advantage of your feelings that way. This is all new for you. You need to figure out what you want—not just in the short term and not in the heat of the moment. There's a lot at stake for you—your reputation, your career. I'm not telling you not to follow your heart—I'm just saying I want you to be very sure this is something you want to pursue and not a simple physical attraction."

Tears perched on C.J.'s lashes. "What about you, Trystan? What do you want?"

"It's complicated for me, too."

C.J. stared into Trystan's eyes. "Is that a nice way of letting me down?" Her words were barely more than a whisper.

"No, it's not." She took C.J.'s hand. It was trembling. "Being with me would affect your image—I have to think about that as much as you do."

"That's my problem," C.J. answered defensively.

"No, that's our problem," Trystan corrected. "Then there's the question of my job…"

"What about your job?"

"If I were to have a relationship with you, it would call into question my objectivity where the other players are concerned."

"You're a professional. It wouldn't affect your performance."

Trystan smiled. "I know that, and I'm glad you believe it, too. But we're not the ones who count here—it's the powers that be at the WTF."

"No one needs to know," C.J. said frantically. She felt a wave of dizziness and swayed as she felt her world crumble.

Trystan squeezed C.J.'s hand and looked at her kindly. "If we kept it from them and Trudy found out, we'd both be in serious trouble. If we were to decide we wanted to move forward, I would have to disclose our relationship to Trudy. Beyond that, as you found out, I'm a notorious lesbian—even being friends with me will tar you with the same brush by association. You need to be sure that's something you can live with."

"I don't care what people think."

"C.J., that's your heart talking, not your head. You've spent years building your image. It could take less than a day, or one incident, to destroy it." Trystan looked at her fondly. "As I said, this isn't something to jump into without thinking it through."

C.J. sat back heavily. Her whole body began to shake. *Why can't I have this? Why can't it be simple? I don't know how to shut this off.*

After several minutes, she said, "If we pursued a relationship, what would happen to your job?"

"That depends on Trudy and how much faith she has in me to be professional. She doesn't know me very well—after all, she practically just hired me. She might decide to fire me."

"She can't do that."

"Yes, she can. She probably would have cause under the terms of my contract."

C.J. felt anxiety clawing at her throat as each option seemed to fade away. "To hell with working for the tour. You could travel with me."

Trystan clearly reined in her temper. "I have a career, too. I can't just toss that aside to travel the world as your concubine, C.J."

Shock rippled through C.J. "I wasn't suggesting…"

"Yes, you were, even though you didn't realize it, I'm sure."

C.J. pursed her lips and considered. *She's right.* She straightened up and collected herself, trying desperately to stuff her emotions back inside. Every nerve ending, every synapse told her to stand and fight for Trystan. Yet looking at Trystan's closed face, she could see no evidence that it would matter.

"I don't want to cost you your career. I won't be responsible for that." She put trembling fingers to her mouth. "So I guess there's nothing for me to think about," she said, choking on the words. She rose abruptly and ran into the house.

"Damn it all to hell," Trystan said into the silence. Her throat was tight with unshed tears. She fought desperately with herself not to go after C.J. *It's better this way, Trys. Her image, her career, her innocence—she could lose all of that. Let her go—be the bad guy—you're used to that.*

Trystan jumped down off the deck, retrieved her hiking boots from the car, and set out to climb the steep, slick surface of Cathedral Rock. She hoped the power of the vortex and the difficulty of the ascent would help soothe her raw edges.

The sun had almost set as Trystan reached the top. She hadn't stopped to rest at all during the climb, instead using the physical challenge to keep her mind off what had just happened.

Her chest heaved, her legs burned, and her body was shaking. She bent over double trying to catch her breath. "Stupid, Trystan. That was just plain dumb." She found a rock to sit on and took a pull on her water bottle.

For several moments, she sat watching the beauty of the sunset, caught up in the magic of the scenery. She breathed deeply, inhaling the scents of a summer evening, and allowed the power of the vortex to calm her jangled nerves.

It was atop places like Cathedral Rock that Trystan felt closest to her heritage. The energy from the rocks, the peacefulness of being with nature, the pull of the vortex—all of it surged through her. She closed her eyes and emptied her mind.

By the time she opened her eyes again, darkness had fallen. She groaned. "What were you thinking, Trys?" She took stock of her surroundings—it was too dark to attempt the descent. She cursed her stupidity again.

Trystan located C.J.'s house set in the rocks across the way. There was a light on in what Trystan thought was C.J.'s bedroom. Her heart tripped. For a very long time, she simply sat watching the lights in the house, wishing more than anything that she was in C.J.'s bed, holding her close.

"Maybe it's a good thing it's too late for you to go back." Trystan found a flat rock and settled in for the night.

"I was worried sick about you," C.J. blurted, answering the door before Trystan could even knock. "You took off without saying anything—you didn't even leave a note. And you didn't come home all night."

"I'm sorry." Trystan took in C.J.'s haggard appearance. She was sure she didn't look much better. "I didn't think about the time…"

"You didn't think—you got that part right. Where did you go? Are you all right? Did you get any sleep?"

"I'm fine—really. I slept on Cathedral Rock."

"You stayed up there all night?"

"Yes."

"That's dangerous."

Trystan shrugged. "I grew up on the reservation. It's not the first time I've slept outside."

"For future reference, I've got three bedrooms." C.J. felt anger bubbling inside her. *How can you be so cavalier? I was terrified I'd lost you.*

"I'll keep that in mind." Trystan motioned to her watch. "It's time for your PT."

"Is that why you came back?" C.J. scanned Trystan's face for any flicker of emotion. *Give me a sign and I'll fight for you, damn it.*

Trystan regulated her breathing and forced herself to be stoic. The hurt in C.J.'s eyes was more than she could bear. *You're breaking her heart and it will destroy you.* She closed her eyes briefly. *If you let this relationship go forward, it could destroy* her. Trystan forced herself to assume a blank expression. "Yes. I have a job to do."

"And you are a woman who honors her obligations." C.J. retreated farther into the house. "I'll get my stuff together. Feel free to take a shower if you want one. There's a bedroom suite down the hall to your left."

When she was safely inside the sanctuary of her bedroom, C.J. fell on the bed sobbing. Her chest was near to exploding. Her fingers tingled and her upper back muscles clenched painfully from hyperventilating. *What's happening to me? Pull yourself together, Ceeg.* Anguish was like a hot knife in her heart.

All night C.J. had waited for Trystan to break down her door, take her in her arms, and tell her she'd give up everything so they could be together. She knew it was a childish romantic fantasy, but she couldn't help herself.

In the cold light of day, the truth was too apparent to ignore—their relationship was to be nothing more than a business arrangement. *She's not going to fight for you. You don't matter to her the way she does to you.*

C.J. spent several minutes erasing the evidence of her tears. She recognized her efforts wouldn't fool Trystan, but dignity pushed her to try anyway.

Trystan's touch on her back during the massage portion of her treatment nearly undid C.J. *This is the closest contact we'll ever have.* She choked on the thought.

"Am I hurting you?" Trystan asked, hearing C.J.'s muted cry.

"I'm fine," C.J. answered shortly. She didn't trust her voice.

"Are you feeling any relief at all?"

My heart is shattered and I can't seem to stop crying. What relief is there for me? "It feels about the same."

"What time does Grant arrive?"

"Lunch time."

"Do you still want me to sit in on your meeting?" Trystan asked shakily.

"If you're willing."

Grant looked from C.J. to Trystan and back again. Something was wrong. Both women looked positively miserable, and neither would make eye contact with the other. He decided to ask C.J. about it later.

"You mentioned using the therapy ball, and something else I never heard of, for C.J. to strengthen her core," he said to Trystan.

"That's right—a stability ball and the Katamibar." Trystan shifted into her professional persona. "It's my opinion that developing a program around those things would increase C.J.'s core stability and decrease the likelihood of further injury."

"Explain," C.J. said, leaning forward.

"I like the Katamibar system because it combines so many of the things you use when playing a match. It's sort of a cross between pilates, gymnastics, yoga, aerobics…you get the idea. It's a straightforward program and it won't take you more than an hour per workout. You've got to focus on your abs, back, hips, and pelvis—that's what you need with your new style of play, and that's what this regimen gives you."

"I've never heard of the—what is it?"

"The Katamibar. I'm not surprised—but you will." Trystan pulled a laptop out of her briefcase and hooked into Enchantment's wireless network. She turned the screen around so Grant and C.J. could see what she was talking about.

"That makes sense," C.J. said after watching the screen for several moments.

"Would it replace her regular weight training?" Grant asked.

"That depends on you," Trystan said. "It could—or you could supplement one with the other. The bottom line is the core muscles are the key to C.J.'s health and her success."

Grant chewed his lower lip. "It's Saturday. We have to make a decision about next week."

"It would be a mistake to play," Trystan said, brooking no argument. "C.J. is still in significant pain. I haven't been able to get the PSIS back into alignment, and she hasn't had a chance to work on strengthening the muscles she'll need to compete without injury."

"There are only two weeks until the Open," Grant said.

"I understand that," Trystan snapped. "I thought the idea was to win the Open, not just show up on the court."

"Of course it is," Grant responded, his face reddening in anger.

"Then give her the best possible chance. If you send her back out there before she's ready, she'll only aggravate the injury, or worse, she could injure something else."

Trystan and Grant were practically nose to nose across the table.

"Hold on," C.J. said, looking from one fierce face to the other. "I don't see any way I can play Toronto. It won't make any difference in the standings, and I'd rather spend the time getting healthy and preparing for the Open."

"What about the Pilot Pen on the 22nd? It's the last tune-up before the Open," Grant pointed out. "You need the work, C.J."

"I'd like to hear what Trystan thinks." C.J. was still looking at Grant when she said it.

"I want to take another shot at moving the PSIS this afternoon. I think there's a chance I can get it to go. If I can make the adjustment before I leave tomorrow afternoon, I think you should spend next week doing light drills, start some of the less strenuous exercises with the Katamibar, and continue PT treatments with Eric."

There was a roaring in C.J.'s ears. She swallowed back a sob. "Okay. What about the Pilot Pen?"

"It's too early to tell." Trystan finally met C.J.'s eyes. The pain in their depths made her heart stop. "One day at a time. One hour at a time if need be, but I suspect you'll have to skip it."

"Do you want me to be your coach or not, C.J.? Because if you don't, let me know now."

"What are you talking about?" C.J. asked Grant after Trystan had left the room.

"If you want Trystan to be in charge of your schedule and training, fine. But it would be nice to know that."

"I don't want… Where did that come from?"

"You undermined my authority in there."

"It wasn't about your authority, Grant. I wanted to get Trystan's input so we could make the best possible decision for me. She has an expertise you and I don't share. That's all. I thought that was what you wanted, too."

"What exactly is going on with you two? You were as jumpy as a couple of rabbits."

C.J.'s stomach dropped. "Nothing. There's nothing going on."

"Come on, C.J.," Grant softened his tone. "Something's different between you two—I can feel it."

"Trystan and I have a professional relationship. Period. There's no difference."

"I thought you were getting to be pretty good friends. Now she's like Frosty, and you look like your dog died. So don't tell me nothing's changed."

"Drop it, Grant."

"Okay." He put a hand on her shoulder. "I'm here for you, C.J., if you need me."

"Thanks." She offered him a brief smile.

"Thanks for getting my PSIS back in alignment." C.J. said. The joint mobilization Trystan had tried in her final treatment had finally done the trick. "I really appreciate that you took part of your vacation week to come down here." C.J. stood awkwardly at the door to Trystan's car.

"I'm glad I was able to fix it. Don't overdo it, C.J. I've given Eric a specific protocol to follow—he's good—you can trust him. Don't go full out on the training or the drills. Slow is fast in this case."

"Will you…" C.J. swallowed hard, her composure slipping. "Will you check in on me this week?"

Trystan's resolution wavered. Her fingers flexed at her sides as she fought a powerful urge to take C.J. in her arms. *Finish it off, Trys. She'll be better for it. One last hurt, then she can heal.* "I'll talk to Eric and Grant to make sure you're on track."

C.J. merely nodded. No words would come. *There it is, Ceeg. There's nothing left.* She covered her mouth with trembling fingers, unable to suppress a sob. She turned and ran inside.

Trystan started the engine and roared away. Less than a mile up the road, she pulled over. Her hands clutched at fistfuls of hair. She rocked back and forth, her teeth clenched tightly together to keep in the pain. *I love you, C.J.*

CHAPTER TWELVE

Trystan slammed the towels down on the counter. Her head felt like it would explode any second. She'd done nine treatments in ten hours, she was exhausted, and none of the players was C.J.

"Damn it all to hell."

"I see your humor isn't improving."

Trystan's head snapped up. "Bec! What're you doing here?"

Becca shrugged. "You wouldn't come to me, so I figured if I wanted to see you, I'd better come to you."

Trystan enveloped her best friend in a bear hug. She stepped back and gave Becca an appraising glance. "You look great."

"Yeah? Well, you don't."

Trystan nearly choked. "Next time, tell me what you really think."

"I calls 'em like I sees 'em, champ. You look awful."

Trystan glared at Becca and shrugged. "*You* treat all these whining women and tell me how *you* feel at the end of the day."

Becca held up her hands in a gesture of surrender. "No, thank you. I'm sure it's no picnic."

"No, it's not."

"I'm not arguing with you, Trys, so why the defensiveness?"

"I'm not being defensive," Trystan snapped.

"Hello?" Becca raised her eyebrows.

Trystan clamped her mouth shut and went back to tidying the treatment area.

Becca tried a different tack. "I'm glad to see you, too, Trys. Thanks for the warm welcome. Where am I staying? Thanks for asking. I'm staying at the host hotel, where I assumed you'd be staying, too." Becca kept up the monologue. "Dinner? I'd love to have dinner with you. What a splendid offer. Maybe you could introduce me to C.J. Winslow."

An arrow pierced Trystan's chest at the mention of C.J.'s name, and she spun around, ready to lash out. Her face was a mask of fury. When she saw Becca's knowing expression, she changed her mind and stalked out of the room.

Becca threw her hands up in the air and followed. "Trys? Hey, slow down."

"Why, so you can poke at me some more?"

"Poke at you?"

"C.J. isn't here, okay? Are you satisfied?" Trystan felt as if her pain was laid bare for everyone to see.

"Easy, tiger. I was just asking a question."

"The hell you were. You were digging."

"Okay, I admit—I want to know what's going on. Last time I talked to you, I couldn't even bring her name up. Then I see you and you're a mess. Trystan, I'm worried about you. I've never seen you look out of sorts the way you do now."

"I appreciate your concern, but I'm fine," Trystan said, gritting her teeth.

"Could've fooled me," Becca mumbled. Out loud, she said, "Will you have dinner with me?"

Trystan took a deep, centering breath and shoved aside her foul mood. "Of course. I'm really glad you're here, Bec."

"Ah, there's my best friend. How much longer are you going to be here? I'm starving."

"When aren't you?" Trystan asked, laughing at Becca's predictability.

"Very funny. Answer the question."

"Three minutes, I promise. Then I just have to make one phone call before we go."

Becca tapped her watch. "You're on the clock, Lightfoot. Better hustle."

"Yes, ma'am." Trystan saluted. She finished straightening up, went in her office, closed the door, and picked up the phone.

"Enchantment Physical Therapy Department, this is Eric speaking. How can I help you?"

Trystan tightened her grip on the phone. "Hey, Eric. It's Trystan. I'm checking in to see how C.J.'s treatment is coming."

"Hey, Trystan. She's doing okay. Seems to be following instructions, and her PSIS is still level—she says her pain is about a three out of ten. I've given her the exercise routine you designed and she's been faithful about keeping up with it. She says she's doing light drills—nothing too strenuous at this point."

"How's her attitude?" Trystan asked, closing her eyes and holding her breath. She knew it was a stretch to ask, but she had to know. And attitude, at least tangentially, affected treatment. *Are you as miserable as I am, C.J.?*

"Funny you should mention that—she seems kind of down, you know? Listless, I guess, is the word I would use."

She's depressed and it's your fault. Trystan tried to swallow the lump in her throat. "Okay, well, keep up the good work, she'll come around. It's probably just that she wants to be going full speed ahead."

"Yeah, I'm sure you're right."

"Thanks, Eric—you're doing great."

"Well, I'm not you, but…"

And C.J. is better off that you're not. Trystan hung up, staring at the phone in the cradle. The urge to call C.J. was almost overwhelming. *It'll only be harder for both of you if you do. Let her be.* Trystan buried her hands in her hair, thinking about C.J. sleeping alone, perhaps having nightmares from which no one would protect her. A small cry escaped her lips.

"This place is great. The food is fantastic," Becca gushed. She noted that Trystan had barely touched her dinner.

"It's all right."

"Want to try this?" Becca asked, indicating her veal parmesan.

"No, thanks."

"Check out that woman over there," Becca inclined her head in the direction of a buxom blonde sitting in the corner.

Trystan turned subtly toward her and back toward Becca. "That's Leslie Karivago."

"She a player?"

"Yes. I treated her today for a sore hamstring."

"Boy, you *are* in the right business. I got to get me a gig like yours. You could have a different woman every night."

Trystan set her fork down deliberately. "I'm pretty sure it's a violation of my contract to 'fraternize' with the players."

"Since when have you ever let rules get in the way?" Becca asked, probing deeper.

"Since I care about my job," Trystan shot back, a spark of anger flaring in her eyes.

"All work and no play makes Trystan a dull girl," Becca teased, intentionally trying to goad Trystan. *Let go and tell me what's really going on, Trys.*

"Yeah, well. Story of my life." Trystan stared at her plate.

"I don't believe that. The Trystan I know is always up for a challenge and could find a way around any set of rules."

"Maybe that Trystan grew up and learned that sometimes you have to play by the rules." There was a hint of bitterness in Trystan's voice.

"Or maybe that Trystan gave up and gave in."

Trystan shot up from her chair. "You don't know anything about it, Becca. Let it go." She threw several large bills on the table and walked out.

"That went well," Becca said to no one in particular.

"Trystan, answer the door." Becca knocked for the third time. "I know you're in there—don't make me huff and puff and blow the door down." She leaned against the doorjamb. "Please, Trys? I came a long way to talk to a faux wooden door."

Trystan opened the door, walked away, and dropped facedown onto the bed.

"Thanks," Becca said. "The neighbors were starting to wonder."

"Becca, why did you come here?"

"You mean, other than to see my best friend about whom I've been truly worried? No reason."

"I'm fine."

"No, you're not, Trys. You're depressed, you're hostile, you're uncommunicative…"

"You paint a lovely picture."

"Am I wrong?" Becca sat on the edge of the bed. "You know I love you, right?"

"You have a funny way of showing it."

"Sometimes tough love is the only way. Trys," Becca tugged on Trystan's hip to turn her. "It's plain to me that you're in love. Although I admit I've never seen it before, only Trystan in love could be as miserable as you are."

Trystan grunted noncommittally.

"I'm not stupid." Becca started counting on her fingers. "C.J.'s not here and you are. I mention her name and you go ballistic. I make vague references to dating women on the tour and you practically throttle me. C.J. is the only woman you've talked about for weeks—very uncharacteristic—and you're suddenly so closed-mouthed, dental floss couldn't get through your lips."

"Cute."

"Thank you. I just thought that one up. Come on, Trys—let me in. This is me, remember? Your we-share-everything friend? What happened?"

Although the silence stretched several minutes, Becca knew from experience that waiting patiently would reap rewards.

Trystan sighed heavily. "There's nothing to talk about. It can't be."

"Why not?" Becca asked quietly.

"First of all, it would be ethically wrong. Second, it violates my contract. Third, it could ruin C.J.'s image and career. Fourth…"

"Yes?"

"Fourth, C.J.'s never been in a relationship before."

"Neither have you," Becca said softly. "You've had lots of women but never anyone who mattered the way C.J. seems to matter to you."

Trystan blew out an exasperated breath. "We don't even know that she's a lesbian."

"Does she think she is?"

"Damned if I know. More importantly, damned if *she* knows. She says she's never felt about anyone the way she feels about me. But that doesn't make her a lesbian, now does it?" Trystan looked at Becca, confusion in her eyes.

"Not necessarily. But it doesn't mean she's not, either."

"It's like—she hasn't even thought about that part."

"Maybe it's not a big deal to her," Becca said.

"How can it not be? Do you remember when you figured it out?"

"Oh, yeah. It was a big deal to me."

"Exactly my point. She doesn't seem the least bit fazed by it."

"Trys, she's been around it all her adult life. You and I both know how many players, coaches, and hangers-on are lesbians. Is it possible it doesn't hold the same charge for her that it did for us?"

Trystan considered. "I suppose that's possible. But still…why on Earth would she want me?"

"Because you're kind, sensitive, caring, intelligent, and gorgeous?"

"Get real," Trystan said.

"I mean it, knucklehead. You are all those things. Good Lord, Trys. How many women over the years have wanted you?"

"That's different—that was about sex."

"That's because sex was all you would let them have of you. It sounds to me like C.J. is different. You've let her inside in a way you've never let anyone else, haven't you?"

"Yes. There's something so strong and yet so vulnerable about her. It's like I'm drawn to her…"

"Then why are you here, and she's…somewhere else?"

"Because it's better for her, that's why."

"Says who? You? Who died and left you the boss of her?"

"She's naïve, Becca. She has no idea what being with me would be like or what it would do to her image."

"She's a champion—a woman used to the spotlight. You think she doesn't know how to deal with publicity?"

"You didn't see her that day she was surrounded by the media after the picture of her and Grant came out. She was petrified."

"Have you asked her if she's worried about her image? Have you given her any options at all?"

Trystan thought back to their conversation. *You cut her off, Trys. She said it was her problem, not yours, and you cut her off.* Trystan frowned. "We got distracted by the issue of my job."

"So what you're saying is, you didn't leave her any room at all to make up her own mind."

"It was a moot point. I said we'd have to disclose the relationship to my boss and that I could be fired. She told me to quit and travel the world with her…"

"That sounds like a great option," Becca interjected.

Trystan glared at her. "Being a kept woman might work for you, Bec, but not for me. I've worked hard to get where I am. Damn hard."

"Good for you, Trystan." Becca's temper started to boil over, and she raised her voice. "Do you want to spend the rest of your life alone? All the time I've known you, it's always been about your career. You've worked yourself to death and avoided anything that remotely smacked of a personal life. Don't you think it's about time you stopped to enjoy yourself?"

"I have been enjoying myself," Trystan practically yelled.

"You haven't allowed yourself the most basic human need, Trys—love. You haven't lived."

"I've done just fine, thank you."

"I'll ask you again—do you want to spend the rest of your life alone? There's a woman out there who loves you and is willing to put her career on the line for you. Do you love her?"

"What?"

"Do you love C.J., Trystan?"

Perhaps it was the bluntness of the question, but for Trystan, it was like being hit with a two-by-four. All the anger seeped out of her. She stared slack-jawed at Becca as the simple truth washed over her. Her face and fingers began to tingle; she gulped in huge gasps of air. She closed her eyes and tears leaked out the corners. "Yes," she whispered. "I love her with an intensity that scares me."

"Good," Becca said, smiling. "Now you're talking."

Trystan took several moments to compose herself. Her hands were shaking so badly she sat on them. "But that doesn't change the facts. Being together means I lose my job. Worse, C.J. stands to lose millions of dollars in endorsements and potentially her privacy."

"Have you even tried to figure out a way it could work?"

"It can't."

"So you've said, but have you even tried to figure out a way it could?"

"There isn't one."

"Of course there is, Trys. Your heart is so wrapped up in C.J. you're not using your head. Since coming to the WTF, have you been doing a good job?"

"What kind of question is that?" Trystan asked indignantly.

"Right. So chances are your boss isn't going to want to lose you."

"I'm new here, I seriously doubt she's all that attached to me yet."

"True or false: she went out of her way to find you and hire you as their first on-staff PT."

"True."

"True or false: you've more than justified her faith in you."

"True."

"True or false: she'd have a hell of a time trying to replace you this close to the Open."

"True, although she'd most likely go back to using local help during the tournament."

Becca nodded in acknowledgment. "True or false: you have some leverage to use with her."

"Like what?"

"Like the fact that you're an asset she's not going to want to lose."

"Even so, can you imagine what the other players would say if I was working on them before they were to play C.J.? I can imagine what I would say if it were me—'She can't be objective. I don't trust her.'"

"Okay, what's your solution?"

"What?"

"You've presented a viable scenario that could be troublesome. What's your solution?"

"I don't have one."

"Come on, Trys. You're not thinking. If you didn't treat C.J.'s immediate opponent on match day, would that solve the problem?"

"I don't know. What're you suggesting, her opponent get no treatment on match day just because C.J. is sleeping with me?"

"No. I'm suggesting you maybe get an assistant who can treat her."

"That's nuts. What makes you think the WTF is going to want to take on another salary just to accommodate me?"

"Aren't you the one who told me earlier today that you were exhausted because you'd been on your feet doing treatments for ten hours?"

"Yes."

"And you don't think you can make an argument for needing an assistant?"

Trystan chewed her lip thoughtfully.

Becca pressed on. "How many locals did the WTF use during any given tournament before they hired you?"

"Three."

"Three? And now they've got just you working with the players?"

"Yes." Trystan mulled that over. "I'm just not sure I'm comfortable kicking up a fuss this early in my tenure on the tour."

"Let me tell you something I've learned—your boss is a businesswoman, right?"

"Yes."

"In essence, she runs a large corporation."

"More or less."

"Talk numbers to numbers people," Becca murmured.

"What?"

"Show her it's still more cost-effective to have you and an assistant than it was to hire three locals every week."

"Is it?"

"How would she have paid them, per diem?"

"Yes."

"Take that figure, multiply it by the number of days and the number of PTs she was using."

"Okay."

"Then take your weekly salary and whatever you think the assistant would cost per week. Add those together and subtract it from the per diem costs of local help."

"Huh."

"Exactly. You can prove to her that you're still more cost-effective, and the players won't be able to accuse you of favoritism."

"What about my contract?"

"What about it?"

"It states no fraternizing with the players."

Becca shrugged. "Stuff happens and wording can be a tricky thing. Contact your lawyer and ask whether you'd be in danger if you and C.J. became a couple."

Trystan sighed heavily.

"Why are you throwing up roadblocks, Trys? I've never known you to back down from something you wanted. It's like this thing with C.J. has you scared to death."

"I never meant to fall in love," Trystan blurted, her voice thick with emotion. "I did that once and it ripped me to shreds. I'm not ready to go there again." She buried her face in her hands.

"Hey, hey, there, girlfriend." Becca rubbed Trystan's back. "We don't choose love, it just finds us."

"Yeah? Well, let it go find someone else, I'm not interested."

Becca laughed. "I don't think it works that way, champ."

"What am I supposed to do now?"

"Get your head out of your butt and go find C.J."

"It's not that simple."

"You have to make it that simple, Trystan. People like C.J. don't walk into your life every day."

Trystan thought about C.J. and her heart leapt. *You're right about that.* In her head, she contemplated what it would take to change her travel plans at the end of the tournament. *Toronto to Sedona to New Haven, Connecticut. Yeah, that'll work.*

CHAPTER THIRTEEN

"Come on, C.J. This isn't rocket science—it's a damn agility drill."

C.J. glared at Grant. "I know that," she snapped.

"Forget it." Grant tossed his racquet on his bag and walked around the net to where C.J. stood. "This is ridiculous. I don't know where your head is, but it sure isn't here. There's no point in drilling if you're not going to pay attention."

A flicker of guilt skittered through C.J. She hadn't been able to focus at all since Trystan's departure. "I'm sorry. I'll try harder."

Grant let out an exasperated sigh. "Look. We can't get anything done when you're this distracted. Whatever's on your mind, you need to deal with it. The Open's coming up in two weeks, C.J. It's bad enough we have to work around your injury. We can't work around this, too. How about if you call me when you're ready to get your head in the game."

Grant moved to the side of the court to gather his things.

C.J. chewed on her lower lip. "Wait," she called. When Grant turned around, she said, "I-I need someone to talk to—someone I can trust who would understand." Even as she said the words, her stomach lurched wildly, and she thought she might be sick.

"I told you before, C.J., I'm right here."

"I don't know what to do." C.J. picked at some imaginary lint on her shorts and studiously avoided looking at Grant. She tried to formulate her thoughts.

"It's about Trystan, right?"

C.J.'s head snapped up. "How do you know that?"

"Because it was obvious to me the other day that something happened between you two, and you haven't been the same since."

"Oh."

"So what is it?"

C.J. began pacing. "I can't explain it. I have…" She swallowed hard. "I have these feelings for her. I've never felt this way about anybody."

"You're in love," Grant marveled quietly.

"What?"

"You're in love with Trystan."

C.J. paused mid-step, her heart stuttering. "Well, I… Yes, I suppose I am," she finished, a note of wonder in her voice.

"I didn't know you were a lesbian, C.J."

"I'm not—I didn't—am I? A lesbian?"

Grant raised an eyebrow. "What do you think?"

"I don't know what to think," C.J. answered, flustered. "This is all new to me. All I know is I can't stop thinking about her, and when I'm near her, my heart races in a way it never has before."

"That's love for you," Grant sighed dreamily. "Does she feel the same way?"

"I don't know. I thought maybe she did, but then she just closed down and shut me out."

"Any particular reason?"

"She said it would adversely impact my image and that I didn't really understand what it would mean. She said it would violate her contract and Trudy would fire her."

"And?" Grant asked, clenching his fists.

"And I told her my image was my problem and that she could quit the tour and travel with me."

Grant groaned. "I bet that went over well."

"Like a lead balloon. Then she took off. When she came back, she was all business." *And she broke my heart.*

"Like she was at the meeting."

"Exactly," C.J. said glumly.

"Is that the last discussion you had with her about it?"

"Pretty much."

"Did you try to talk to her after that?"

"She wouldn't even give me a chance."

"How hard did you try?"

"She wasn't interested, Grant." C.J.'s voice rose. "What was I supposed to do, chase her?"

"If you love her, and it sure sounds to me like you do—then, yes."

"Yes?" A glimmer of hope touched C.J.'s heart.

"When you think about her, does your pulse speed up and do your palms get sweaty? Do you get a feeling like little happy bubbles live inside you?"

"Yes." *When I think of her, I can't stop smiling.*

"When she's not with you, is she all you think about?"

"Mostly." *When I think of her, nothing else matters.*

"Do you find yourself daydreaming about her? Picturing her hands, the way she looks at you..."

"Yes," C.J. said. *Her eyes melt me.*

"C.J.—if she's your future, if she's what you want, you've got to fight for her just like you'd fight for a match. You've got to want it with everything you have and be single-minded about getting her back."

C.J. nodded. "I have to win."

"Yes," Grant said softly. "You have to win. But you're not going to get there by sitting around here mooning about her. Go get her, for heaven's sake."

"Go get her?"

"Yes. You're useless here. I don't want to see you again until you've straightened this out between you. Go tell her how you feel, and don't take no for an answer. I'm sure you two can find a way to make it work."

"Really? You think I should go to Toronto?" C.J.'s heart hammered in her chest.

"I think she's worth fighting for, and I don't know anyone who's a better fighter than you are."

C.J. jumped into Grant's arms and gave him a big hug. "Thank you," she whispered with feeling. "Thank you."

"You're welcome. Now if you don't get out of here, we're both going to turn into sentimental fools. Get going."

"Okay," C.J. said as she grabbed her practice bag and headed for the parking lot. "I'll call you."

"I'll keep my fingers crossed," Grant answered. "God speed, C.J. Good luck."

C.J. inhaled deeply through her nose and exhaled through her mouth. *Center yourself.* She continued the breathing exercise for several more seconds. *You can do this.* When she thought she might chicken out, she knocked on the door.

"Just a minute."

C.J.'s eyes widened in trepidation at the sound of Trystan's voice on the other side. Part of her wanted to flee; she took another deep breath.

"I didn't order…" Trystan's voice trailed off at the sight of C.J. standing in the doorway, looking painfully vulnerable and positively beautiful. Trystan closed her eyes involuntarily as a shiver of naked desire coursed through her. Her knees went weak.

"Hi," C.J. squeaked out, her throat suddenly dry. Trystan's hair was down and splayed over her shoulders. *You're magnificent.* "I was in the neighborhood."

The most Trystan could manage was a raised eyebrow.

C.J. squared her shoulders. "Can I come in?"

Trystan merely stepped aside.

"I hope I'm not interrupting, but I need to speak to you."

"Are you okay? Eric said you were doing fine with the PT…"

"It's not about that," C.J. cut Trystan off. She walked over to the window and looked out at the lights of Toronto in the dark. She could see Trystan's reflection in the glass.

Now or never, Ceeg. "I want to talk about us."

"I…"

"Just hear me out, please, Trystan. This isn't easy for me—coming here like this."

Trystan's jaw clicked shut. This was not the same C.J. she had left in the driveway earlier in the week.

C.J. took another deep, steadying breath and ignored the butterflies wreaking havoc in her belly. "I know you said I needed time to figure out what I wanted, and I know you think nothing can happen between us because it could hurt my image and cost you your job. I know all that."

C.J. stared straight ahead at the reflection in the window and watched Trystan shift uncomfortably behind her. She pivoted to face her. "I don't care about any of it." *Say it now, Ceeg, or you never will.* She clasped her hands together to stop them from trembling.

"I'm in love with you, Trystan. And if you feel the same way, we can overcome any obstacle." C.J. stood there, her heart laid bare, and searched Trystan's eyes for an answer.

Trystan tried to speak around the lump in her throat, but no words would come. On shaky legs, she crossed the room toward C.J., took her by the hand, and led her to the nightstand. From the top drawer, she removed an envelope and handed it to C.J.

"What's this?"

"Open it," Trystan managed.

C.J. flipped open a travel itinerary and began to scan it. "Toronto to Sedona, Sedona to New Haven?"

"Yes."

C.J.'s stomach flipped. "Not exactly a direct route."

"It is if you've realized what a fool you've been and you plan to correct your stupidity." Trystan took the papers from C.J.'s pliant fingers and linked their hands together. "I was coming to Sedona to tell you the same thing."

C.J.'s heart jumped. "The same thing?" she repeated dumbly.

"Yes." Trystan swallowed a lump of fear. *She needs to hear the words, Trys.* For the first time in many years, she allowed her emotions to show. "I love you, C.J., and together we *will* find a way."

The intensity of Trystan's gaze made C.J.'s whole body tremble in a completely different way.

Feeling the tremor, Trystan gathered C.J. in her arms. *Go slow, Trys—this is new for her.* She captured C.J.'s lips gently and lingered, savoring the silky texture.

C.J. returned the kiss with fervor, exploring with her tongue. Her hands found purchase in Trystan's hair, reveling in the softness of it. When Trystan moaned into her mouth, C.J.'s legs buckled. She backed them to the bed, pulling Trystan down with her.

"C.J.," Trystan started to say. Her words were suffocated by another scorching kiss. She lost herself in the moment, matching C.J.'s tempo and heat with equal passion.

C.J. insinuated her thigh between Trystan's legs and urged her downward. She could feel Trystan's arms shaking as she struggled to hold herself up, and it only served to fuel her desire more. She reached underneath Trystan's shirt, desperately seeking skin. Her fingernails scraped along Trystan's spine.

The sensation was like lighting a match underneath Trystan's skin. She temporarily forgot the restraint she had intended to show. With one hand, she tore at the buttons on C.J.'s shirt, popping several of them and laying open smooth, tender flesh. She unleashed some of her hunger, sampling skin with tiny bites and licks.

C.J. felt the flames licking at her self-control. She arched up to meet Trystan's questing mouth.

The motion drove Trystan to new heights. In one fluid move, she captured C.J.'s wrists and pinned them over her head.

C.J.'s eyes, clouded with passion just seconds earlier, burned bright with fear. *No. No. Don't.*

She struggled briefly, whipping her head from side to side, desperate to break free. *The wind howled, bending the arms of the old oaks and maple trees. The branches reached out, grabbing at the car windows. C.J. could hear the scrape, scrape of wood against glass. She whipped her head from side to side as rough hands clamped her wrists over her head. She tried to free herself, but the pressure was like a vise.* C.J. gathered herself and pushed upward…

The move caught Trystan off-guard, and she bounced once on the edge of the bed before falling to the floor. She scrambled back up to find C.J. gasping for air, tears streaming down her cheeks. Panic made Trystan's head spin. *Did I do that? No, please say I didn't.* C.J.'s sobs tore at her heart.

"Hey, baby. C.J.? What is it?" C.J. seemed to be lost in another world. "C.J.? It's me, honey. It's Trystan. You're safe now. Come on, let me in."

C.J. didn't immediately respond.

"Please, C.J. Whatever you're carrying, I want to be here for you. You don't need to do this alone." *If something I did caused this, I'll never forgive myself.*

C.J. looked at Trystan out of the fog of her memory. "Oh, God." The words were a plea and a cry. She threw herself into Trystan's arms, burying her face in Trystan's shoulder.

For several minutes, the stillness was broken only by the sounds of C.J.'s sobs and Trystan's words of comfort. When she began talking, C.J.'s words were barely a whisper. Trystan strained to hear.

"I was twelve. Jonas was away with another of his players at a tournament. Since it was important for me to keep up with my training, Jonas had his new assistant Terrance watch out for me. On Thursdays, I always drilled with six other kids at a clinic another pro ran nearby. Terrance drove me to the clinic."

Listening to C.J. and watching her face, it was clear to Trystan that she was already lost in the memory again. Trystan just held on tightly, rocking C.J. slowly. *Nothing bad can happen to you now—I won't let it.*

"We were doing a serving drill—the other pro, Larry, would line balls up on all the lines of the service box. We had to hit every ball with a serve before we could be dismissed. I went last." C.J. took an unsteady breath. "With three target balls left, I remember looking up as I was serving. Terrance was standing up in the observation area one flight up, watching me through the glass." C.J. shivered.

Trystan rubbed her back in circles. "He can't hurt you now, C.J. I'm here."

If C.J. heard Trystan, she made no sign. "I don't know how I knew what was going to happen, but looking up at him, I just did." Her body convulsed.

"I've got you, baby. It's okay."

"I didn't want to finish the drill—I didn't want to get off the court. I knew Larry would never let me go until I hit every one of the targets, so I began to miss intentionally. I glanced up again, and Terrance had this look on his face I can't even describe. It was as if he knew what I was doing, and it thrilled him even more." C.J.'s teeth were chattering.

"After about twenty misses, Larry got fed up with me. He told me to go. I told him I'd rather stay until I finished, but he was already turning off the lights. It was late—11:00 p.m.—and the club was closing for the night.

"The stairs were camel-colored. I remember because I wouldn't take my eyes off them. I didn't want to look up because I knew." She shuddered in Trystan's arms. Her voice took on a far-away, flat tone. "We walked to the car. He had parked it in a remote part of the lower parking lot, which was deserted. The car was an olive green Chevy Impala. You know, the kind with the three round taillights on each side."

"I know the model," Trystan said, hoping by answering she might ground C.J. in the present.

"I didn't want to get in. I stood next to the passenger door. Terrance looked around to make sure nobody could see and slammed me into the door. Then he opened it and shoved me inside, locking the door before I had a chance to get out."

Trystan's nostrils flared as she anticipated where the story was going. She struggled to control her own anger, knowing instinctively it would only add to C.J.'s fear.

"He ran around to the driver's side before I could crawl out that way." C.J. looked at Trystan without seeing her. "Terrance was a big man—probably three hundred fifty pounds or more. I was no match for him. He yanked my legs until I was lying down on the bench seat and pinned my wrists over my head."

It was Trystan's turn to shudder, realizing with a jolt what had set C.J.'s memory off. Her stomach roiled and a wave of nausea washed over her. *Oh, C.J. I would never have done that if I'd known.*

"He tore my underwear, pawing at me. I twisted and turned but couldn't get away." C.J.'s voice broke and the tears began anew. "He put his full weight on top of me and stuck his fat fingers inside me, but that wasn't enough. I remember him fumbling with his belt and zipper, pulling his pants down. I thought I might get a break then and tried again to get my arms free. That made him even angrier. He called me a cheap whore." C.J. stumbled over the word. "Then h-he raped me." Her cry pierced the quiet of the hotel room.

Trystan's jaw set and her eyes narrowed to dangerous slits. It was all she could do to contain her fury.

C.J. continued. "I tried not to pay attention to what he was doing. I looked backward—over my head—so I didn't have to watch. It hurt so much." C.J. ran trembling fingers over her eyes. "All I could see were the branches of these old oak and maple trees scraping against the car windows. I could hear the wind howling. My head hurt because every thrust smashed my skull into the knob of the window crank handle."

"Oh, baby," Trystan murmured, cradling C.J. in her arms. "I'm so, so sorry."

"When he was finished with me, he shoved me into the passenger door and told me to straighten myself up and make myself presentable. He zipped his pants as he started the car. When we were on the way to my house, he told me if I ever told anyone what had happened, he'd kill my mother."

Trystan's growl was audible.

"I believed him," C.J. said, shrugging. Her tears were once again flowing freely. "So I never told. Not ever—not to anyone. Until now." Finally, she looked up at Trystan, as if realizing for the first time that she was there.

"Thank you for your trust, C.J. Thank you for telling me. I'm so, so sorry if I scared you earlier. I would never, ever hurt you. I want you to know that."

"I know," C.J. agreed, nodding sadly. "It's just that sometimes things happen that remind me of then, and it feels like I'm back there all over again."

A light bulb clicked on in Trystan's head. "Did something like that happen during your match against Monica?"

C.J. considered for a moment. "Yes. A fan yelled out words similar to something Terrance said to me." She blushed, embarrassed. "I know it must sound crazy, but things like that still get to me. Every now and again—more often than not lately—something triggers me and it affects my serve. When I'm about to close out a match, my serve goes to hell and I begin blowing points. I think it's almost as if part of me is still that young girl who's afraid to get off the court. I'm not missing serves intentionally—it's just that I panic when I have to hit it."

"Have you ever thought about seeing a therapist, C.J.?" Trystan asked quietly.

"I've thought about it. But I'm never in one place long enough to keep regular appointments."

"Maybe I can find someone who can help you at least get past the serve thing."

"How?"

"There are some interesting newer techniques in thought field therapy that might work for you."

"Thought field therapy?"

"Yes. It's especially effective with trauma victims, and it's something you can do yourself—like before a match. If you're interested, I think my mother has a friend who specializes in it."

C.J. chewed her lower lip. *It can't hurt you, Ceeg. You know you need the help. You were lucky to win some of those matches in San Diego. You won't get away with that at the Open.* "Okay. I'd at least like to hear a little bit more about it."

"I'll talk to my mother in the morning."

"I'd like that." C.J. paused, her fingers playing with the bedspread. "About earlier, Trystan. I'm really sorry. I didn't mean to hurt you. I just…"

Trystan put her hand over C.J.'s to stop the nervous motion. "Don't apologize, C.J. You don't have anything to apologize for. Now that I know the root cause, it's easier to understand why you reacted the way you did." Trystan weighed her next words carefully. "The nightmares you've been having, are they related to what you just told me?"

C.J. frowned. "Yes. Bits and pieces, unrelated fragments—they seem to seep into my subconscious mind and wreak havoc in my dreams."

"Has that always been the case?"

"It's been true for many years—but it's been even more true lately."

"That explains a lot."

"I'm sorry I didn't say anything earlier."

Trystan cut C.J. off with a wave of her hand. "You don't have to apologize for that. It was very hard to tell me what you did tonight. I understand that, and I'm honored that you would share it with me."

"But I should have told you…"

"You did tell me—when you were ready. I wouldn't have wanted to rush you into that, C.J. I don't think you were ready."

C.J. gazed at Trystan with a mixture of relief and thanks. "I can't believe how understanding you are of all this."

"If you let me, I'll be right here beside you, working through it with you, always." *Please, let me take care of you.* Trystan held out her hand.

C.J. took it, lifting it to her lips and kissing it. "How did I ever get so lucky?"

"I'm the lucky one, C.J." Trystan noted the exhaustion in C.J.'s face. "Where are you staying?"

C.J. looked at Trystan blankly. "I hadn't thought that far in advance."

Trystan laughed. "You mean to tell me you just picked up and booked a flight to Toronto with no plan?"

"My plan was to come find you and convince you that we belong together. I didn't think beyond that."

"You're amazing, you know that?" Trystan turned C.J. slightly and kissed her on the nose. "Did you at least bring a suitcase?"

"Oh, my God," C.J. exclaimed, jumping up. "I left it in the hallway. I hope it's still there." She ran to the door and flung it open. The duffle bag was sitting right where she'd left it, just to the left of the opening. She pointed a warning finger at Trystan, who was trying hard not to laugh.

"I don't suppose I could stay here with you?" C.J. asked.

"I can't think of anything I'd love more," Trystan answered, meaning it. She watched as C.J. carried her bag into the bathroom, then readied herself for bed.

Trystan's head was spinning; she wanted to weep for that little girl. She also wanted to seek out and destroy Terrance. Her jaw muscles stood out in sharp relief as she considered what he'd done. She satisfied herself temporarily with visions of the many ways in which she would castrate him if ever given the chance.

C.J. leaned on the bathroom sink. She didn't need to look in the mirror to see exactly how tired she looked. Her muscles were strung tight as a bow and her neck ached. She finished washing her face, brushing her teeth, and changing her clothes. It wasn't until she stood at the foot of the bed that nerves got the best of her. She looked at Trystan, who had thrown back the covers for her to climb under. *Can you really still want me after what I told you? I'm damaged goods.*

"Come here, honey." Trystan held her arms open.

C.J. hesitated for a split second, apprehension giving her pause, before tumbling gratefully into Trystan's arms.

Trystan closed her eyes and kissed C.J. on the top of the head, then the forehead. "I love you, C.J. Nothing you've said tonight changes that."

Tears sprang to C.J.'s eyes. "I can't believe how lucky I am."

"I told you, I'm the lucky one."

C.J. settled into Trystan's arms as she pulled the covers over them. For the first time she could remember in ages, she felt at peace.

C.J.'s breathing evened out into the sweet cadence of sleep. Trystan lay there for a few moments listening to C.J. and feeling their hearts beat together. She tightened her hold, tucked C.J.'s head under her chin, and joined her in slumber.

CHAPTER FOURTEEN

Trystan rolled over and took C.J.'s hands. It was early—the sky through the still-open drapes was barely turning pink. She smiled and kissed C.J.'s forehead. "I can't believe you're here."

"It feels like a dream, doesn't it?"

Trystan nodded. "That's exactly how it feels. I'm trying to remember why I thought this," she indicated their entangled limbs, "was a bad idea."

C.J. chuckled. "I'd prefer if you didn't figure that out, thank you."

"Good point," Trystan agreed. She shifted so she could better see C.J.'s eyes. Her expression turned serious. "I want you to know you will always be safe with me."

"I know that. The day you rescued me from that pushy pack of reporters, you took my breath away."

"Why?"

"You walked right into the middle of a mob and took charge just so I could get away."

Trystan shrugged. "I just did what needed to be done."

"Then," C.J. continued, "when you held me all night after my nightmare, I couldn't stop thinking about how safe and comfortable you made me feel. Nobody's ever made me feel that way before." She rested a palm on Trystan's cheek. "Now you're all I think about. When I'm with you, I'm the happiest I've ever been. When we're apart, all I do is think about you and wonder where you are and what you're doing."

"I feel the same way," Trystan said. "I've been fighting it, I think, since the very first time I saw you." Trystan squirmed. "I've never really had a relationship—not a real one, C.J., and I'd be lying if I told you I wasn't scared to death."

"I'm scared, too. I probably wouldn't have come here except that Grant kicked me out yesterday—he told me I was useless and that he didn't want to see me again until I'd worked it out with you. He gave me the courage to come after you."

"Remind me to send Grant a present," Trystan said, smiling.

"We'll send him one together." C.J. turned in Trystan's arms to see her better. Her stomach fluttered. "I know I love you, and I know I want you, but I'm not sure how prepared I am to have sex."

The uncertainty on C.J.'s face melted Trystan's heart. "We'll take it slowly, C.J. There's no rush. We'll go at your pace." *I've waited for you all my life. Waiting a little longer won't kill me.*

"I can't believe how lucky I am."

"You've got to stop saying that. I'm the lucky one."

"What are we going to do about your contract?"

"I think I may have a plan," Trystan answered, and explained what she and Becca had discussed.

Trudy's expression was sour, her cheeks pinched together. The effect magnified her bird-like features. "The terms of your contract are very clear. There was to be no fraternization with the players."

Trystan sat across the desk in Trudy's on-site office, her arms folded across her chest. C.J. was standing at the window, watching the matches below.

"Actually, the contract does not speak specifically to the issue of falling in love with a player." Trystan had spent an hour on a conference call with her attorney after breakfast. Together, they'd mapped out a strategy and answers to issues Trudy was likely to raise.

"We're disclosing this to you in good faith and because my sense of professional ethics won't permit me to do otherwise. I've offered you a viable solution—one that takes into account the needs of the WTF and the confidence of the players in the integrity of their treatment."

"You've presented me with an ultimatum."

Trystan shrugged. "Only if you choose to view it as such. The players are getting consistent, top-quality care and the tour is saving money by not having to hire per diem PTs at every stop. I've offered you a way to maintain the cost savings and the integrity of the care. I don't believe that's an ultimatum—just smart business."

Trudy frowned. "I want time to think about this. I'll discuss it with my lawyers and the board. In the meantime, I have no choice but to suspend you until further notice."

C.J. whipped around, anger snapping in her eyes. "You can't do that. Trystan hasn't done anything wrong."

"C.J.," Trystan said in a low, warning tone.

"No." C.J. walked over and put a hand on Trystan's shoulder. "You haven't done anything except be honest and aboveboard." She squared her shoulders and addressed Trudy. "I can't see what issue you could have as long as Trystan doesn't treat my opponent on match day."

Trudy sat up straighter. "As I said, we'll consider it. As for you," she clucked her tongue disapprovingly at C.J., "do you have any idea what this could do to your image? Have you considered what the tabloids will do to you? You have everything right now—fame, endorsements, a golden girl image—you're just going to toss all that away."

Trystan gripped the arms of the chair to keep from lunging across the desk at Trudy. *You're just afraid you'll lose your poster girl and it'll be bad for the tour's image, you snake.*

Trystan's muscles tensed under C.J.'s hand. C.J. patted the shoulder reassuringly. "Trudy, I've considered all of those things. The fact of the matter is, I'm the same person I was yesterday, and last week, and the last time I won Wimbledon. I'm a champion with a deep respect for the traditions and history of our sport. I've always represented it well and that isn't going to change any time soon."

"I'm not questioning your loyalty to the game, C.J. I've been at this a very long time. I've watched women's careers derailed by the mere whisper of lesbianism."

"I'm not foolish or naïve enough to believe I'll be universally accepted if our relationship becomes public knowledge. But I'm also no longer willing to put my own happiness on hold for the sake of 'propriety.' I'm thirty-four years old, in love, and willing to live with whatever the fallout is."

"I wonder if you really are," Trudy said.

"I guess we'll find out," C.J. answered, her jaw firmly set.

"Very well." Trudy sighed. "I can't stop you. I will tell you this, though. If you do anything that reflects badly on the game or the tour, there will be consequences."

Trystan started to rise from her chair. C.J. applied light pressure to keep her in the seat. "I'm not worried," she replied blithely.

Trudy narrowed her eyes and returned her focus to Trystan. "I suggest you head out this morning. I'll call you when we've had a chance to discuss your disposition."

"I'll look forward to it," Trystan said, smiling grimly and nodding at Trudy as she and C.J. left the room.

"That went well," Trystan said sarcastically, when they'd gotten some distance away.

"Don't worry. Trudy is a hard-ass, but she's also a realist. She needs me because I'm good for the game and she needs you because you're the best at what you do. She'll come around."

Trystan grunted her agreement. "Seems to me we have some time on our hands."

"I guess we do. I should get back to practicing and PT. Will you come back to Sedona with me?" C.J. asked.

Trystan considered. "I'd love to go home with you. Is there any chance you could take the weekend off first?"

"I'll ask Grant what he thinks, but if my PT thought I should take a break, then…"

"It wouldn't hurt you to have a couple of days where you just worked on your fitness and strength," Trystan said.

"What do you have in mind for the weekend?"

"I'd like to introduce you to my mother and show you the canyon."

C.J.'s eyes lit up. "I'd love that."

Trystan smiled at her and squeezed her hand. "You and my mother are going to love each other."

"I'm sure you're right."

C.J. sat at Terri Lightfoot's kitchen table, her hands wrapped around a cup of coffee. Trystan had just left for her run. "Thank you again for having me here, Dr. Lightfoot."

"You must call me Terri."

"Terri, then."

"I want to thank you," Terri said, sitting down across from C.J.

"Thank me? For what?"

"It's been many years since I've seen Trystan truly happy. There's something new in her eyes, and I can see that you're the cause." Terri smiled.

C.J. blushed. "She's very, very special—not like anyone I've ever known."

"It's been too easy for her to lose herself in work and ignore her heart." Terri searched C.J.'s face and made a decision. "Trystan is a very sensitive person—a fact she generally hides well. There was a time long ago when she wore her heart on her sleeve."

"What happened to change that?" C.J. asked softly.

"She fell in love."

"Oh," C.J. said, discomfort evident in her expression. "Unfortunately, the circumstances were very complicated, and Trystan was badly hurt." Terri thought about how her choice of words must have sounded to C.J. "Please don't misunderstand me. Neither Trystan nor Jay, the woman Trystan fell in love with, did anything they shouldn't have—it simply wasn't meant to be." Terri shrugged. "Sometimes you just meet the right person at the wrong time. Trystan was devastated."

"That's awful," C.J. breathed.

"You are the first woman since Jay who Trystan has allowed inside," Terri continued. "You've touched her in a way not even Jay could—you've breathed life into her soul—I thought I could see it in her eyes the last time she was home, and now happiness radiates from her being. I've been waiting a long time for someone who could renew her spirit, so has she, although I imagine she didn't know it."

"I guess in a way, your daughter and I are a bit alike. I've spent my whole life focused on my career, too. Until Trystan came into my world, I hardly noticed how lonely I really was. I thought it had to be that way for me to compete—to succeed."

Terri nodded. "Yours is a very competitive field. I can understand that kind of single-mindedness."

"Since I met Trystan, though, I've discovered that it doesn't have to be like that. At the tournament in San Diego, toward the latter rounds, I found myself looking for her in the crowd. Somehow her being there settled me in a way nothing else did."

"Like a touchstone, I suppose," Terri offered.

"Yes, something like that."

Terri reached out and covered C.J.'s hands with her own. "You're good for each other then."

C.J. smiled. "I'd like to think so."

"Speaking of your tennis… Trystan's told me that Andrea might be helpful to you," Terri said.

"Andrea?"

"My friend, the psychologist." Terri felt C.J.'s hands go tense under her own.

"Oh. Thought field therapy," C.J. mumbled, looking at a spot on the wall.

"C.J.," Terri squeezed her hands, "you should know that Trystan's told me nothing more than that she thought Andrea might be able to help you with a tennis issue." Terri looked at C.J. with compassion and understanding. "That's all I need to know. Whatever the issue is, Trystan would never violate a confidence."

C.J. smiled wanly. "I should've known that."

"I've spoken to Andrea. It seems her schedule is clear and she could be here tomorrow if that was something you wanted."

"She would come to me?" C.J. asked incredulously.

Terri smiled and chuckled, intentionally ignoring the look of mild panic on C.J.'s face. "Andrea's one of my best friends—we go back a very long way. If it's important to me and to Trystan, it's important to her. Besides, I've been trying to get her up here forever. This is just the excuse I needed. You'd be doing me a favor. There's no pressure to say yes, child. Just know that whatever troubles you, it's easier to share the burden than to carry it alone. Andrea is the best there is—she's taught many athletes cutting-edge techniques to help improve their focus." Terri could still see the uncertainty in C.J.'s eyes. She watched as C.J. appeared to struggle internally with her decision.

C.J. nodded, seemingly to herself, before focusing on Terri's kind face. "I'd like that very much," she said quietly.

Terri squeezed C.J.'s hands again before releasing them. "You have much courage, child. It radiates from inside you. I imagine that's part of what makes you such a great champion."

C.J. smiled shyly. "I can see where Trystan gets her big heart and her intuitiveness. You're very sweet."

"I speak only the truth."

"What truth is that?" Trystan asked, bursting through the door.

"That you need a shower," Terri said, ruffling her daughter's damp hair as she rose to clear the coffee cups from the table.

"My mother tells me Andrea will be here early tomorrow," Trystan said as she and C.J. walked along Trystan's favorite creek.

"Yes. Thank you for taking care of that for me."

Trystan took C.J.'s hand. "I know it won't be easy for you, honey."

C.J. pulled Trystan to a stop and faced her. "No, it won't—but I want my life back. I'm tired of being afraid. I'm sick to death of letting Terrance have that kind of control over me, and I want more than anything else for us to be together." She pressed Trystan's hands to her lips. "In every way. We can't do that if he's standing between us."

Trystan swallowed the lump in her throat. "You are the bravest person I know, C.J. Winslow."

C.J. shook her head. "I just know what I want, and I'm not going to let anything stand in the way." She leaned forward and captured Trystan's lips. As the kiss deepened, their bodies melded together, fitting perfectly. C.J.'s hands sought skin. She pulled Trystan's T-shirt from her shorts, running her palms over taut stomach muscles.

Trystan moaned into C.J.'s mouth, scraping her teeth across C.J.'s lower lip. When C.J. trembled against her, she allowed her hands to roam freely over firm buttocks and tapered hips.

When they pulled back, both women were breathless. C.J. pressed her lips to Trystan's forehead. For several moments, they simply stayed like that, swaying to the music of the canyon.

"This is a beautiful spot. Growing up here must have been incredible."

"It had its pros and cons. There was no better playground, that's for sure. But it was also a lonely place for someone like me."

"Do you come back here often?"

Trystan felt the familiar pang of sadness. "Not very much anymore, no."

C.J. debated whether to mention her conversation with Terri and decided against it. They walked for several more minutes in companionable silence.

"C.J.?"

"Yes?"

"What made you want to play tennis?"

"Originally?"

"I guess."

C.J. shrugged. "I played lots of sports growing up—basketball, softball, and field hockey. But tennis was different. I picked up a racquet when I was eight, and it was like an extension of my arm. I don't know how to explain it."

"You were meant for the game."

"In a way, I suppose I was. I was a shy kid, so I didn't have a lot of friends. That didn't matter on the tennis court. It was such a clean, clear-cut game, with well-defined boundaries and rules. I knew what was expected of me."

"I can appreciate that."

"And then there was the strategy piece of it. In many ways, tennis is like mental chess. When you reach a certain level, everyone can hit the shots. The difference between winning and losing, champions and second-tier players, is mental toughness and the ability to outthink your opponent. That's my favorite part of the game."

"It shows," Trystan said. "Do you remember? It was one of the first things I told you—I'm awed by the way you think on the court."

"I do remember," C.J. said. "You made me blush."

"People must tell you that sort of thing all the time."

"People," C.J. emphasized the word, "aren't you." She took her time kissing Trystan thoroughly.

"Thank goodness for that," Trystan said when they parted. "We should probably head back."

"This place is magical. Thank you for sharing it with me."

"I'm pretty sure you brought the magic," Trystan answered. For the first time in more years than she cared to count, she felt happy and at peace by the creek. It was a marvelous feeling.

"To move you past the memory, we have to take the power out of it." Andrea Marsden unfolded her legs and planted both feet on the floor. She'd been listening to C.J.'s story intently for the previous half hour, asking questions where appropriate.

"What do you mean 'take the power out of it?'" C.J. asked.

"When you were raped, your body shifted into fight or flight mode, and your brain released certain chemicals that helped you to survive the ordeal. In your case, the chemical release prevented your brain from helping your body recognize that the event was over, and the trauma got stuck inside you. As a result, certain things will trigger you and bring the trauma back."

"Like when that man shouted at me from the stands right before I served," C.J. said.

"Exactly," Andrea nodded. "His words triggered the memory and made it real again. I can show you techniques that will help you essentially disconnect the trigger from the memory."

"How?"

"Energy psychology. By working with the meridian points in your body, we can calm the limbic system—the part that goes into fight or flight mode."

"Whoa," C.J. said, her mind a jumble. She mentally shook herself. *This is not your mother's talk therapy, Ceeg.* "Meridian points?"

"Have you heard of acupuncture?"

"Like the Chinese do with needles?"

"Yes," Andrea nodded. "The spots where the acupuncture needles are placed correspond with the meridian points—sort of like the body's energy bloodstream."

C.J. sat forward, intrigued. "Okay. Does this tie in somehow with the thought field therapy that Trystan was talking about?"

"Thought field therapy involves literally tapping with your fingers on certain meridian points in a specific sequence. I like the technique because you can do it yourself."

"Would it work as part of my pre-match preparation, for instance?"

"Absolutely. We'll work today to take the power out of the memory, then before every match, you can sit and tap on the meridian points to take down any remaining anxiety."

C.J.'s heart lifted. "Is there a chance I can get rid of the memory for good?"

"You'll always remember what happened, C.J. This technique won't erase your memories. What it will do is take the emotional charge out of the ordeal. You'll be able to remember it without the terror you feel now."

C.J. chewed her lower lip. "It would be great if I could get it out of my mind while I was serving in a match—but there's something even more important to me."

"Okay."

"This treatment—will it help in my personal life, too?"

"It will help any time this particular memory would normally be triggered. I assume you're asking for a specific reason?" Andrea probed.

"Mmm-hmm," C.J. managed, crossing her arms and hugging herself. "I want my life back. I want to make love without Terrance coming between us." She began rocking back and forth. "I'm tired of fighting the ghosts."

"That's great motivation, C.J. I think I can help you with all that."

"Let's do it."

C.J. couldn't stop smiling. She felt like a weight had been lifted from her shoulders, even though she knew her work around the rape was just beginning. She and Andrea walked back across the road from Terri's office to the house, where Terri and Trystan were putting together an early dinner.

The conversation flowed along with the food as Trystan and C.J. managed to con Andrea into sharing some amusing stories of Terri's college days.

"I wish you two didn't have to leave so soon," Terri said as they reached the end of the meal. "You just got here."

"Amá, you knew we could only stay the weekend. The Open starts a week from tomorrow, and C.J. has to train."

"I understand all that intellectually, Acheehen, but you can't blame a mother for wanting more time with her child."

"Mother's prerogative, Trystan—don't try to argue with her," Andrea said, waving her hand dismissively. "You can't win."

"I wish we could spend more time here, Terri. You've been wonderful, and I love it here," C.J. said.

"See? Now there's a woman who understands," Terri said, shaking her finger at Trystan.

"She's just a brownnoser," Trystan shot back, ducking to avoid the napkin C.J. threw at her. "In any event, we have to get going." She stood up, taking C.J. by the hand. Terri and Andrea followed them out to the car.

"I can't thank you enough for what you did," C.J. whispered to Andrea as she hugged her goodbye.

"Remember, you can use those tools anywhere. Call me if you need me. I'll be watching the tournament, so you can be sure I'll be available before your matches."

"I may just take you up on that." C.J. gave one last squeeze before letting Andrea go.

"I want a better hug than that," Terri said.

"You've got it." C.J. wrapped her arms around Terri and gave her a heartfelt embrace.

"My home is your home, child."

"I can't tell you what that means to me," C.J. said, wiping a tear from her eye. "I promise to make sure Trystan comes back here more often."

"Not without you in tow," Terri said. "I want to see both of you."

"Cross my heart," C.J. said, "we'll be back soon."

CHAPTER FIFTEEN

Trystan watched C.J. through the floor-to-ceiling glass windows.

C.J.'s face was turned to the rising sun, her eyes were closed, and her legs were crossed Indian-style on a yoga mat. After ten minutes or so, she opened her eyes, smiling as she spied Trystan staring at her. She motioned for Trystan to join her on the deck.

"Hi. I didn't want to disturb you. You looked so beautiful, so peaceful," Trystan said.

"I was trying a new meditation technique Andrea taught me." C.J. pulled Trystan down for a kiss. "Mmm. Yep—it definitely centered me." C.J. smiled against Trystan's lips.

"Keep that up and I may have to try a few deep breathing exercises myself."

C.J. leaned in and kissed Trystan again. *I want you so much, but I'm scared.* She let her lips roam over Trystan's jaw, her neck, her collarbones.

Trystan buried her hands in C.J.'s thick, copper hair, cautiously pulling her closer. They still hadn't done more than kiss and spend the night holding each other.

When C.J. slid her hands under Trystan's T-shirt, Trystan gasped. "Baby, you're making me crazy."

"That's the idea," C.J. murmured against the side of Trystan's neck.

Trystan's pulse raced. "C.J., I want to make love with you, but it's your call. I don't want to push you."

C.J. pulled back and stared deeply into Trystan's eyes. The intensity she saw there made her instantly wet. She swallowed hard, her heart rate accelerating. Without pausing to consider what she was doing, C.J. stood and removed her sports bra and shorts. She reached down, took Trystan's hands, and pulled her up.

"Touch me," C.J. breathed.

Trystan's mouth went dry and her eyes grew wide. "Are you sure?"

C.J. closed her eyes. When she opened them, the look was enough to melt Trystan on the spot.

"Yes, I'm sure." C.J. threaded Trystan's fingers through her own and brought their combined hands to her breasts. "Touch me. Please."

Trystan moaned, need pooling in the pit of her stomach. She brought C.J.'s palms to her lips, kissing and licking each one before disentangling their fingers. Slowly, she brushed the hair from C.J.'s shoulders, placing gentle kisses along her shoulders and throat.

C.J. leaned her head back to give Trystan better access.

"You are so very beautiful," Trystan said, ducking her head to capture a hardening nipple with her teeth.

"Oh, my God," C.J. cried, the sensation sending pulses of fire racing through her body. She surged forward into Trystan's mouth. "That feels so good." She held Trystan against her, wanting—needing—more.

Trystan splayed her hands against C.J.'s bare back, her blunt fingernails digging lightly into C.J.'s flesh. "Let me take you inside," she murmured against C.J.'s breast.

"No, I don't want to stop."

"C.J...."

"Please." C.J. shifted subtly, bringing her hot center in contact with Trystan's pelvis. "Please, baby."

The timbre of C.J.'s voice sent shivers down Trystan's spine. She lowered her hands to cup C.J.'s buttocks, gradually increasing the pressure on her center. "Like that?"

"Oh, yes," C.J. moaned.

"You're so wet for me, love." C.J.'s desire was evident through the satin panties she still wore.

"It's all for you. Everything I have is yours."

Trystan knelt and kissed C.J.'s center through the thin material. She breathed deeply, inhaling the intoxicating, rich scent.

"Argh." C.J.'s fingers dug into Trystan's shoulders. Her legs began to tremble. She tried to formulate the words to ask for what she needed—it all coalesced into a single syllable. "Please." She tore at her own panties, removing the last remaining barrier until she stood gloriously naked, the early morning sunshine glinting off her hair, her head thrown back in passion.

Reverently, Trystan buried her face in C.J., nuzzling the soft folds with her nose, flattening her tongue against C.J.'s clit and running it the length of her center.

C.J. let out a surprised gasp, her body shaking with a need she'd never known. She swayed and pulled Trystan's head closer, her mind struggling to catch up with the rest of her. When her knees would've buckled, Trystan tightened her grip.

"I've got you, love. I'll never let you fall."

C.J. could find no words. A kaleidoscope of colors and shapes formed behind her eyes, bursting forth in unison. She fought desperately to maintain control, panic rising unbidden within. Her teeth ground together and tears leaked from the corners of her eyes. Feelings of shame warred with intense pleasure, and helplessness dueled with joy as the orgasm ripped through her, leaving her breathless. As she struggled to regain her equilibrium, she began to cry great, gulping sobs.

The intensity of C.J.'s reaction made Trystan's head spin. Her heart, which had been filled with joy at bringing C.J. pleasure, constricted painfully at the sight of her lover's obvious distress. She leapt to her feet, gathered C.J. in her arms and rocked her. "What is it, baby? Did I hurt you? What is it?"

C.J. continued to cry and her whole body trembled. Her chest heaved with the effort to bring air into her lungs.

Trystan continued to hold her, whispering soothing words into her hair as her own tears began to fall. *I would never hurt you, never.* "Nothing bad can happen to you, love. Not now, not ever. Not as long as I'm here."

C.J. took a ragged breath and buried her head in the side of Trystan's neck. "I-I c-came."

Trystan smiled in spite of herself. "Yes, you did, baby, and it was beautiful."

"No," C.J. said, shaking her head against Trystan. "T-Terrance. I didn't know what was happening to me. All I knew was how ashamed I felt afterward." She cried harder.

"Oh, baby," Trystan gasped. She tightened her grip even more. "You couldn't help the way your body reacted. That was physiological, honey. It doesn't mean you liked what he did to you."

"I d-don't want to have that between us every time you make love to me."

"It won't be, C.J. I promise you it won't be." Trystan pulled back and lifted C.J.'s chin so that they were eye-to-eye. "Do you love me?"

"With all my heart."

"And I love you with all *my* heart. That's what makes it different, baby. You and I give ourselves willingly, in love. Not in anger, not in hate, not in any sick, twisted way, but because we love each other and we want to express that love."

C.J. nodded and wiped away a tear with the tip of her finger. "Okay."

"How about if we forgive the little C.J. for what she had to do to survive? Can we do that? She was damn resourceful in my book and courageous. What do you say?"

C.J. sniffled. "Do you really think so?"

"I know so," Trystan said.

"I can try."

"That's my girl."

"I love you, Trystan."

"And I love you, C.J."

They stayed like that a few moments longer, bodies pressed tightly together.

"I want to make love to you," C.J. finally said.

"And I want you to, baby. But not right now. We've got a workout to get through, and you've got to get your butt on the practice court."

"But..."

Trystan laughed. "Far be it for me to turn down a beautiful woman who wants to ravish my body, but first things first."

"No fair."

"Life's not fair, C.J. How about if I promise to make myself available for dinner and dessert later on?" Trystan waggled her eyebrows.

"I want a written guarantee that I get to do whatever I want to you later."

"Where's the pen and paper?"

"Sorry, I don't seem to have any pockets," C.J. said, bending over to pick up her clothes.

Trystan slapped C.J. playfully on the butt as the two women walked into the house together, arm in arm.

"Give me ten more, baby."

C.J. shot Trystan a murderous glare.

"It's about strengthening your core muscles, C.J.," Trystan said.

"I don't see you doing crunches while lying on some ball."

"You also don't see me out winning championships. It's all for you, cupcake."

"I'll give you six more."

"Eight and it's a deal—you drive a hard bargain."

C.J. grumbled but completed eight more abdominal crunches on the stability ball.

As she rose from the last crunch, Trystan kissed her thoroughly. "Compliance has its rewards," she said, winking.

"Want another eight?" C.J. asked, laughing.

"Save your strength for later. Right now, if I'm not mistaken, you're expected courtside."

Trystan sat in the small bleachers off to the side of the court with Mitch as Grant put C.J. through a grueling practice.

"I really appreciate C.J. inviting me up here," Mitch said.

"With the tour schedule, I imagine you and Grant don't get much time together," Trystan said. "There's no reason why you two should have to be apart on an off-week. I'm sure that's what C.J. was thinking."

Mitch regarded Trystan thoughtfully. Her eyes hadn't left C.J. since she'd walked out on the court. "The tour doesn't mind loaning you out to C.J. for a week?"

Trystan weighed her response carefully. She didn't want to do anything to jeopardize C.J.'s privacy without talking to her about it first. "It just so happens that I'm off this week, too. C.J. asked me if I would be willing to continue working with her, and I agreed."

"That works out well then," Mitch said agreeably.

"Yes, it does."

Before either one of them could say anything more, Trystan's cell phone rang. "Excuse me," she said, moving away.

"Trystan Lightfoot."

"It's Trudy Skylar, Trystan."

"What can I do for you?"

"Our lawyers and the board have reviewed your *situation*," she said the last word with disdain.

"And?"

"Despite the fact that we feel you've violated the spirit of the contract, technically, you've done nothing wrong. As a result, you will be formally reinstated as of next Monday. I'll expect you in New York for the start of the Open."

Trystan smiled to herself. "What about my proposal with regard to an assistant?"

"Do you have someone specific in mind?"

Trystan had already given the matter a great deal of consideration. "Yes, I do. Her name is Nanette Cooley—I've worked with her before. Her credentials are impeccable, and I like her work ethic. Oh, and for the record, she's straight." Trystan could've sworn she heard Trudy breathe a sigh of relief.

"Can you get her on board in time for next week? You've only got a couple of days..."

"I'll talk to her today. Shall I have her call you?"

"No. The way I see it, she'll be on your staff. You make the decisions—and you're the one who'll be held accountable. I'll fax you a salary range and generic contract. You fill in the blanks."

"Okay, fine."

"Let there be no mistake about it, Trystan, if this doesn't work, we won't hesitate to terminate your contract."

"Understood. You don't have anything to worry about."

"For your sake, I hope you're right."

Trystan clicked the phone shut and tapped it against her chin. Nanette was an old friend, her first roommate when she'd gone back to school for her PT degree. Trystan trusted Nan with her life—it was why she'd been contemplating her for the assistant's job.

Trystan knew there was a chance that Trudy would decide Nan could do the job quite nicely and cut her out of the picture. She also knew Nan would tell Trudy to pound salt if she tried anything remotely like that. Trystan dialed Nanette's cell phone number.

Trystan sat with her back against the house, C.J. snuggled safely in her arms. Candles placed strategically around the deck bathed the side of C.J.'s face in soft light. Trystan kissed her temple.

"I never allowed myself to dream it could be like this," C.J. said softly.

"No?"

C.J. shook her head. "Every time I would start to get lonely and regret the things I was missing, I would remind myself that my existence was about tennis. Period. There would be time for the rest of my life later, after I retired."

"That must've felt very sad."

"It did, but I was so focused, it wasn't hard to redirect my energy toward the game."

"And now?" Trystan held her breath.

"Now I know that I was a fool—love only makes everything sweeter." She shifted her body so that their lips met. The kiss was long, slow, and tender.

"Thank you for letting me in," C.J. said when they finally pulled apart.

"I'm the one who should be thanking you." Trystan twirled a lock of C.J.'s hair around her finger.

"What is a beautiful woman like you doing on the market?" C.J. wondered aloud.

"I'm not on the market anymore," Trystan said tightly.

"I'm okay with that," C.J. said, flashing a sexy smile. She could feel the waves of tension flowing from Trystan. "Now answer the question." She kissed Trystan playfully on the mouth, then moved just out of reach. She hoped the gesture would help Trystan relax.

Trystan sighed. "I've never been much for commitment, I guess."

C.J. shook her head sadly. "I find that hard to believe, love. Something must've happened to make you feel that way."

Trystan bit her lower lip. *If you don't tell her, how can you ever have an honest relationship? Admit your mistakes and move on.* She got up and began to pace, unable to tell the story without separating herself physically from C.J.

"There was a woman once, a very long time ago."

"Tell me about her," C.J. said quietly. She wanted to take Trystan in her arms but sensed that any such move on her part wouldn't be welcome.

"Her name was Jamison Parker."

"The author?"

Trystan nodded. "She was a reporter for *Time* magazine at the time, although I didn't know it then. I'd recently returned to the reservation, and she was a patient of my mother's—she'd been forced off the road in an attempted murder."

"Oh, my God." C.J. put a hand over her mouth.

"She was pretty banged up—broken ribs, dislocated shoulder, and a head injury."

"Ouch."

"That wasn't the worst, though. She couldn't remember anything when she woke up."

"I can't imagine what that must've felt like," C.J. said.

"Mmm. Andrea attributed it to traumatic amnesia. The circumstances of the accident were just too much for Jay's mind to deal with."

"Not surprising—I mean, someone tried to kill her."

"Anyway," Trystan paused to stare out at Cathedral Rock, gathering strength from its solidity. "I was taken with her right from the start. I was in my early twenties, and I'd never known anyone like Jay—she was gentle, pretty, and funny." Trystan gave a self-deprecating half-shrug. "I fell head over heels for her in no time flat."

C.J. sat unmoving, when all she wanted was to take Trystan in her arms and offer comfort. Her heart was breaking for Trystan and for the pain she obviously still carried. *Let her get through it, Ceeg. She needs to do this on her own.*

"I had all sorts of romantic visions of a future together and a lifetime spent loving each other." Trystan shook her head. "I was so naïve and young. I just assumed that's what Jay wanted, too, although she never indicated one way or the other. I thought things were moving in that direction."

"What happened?" C.J. asked.

"Her memory happened," Trystan answered, a trace of bitterness in her voice. "Turns out she had a partner and a life somewhere else."

"I'm so sorry."

Trystan turned to face C.J. "It was a long time ago, as I said."

"But it still hurts." *I can see the pain in your eyes.*

"If it doesn't kill you, it will make you stronger, right? I decided romantic love and real relationships weren't for me. It took me a long time to get over Jay, and I never wanted to go through that again."

"And now?"

Trystan smiled. "Now you've waltzed into my life and stolen my heart quite without my permission." She helped C.J. up and took her in her arms. "I tried to fight this, C.J. I tried, and I just can't. It's too strong." Tears spilled down her face.

"Don't cry, baby. Why are you crying?"

"I'm scared, and there's nothing I can do about it."

"What are you afraid of?" C.J. asked.

"That I'm in too deep. What if you decide this isn't really what you want? I don't think I can take being hurt like that again."

"I'll never hurt you, Trystan. I admit that I'm scared to death—I've never been in love before—but I also know I want to spend the rest of my life with you. I've never been more sure of anything."

C.J. brushed Trystan's tears away with her thumbs, then replaced her thumbs with her lips. She slid her hand down Trystan's bare arm and linked their fingers. "Come with me."

Trystan followed willingly.

"I believe you promised me something this morning," C.J. purred.

"I did?"

"Mmm-hmm."

"My memory's a little foggy—want to refresh me?"

C.J.'s eyes sparkled with desire. She took a deep breath to calm her nerves. *You can do this, Ceeg. Listen to her body and follow your instincts.* Without warning or preamble, she reached out and cupped Trystan through her shorts.

Tendrils of fire licked at Trystan's abdomen. Every muscle in her body tensed until she felt like she was holding herself up by sheer force of will alone. Gasping for air, she pulled oxygen into her starved lungs.

C.J. couldn't tear her eyes from those full, moisture-laden lips. Emboldened, she covered Trystan's mouth with her own, swallowing Trystan's strangled whimper. The sound made C.J. moan and her center turn to molten liquid. With her hands, she pulled frantically at Trystan's T-shirt, desperate to reach the skin beneath. Within seconds, she had divested Trystan of every article of clothing.

Unable to think clearly or act, Trystan's whole world narrowed to C.J.'s next touch. Never in her life had she felt so helpless and yet so safe.

C.J. lowered her head and sucked Trystan's breast greedily into her mouth. She moaned with delight at the exquisite taste and feel of the taut nipple. Wetness coated the inside of her own thighs, yet she ignored her needs, intent only on eliciting more whimpers from Trystan.

Trystan arched back, giving C.J. a better angle. She tried to form words, but none would come. Instead, she surrendered herself, body and soul.

C.J.'s movements became more fevered as a bone-deep yearning to satisfy Trystan stole over her. She buried her fingers in moist folds, sighing with pleasure as Trystan trembled beneath her touch. Impatiently, C.J. removed her own clothes and urged Trystan backward onto the bed.

Trystan cried out at the loss of contact, her body craving C.J.'s touch.

C.J. slid on top of Trystan's sweat-slicked skin, the first sweet brush of flesh against flesh making her body ache with pleasure and nearly causing her to climax. Hungrily, she sucked the hollow at Trystan's pulse point as her fingers once again sought Trystan's center.

Trystan's body thrust upward, pulling C.J. deeper inside. Her hips rocked of their own accord against C.J.'s hand, unsure whether it was release or prolongation they sought. Her fingers clawed at C.J.'s back, bringing their bodies closer. The change in position allowed her to lick at the sweat on a nearby shoulder.

C.J. growled against Trystan's neck, shifting so that her thigh provided additional pressure behind her hand. Trystan reached for C.J.'s hips, bringing their bodies into contact all along their lengths. The shock was like lighting a match to dry kindling for C.J. Her body soared through space, the flames consuming her.

As C.J.'s body shivered against her, the thin thread of control to which Trystan had been clinging snapped, pushing the air out of her lungs. Unbidden, tears sprang to her eyes as her body surrendered its vigilance. For the first time in her life, Trystan allowed herself to be vulnerable. She wept as a huge burden lifted from her soul, leaving her feeling lighter than she could ever remember being.

C.J.'s heart contracted as she felt Trystan sobbing against her shoulder. "Are you okay, love?" C.J. whispered, unsure what to make of the tears.

Trystan nodded against C.J.'s shoulder. Drying her eyes, she murmured, "Thank you."

"Why are you thanking me?" C.J. asked, somewhat confused.

"For giving me back something I didn't even know I was missing."

"What's that?"

"My soul," Trystan answered simply.

C.J. gathered Trystan in her arms, kissing her temple, then her eyelids and forehead. "Thank you," she said, "for helping me to reclaim my life."

Trystan wrapped her arm around C.J., pulled up the blanket, and snuggled close, smiling as she felt C.J. drift off to sleep.

CHAPTER SIXTEEN

Trystan paced back and forth at a LaGuardia Airport security checkpoint, looking at her watch yet again. She and C.J. had arrived forty-five minutes earlier, and she'd sent C.J. into Manhattan in the chauffeur-driven car provided for her by U.S. Open officials while she waited for her assistant PT to arrive.

Trystan hoped C.J. was getting settled into Becca's Upper West Side loft, where they would be staying for the duration of the tournament. She'd given C.J. the key since Becca had insisted on moving out while Trystan and C.J. were there to give them privacy and allow C.J. to focus without distractions.

"Hey, it's great to see you," a stocky, gregarious blonde pulled Trystan into a bear hug.

"Nan, you haven't changed a bit."

Nanette Cooley patted her ample belly. "The hell I haven't, liar."

"You look great to me."

"Thanks for the gig, Trys. I really appreciate it—working in a regular PT office wasn't for me."

"I'm sure the place wasn't big enough for your quiet personality." Trystan winked.

"What're you saying about me?"

"Nothing."

"Good."

"Did you check any luggage?"

"Nah."

"Okay, let's get out of here then," Trystan said, steering Nan down the escalator to the taxi stand.

Trystan gave the driver the address of the tournament's nearby host hotel, then sat back. Nan was staring at her. "What?"

"You look different—happier."

"You think?"

"Yeah, I think. What gives? You didn't say much on the phone."

"There are one hundred twenty-eight players in the draw—I can't possibly deal with all of them."

Nan shook her head. "Okay—that's the company line. Now cut the bullshit and tell me the real reason."

Trystan laughed. "I love that you're always so damn tactful."

"It's part of my charm."

"Yes, it is."

Trystan glanced to the front of the cab. "Not here."

They rode in silence until the driver pulled up to the hotel.

"Coffee?" Trystan asked Nan as they walked through the lobby.

"You know me too well."

When they were settled in a booth, Trystan said, "Politics and ethics."

"What?"

"That's part of the reason you're here."

"Elaborate, please."

"Trudy Skylar, the president of the WTF is very uptight about the perception of the tour as a hotbed of lesbianism. So she does everything in her power to make it look like there are no lesbians in women's tennis."

"Next thing I know, you'll be telling me there's no Santa Claus." Nan laughed.

"What can I say, she lives in her own little world."

"And this has something to do with me, how? I'm here because I'm straight?"

Trystan chuckled. "Let's just say that counted as a bonus when I mentioned it to her." Trystan leaned forward. "You're here because I had the temerity to fall in love with one of the top players."

"You rat—I told you you looked happier. Who's the lucky woman? And please tell me you aren't robbing the cradle."

"No, no cradle robbing. She's C.J. Winslow, and she's incredible."

Nan whistled. "I'll say. Way to go, girlfriend. Nice catch."

"The point is, ethically, it would be wrong for me to treat C.J.'s opponent on match day. Legally, it's not forbidden, but it's frowned upon. I made a case that it would be more efficient for me to hire an assistant and divide up the workload accordingly than for them to fire me and hire per diems."

"Oh, very smooth."

"Well, it's true. I was struggling to keep up anyway."

"I've got to give you props, my friend, for coming clean in the first place. That took guts."

"Not really. It was practical. I value my career—my reputation and integrity are important to me. Not only that, but I would never take a chance on hurting C.J. that way. If it ever came out…"

"I see your point. So I take it you're not going public."

Trystan reluctantly shook her head. "There's a lot at stake for C.J. here, Nan. Sponsorship monies, commercials, the media, the public… Her career has been her whole life. I don't want to mess with that."

Nan watched Trystan closely. "Coming from an out lesbian like you, that's quite a sacrifice. You must really be in love."

"Yeah, I really am."

"I can't wait to meet her."

"You'll love her." At Nan's raised eyebrow, Trystan added, "But in a completely platonic way."

"Glad you added that. Okay, so the deal is, we 'casually' divvy up the assignments like it's just a matter of availability. In truth, we'll scour the draw ahead of time and figure out who you can't treat, right?"

"I knew I liked you for a reason," Trystan smiled.

"No worries, my friend. I've got your back."

"How much time do we have?" Trystan asked as she and C.J. strolled along the streets of Manhattan on their way to ESPN's Times Square studio.

"Half an hour."

"Should we pick up the pace?"

"We're not very far," C.J. answered. She was enjoying the warm late-summer evening, the bustle of the city, and Trystan's company. *I want to spend the rest of my life walking beside you.*

"Grant arrives tonight?"

"Yes. He and Mitch are flying into Newark."

"One of my least favorite airports," Trystan said.

"Mine too," C.J. agreed.

"That reminds me. The other day when Mitch and I were watching you practice, I got the feeling he might've figured it out."

"Figured what out?"

"You and me. He was fishing a little, but I didn't tell him anything. What do you want to do?"

"Do?"

"He's not stupid, C.J. You spend half of your waking hours with Grant and the rest with me. I don't want to make an assumption, but I'm guessing Grant might have told Mitch about your discussion with him. Do you want to tell them explicitly about us or not?"

"Since Grant was the one who sent me after you in the first place, it only seems fitting that we share the great news with him and Mitch," C.J. said.

Trystan squeezed C.J.'s hand. "You want to tell them together? Or do you want to do it yourself?"

"Let's tell them over breakfast tomorrow morning," C.J. said. "Speaking of friends, am I going to get to meet the mysterious Becca tonight?"

"She said she'd stop by the apartment a little later. She's looking forward to meeting you."

"I'm looking forward to bribing her into telling me stories about you."

"Uh-oh," Trystan said. "On second thought, maybe I can get her to stay away."

C.J. pulled Trystan to a stop under the ESPN marquee. "Show time." Suddenly, she was nervous. Her pulse quickened and she bit her lower lip.

"You okay?" Trystan asked, clearly sensing the change in C.J.'s mood.

C.J. nodded. "I'm just trying to figure out what to say if anyone asks who you are."

Trystan's nostrils flared as she fought a flash of anger. "Why don't I just wait out here? Then you won't have to worry about being seen with me."

C.J. cringed as if she'd been struck. "That's not what I meant. I just…"

"It's all right, C.J. You have an image to maintain. I get it. I'll be back at Becca's when you're done." Trystan turned on her heel and stalked away, leaving C.J. standing alone on the sidewalk.

C.J.'s heart sank. She took two steps in the direction Trystan had headed, wanting nothing more than to go after her and set things right. *How are you going to explain blowing off a live interview, Ceeg? You have responsibilities.* Reluctantly, her heart aching, C.J. opened the door and walked into the television station.

"How's the back, C.J.?" ESPN *SportsCenter* anchor Rod Carter sat opposite C.J. on the set. She'd met him once before, at a sports banquet where he'd hit on her.

She tried to relax her shoulders, putting on her best public smile. The combination of Rod's overly familiar style and the argument with Trystan, however, was making C.J.'s nerves jump. "I'm feeling great, thanks."

"So you're one hundred percent for the Open?"

"I'm feeling good, I've been working on my game, and I'm confident."

"There was some speculation that you might retire. Any truth to that? Will we be seeing you in the broadcast booth soon?"

C.J. forced a smile. "I'm still excited about the game—eager to get out there and play every day. Don't count me out yet."

"I think anybody who saw you play in San Diego knows you've still got game. What do you think about your draw?"

"Both sides of the draw feature top-notch players. There are no easy wins anymore in women's tennis, especially at a major like the Open."

"Have you been doing anything different to train for this tournament? I imagine the older you get, the harder it is to keep in shape."

A shadow crossed C.J.'s face and her heart thudded heavily once as she thought about her workouts with Trystan. In her mind, she watched Trystan walk away outside the studio, her face set in an angry scowl. *You can't fall apart now, Ceeg. You'll work it out—have faith.*

"C.J.?"

"Sorry, what was the question?"

"Training—have you altered your routine to compensate for having to play all these youngsters?"

The way you've colored your hair to compete with younger anchors, jerkball? "Today's game is different than it was twenty years ago. Likewise, the equipment and training techniques have changed. Like all the other players, I try to keep up with the latest advances." C.J. managed a chuckle. "This is not your mother's tennis game."

"No, I guess it's not. Should we expect any surprises from you over the next fortnight?"

"Just good, solid tennis."

"A win would vault you back into the number one spot on the tour. Do you think that's a realistic goal?"

C.J. narrowed her eyes. *Asshole.* "I wouldn't be playing if I didn't think I could be number one."

"That's the competitive fire we've come to expect over the years from C.J. Winslow, folks. Good luck at the Open, C.J., and thanks for coming by the studio."

"You're welcome, Rod."

When they were clear, C.J. hastily removed her lapel microphone, intent on finding Trystan and working through their earlier misunderstanding.

"You're looking good, C.J.," Rod said, stepping into her personal space.

"Thanks. I'd love to stay and chat, but I've got to be someplace." She didn't give him an opportunity to respond as she walked off the set and into a waiting elevator.

Trystan watched the interview live on the large-screen plasma TV in Becca's living room. She was pacing while Becca sat on the leather sofa.

"Sit down, will you? You're making me dizzy."

"See that? Her jaw muscle bunched."

"My jaw muscle would bunch, too, if I had a loser like him asking me ridiculous questions," Becca said.

Trystan wheeled around to face Becca. "I thought you were my friend."

"I am your friend. What do you want me to say? You want to know that C.J.'s unhappy—that she's pining for you because you blew your cork at her? Is that what I'm supposed to be seeing in her face?"

Trystan pivoted and resumed her pacing. "Can you look at her and tell me you don't see tension there? And she was completely distracted when he asked her about her training routine."

"What is it you want from her, Trys? You want her to be contrite for worrying about her image? For being honest in telling you what was on her mind?"

Trystan growled.

"Listen, friend. C.J. does have a reputation to maintain—there are millions of dollars in endorsement deals at stake and thousands of little girls who want to grow up to be just like her. Getting mad at her for taking all that into consideration hardly seems fair to me."

Trystan stopped in the middle of the floor. "You think I was wrong."

"I think this is all new to C.J. and probably more than a little overwhelming."

"And it's not to me?"

"You've been an out lesbian for a long time, Trys."

"I don't have any experience at relationships."

"Not a lot, no, but you have some, which is more than C.J. has. Beyond that, I think she's under a ton of pressure right now—the U.S. Open, in case you haven't heard, is a pretty major tournament. She's just coming off a bad injury, she's got a new coach, a new relationship, a new sexuality… Yeah, I think you might have been a little hard on her."

Trystan plopped down on the sofa and ran her fingers roughly through her hair. "I flew off the handle."

Becca nodded. "Yes, you did. It's going to take time, champ, for you to get used to each other and to work through these kinds of issues. Running away every time your feelings get hurt isn't going to help."

Trystan started to defend herself, then clicked her jaw shut. When she did open her mouth to speak, her tone had changed. "I was an asshole, huh?"

"I think you were a tad insensitive to C.J.'s plight."

Trystan nodded. "I was an asshole."

"If you say so," Becca agreed.

They watched the rest of *SportsCenter* together, then a show about octopuses in which scientists explained why they were the most intelligent invertebrates on Earth.

A hesitant knock on the door brought Trystan to her feet. "I'll get it," she said.

Becca watched with amusement as Trystan practically ran to the door. She gathered her duffle bag and keys from the foyer.

"Hi," C.J. said tentatively when Trystan opened the door.

"Hi," Trystan answered, pulling C.J. inside and into a hug. "I'm sorry, I was a jerk."

"I'm sorry, too," C.J. said. "All I want is to have you by my side. I can't imagine my world without you, and I'll do whatever it takes to make this work."

"No. Your concerns were real, and I was being selfish. I had no right to be angry." Trystan kissed C.J. on the forehead.

"If you all will excuse me, I'll just sneak right on past you," Becca said, maneuvering her way around the couple.

"Oh, no you don't," Trystan said, releasing C.J. and grabbing Becca by the back of the shirt. "You're not going anywhere until proper introductions have been made."

"Seems to me you guys have better things to do than make small talk with me."

"C.J. Winslow, this is my best friend, Rebecca Hamilton—Becca. Becca, this is the extraordinarily talented and sexy C.J. Winslow."

"It's a pleasure to meet you," C.J. said, blushing.

"I'm the one who should be honored. Any woman who can tame Trystan Lightfoot deserves to be revered."

C.J. laughed. "I'm fairly certain I haven't tamed Trystan."

"Yet," Becca said, winking. "But you have captured her heart—a feat no one has ever accomplished—very impressive."

Trystan reddened and slapped Becca playfully on the arm.

"I'd love to stay and chat," Becca said, "but I'm off on a great adventure."

"You're leaving?" C.J. asked.

"Yep," Trystan jumped in. "Becca has some crazy notion that we'll be needing privacy over the next two weeks."

"I won't be responsible for kicking you out of your own home," C.J. said. "That's ridiculous."

"My choice, C.J., I assure you. I've been wanting to take a vacation for months. You've just given me the excuse I was looking for."

"Why is it I don't believe you?" C.J. said, narrowing her eyes.

Becca affected her best wide-eyed innocent look. "I don't know what you're talking about. Gotta run, ladies. Ta ta for now." She glided out the door, leaving C.J. and Trystan alone.

"Are we okay?" C.J. asked, wrapping her arms around Trystan.

"We're better than okay," Trystan answered, kissing C.J.'s forehead, eyelids, and chin before claiming her lips in a tender gesture of truce.

"Mmm," C.J. hummed against Trystan's mouth, relief giving way to desire. "How is it that I can't seem to get enough of you?" She surged forward, pressing her body hard against Trystan. Her hands found the back pockets of Trystan's jeans as their hips melded together. "I'm so wet for you," C.J. panted. "Always."

"I'm glad," Trystan said, guiding them to the floor, "because I'm addicted to you."

C.J. gasped as Trystan nibbled on the tender skin at her pulse point. "I love you, Trystan."

"I love you, too, C.J."

Grant and Mitch had just been seated when C.J. and Trystan joined them in the restaurant at Trump Towers.

"Good morning, guys," C.J. said brightly. "How was your flight?"

"Long," Mitch answered, his gaze shifting from one woman to the other and back again. "But you two look refreshed."

C.J. and Trystan exchanged a knowing glance. "That's because we took the earlier flight," C.J. said. "Did you see the ESPN interview?"

"We caught some of it in the airport," Grant said. "What's Carter's problem with you anyway?" he addressed C.J.

"I turned him down."

"Ah," Mitch said, "nothing like a blow to a stud's ego to bring out the catty bitch in him."

"Was it obvious how uncomfortable I was?" C.J. asked.

"No. I thought you handled him well," Grant said. "You didn't take the bait, you were gracious, and you were confident. I hope Duchan, Ries-Mantonia, Quick, Duschene, Pace, and Meritsa were all watching."

"Foster's the only one I care about," C.J. said, referring to Sylvia Foster, currently ranked first in the world.

"Let's worry about your side of the draw before we get too far ahead of ourselves," Grant cautioned.

"You and I both know she'll get to the finals. She's standing between me and the championship." *And the number one ranking.*

"Her and your entire side of the draw. We can't overlook any of these matches, C.J."

C.J. sat back, rotating her shoulders. "I know."

"Look, I understand how you feel about Foster—really, I do," Grant said. "She's an arrogant little vamp who'd feed her mother to a rabid dog if it got her more publicity. She's not worthy of a number one—I get it. But there are six matches before you reach the finals. The path to Foster runs through your half of the draw."

C.J. searched Grant's face. "Are you worried I won't get there?"

"No." He looked her directly in the eyes. "I think if you stay healthy and focused, you can beat anybody."

"Yes, I can. And I will."

"The workouts are going well. I can't say it's impossible that the PSIS could give C.J. trouble again," Trystan said, "but I'm confident that the original injury is healed. We've just got to keep up with the core strengthening program."

"I've reserved court time for us later this morning over at the Manhattan Tennis Club," Grant said. "I thought it would be nice to work away from prying eyes for a day."

"Sounds good," C.J. said. She glanced over at Trystan, a question in her eyes.

Trystan nodded.

"There's something we wanted to talk to you about," C.J. began, a smile playing on her lips. A warm hand closed over hers under the table. "You guys are part of my family now."

"And you're part of ours," Mitch said, regarding C.J. shrewdly. "So tell us you two are in love already and get it over with so we can eat."

C.J. knew her mouth was hanging open, but she couldn't help it.

Trystan threw back her head and laughed, as did Grant.

Mitch looked around the table at all three of them. "What? Am I wrong? You two have been mooning over each other for weeks. Now you've got that certain…glow about you that just screams love. I call it the way I see it." He shrugged.

"I guess I should thank you for making that so easy, but honestly, that isn't quite the way I envisioned telling you," C.J. said, joining in the laughter.

"It's great to have company in love—I just couldn't wait anymore for you to beat around the bush," Mitch said.

"C.J., Mitch and I have never been able to be ourselves anywhere. You accepted us as a couple and gave me a place where I could actually be myself," Grant said.

"Yes, having to be a macho stud can be so tiring," Mitch threw in.

Grant gave him a mock glare. "I can't tell you what that means to us. We think it's great—you guys make an awesome couple."

C.J. melted into Trystan's eyes. "Yeah, we do, don't we?"

CHAPTER SEVENTEEN

Monday dawned bright and clear. C.J. sat cross-legged in the middle of Becca's living room rug; the sun pouring in through the windows bathed her in bright light. Her eyes were closed and she was concentrating on her breathing.

Trystan, who was becoming accustomed to this sight, tiptoed into the kitchen in a T-shirt and panties to start the coffee brewing.

"No need to sneak around, Lightfoot, I know you're there," C.J. said, without opening her eyes.

"You do, do you?" Trystan moved closer to C.J. but remained just out of reach.

"Yep. I do." C.J. opened her eyes and quick as a cat, pounced on Trystan's legs, forcing her to the floor.

"Hey!" Trystan yelped as C.J. straddled her.

"Are you complaining?" C.J. asked in a low, seductive whisper as she pinned Trystan's arms to the floor.

Trystan arched an eyebrow. "I guess that depends on your intentions."

"What do you want my intentions to be?" C.J. laughed and pulled her head back as Trystan tried to rise up for a kiss. "Use your words, strong girl."

Trystan tried once more unsuccessfully to leverage herself up.

"Some people are slow learners." C.J. shook her head. "What do you want, baby?" she cooed.

Trystan licked her lips. *You are the sexiest woman alive.* "I want you to take me, any way you want to take me."

C.J. swallowed hard as her pulse jumped. *You started it, Ceeg. You're the one playing with fire.* She swooped in and kissed Trystan on the mouth. As she felt her yield, C.J. released one of Trystan's arms. With her free hand, she stroked first one breast, then the other as she deepened the kiss.

Trystan willed herself to relax. She'd never allowed another woman to take control during lovemaking, but C.J. wasn't just any other woman. *She owns your heart, Trys, and she doesn't seem to be afraid or holding anything back anymore. You don't need to be in charge all the time.*

C.J. rose off her to remove their clothes, and Trystan immediately felt the loss. She groaned.

"Miss me?" C.J. asked playfully. She made a show of disrobing, taking her time. She watched Trystan's eyes follow her every move, her skin flushing from the heat of her lover's gaze. "No touching me when I take your clothes off, hot stuff," C.J. said before peeling Trystan's underwear and T-shirt off.

Trystan growled when C.J. pinned her arms again and slid along her abdomen, leaving a trail of wetness in her wake.

"Does that feel good, baby?" C.J. asked, leaning forward so that her breasts swayed just out of reach of Trystan's mouth. C.J. was having a hard time focusing. The velvet feel of her lover's soft skin against her center melted her insides.

"Mmm." Trystan was mesmerized—her body was aflame. The feel of C.J.'s slick folds against her left a trail of gooseflesh all along Trystan's abdomen. She flexed her fingers and struggled against the restraining bonds of C.J.'s hands. "Can I have my hands back? I want to touch you."

"Not yet," C.J. said, her eyes twinkling. "I'm just getting started. I'm going to let go of you, but I want your word that you won't move your hands or arms from their current position."

"That's not fair," Trystan said.

"Promise me," C.J. said in her most persuasively seductive voice. She planted a trail of kisses down the center of Trystan's body, pausing to nip at her bellybutton, suck on her pelvic bones, and kiss the insides of her thighs.

"I don't know if I can promise you that, but I'll try," Trystan choked out.

"You did say it was my show, didn't you?" C.J. said as she felt Trystan squirm. "Well, didn't you?" C.J. asked again, as she ran her tongue along the length of Trystan's clit and cupped her ass with her hands.

Trystan gasped and lifted her hips to prolong the contact with C.J.'s mouth.

"Mmm. You taste wonderful." *You're so wet for me, love.* C.J. kissed Trystan's clit and licked her again. "You were the one who said I could do anything I wanted, right?"

"Ugh."

"I'm sorry, I couldn't make out what you were saying." C.J. smiled. "Care to repeat yourself?" she asked, dipping her head for another taste.

No one's ever done this to me before—not this way. I'm going to explode, love. "You're killing me."

"I certainly hope not." C.J. settled in to devour her lover.

Trystan arched upward, body taut, pulse racing, her heart full. "Oh, C.J., right there. Don't stop."

C.J. felt elated. *I won't, baby. Not now, not ever. I love you.* She savored the moment as Trystan came.

"We'll be inviting scrutiny if we show up together," Trystan argued as she and C.J. sat on the sofa watching footage of Cynthia Quick, C.J.'s first-round opponent.

C.J., her hair still damp from the shower, nuzzled Trystan's neck. "All I want is to be with you as long as possible."

"I feel the same way, babe, but we have to be practical here. I have to be in the treatment room and ready to work at 8:30 a.m. Your match isn't until 11:00."

"I have to be there early to stretch and practice—we'll be getting there at the same time anyway."

"Maybe so, but you and I both know arriving at exactly the same time would be like waving a red cape in front of a bull. Work with me here, C.J. This isn't what I want, either."

C.J. turned to face Trystan fully. "This is going to be hell, isn't it—pretending like I'm not madly in love with you and you're not my world?"

"Tell me about it," Trystan agreed. "But right now it has to be about your tennis. This is everything you've been pointing toward. We can be together every night and wake up together every morning, but while the tournament's on, it's got to be all business."

"I don't have to like it," C.J. said, pouting.

"Neither do I, but we've both got jobs to do. Trudy's going to be watching me like a hawk, for one thing. And for another, I won't be a distraction for you. You need to focus on winning the championship."

"I won't lose sight of that—you know I won't. You're right, it's what I've been working toward all season. I promised myself I'd win my eighth Open. Not only that, but I swore I'd knock snide Sylvia into next week and regain my ranking. It's just that…"

"What?" Trystan's heart melted as she noted the sadness in C.J.'s eyes.

"Tennis has always been the most important—no, the only thing—for me. That's not true anymore. It doesn't mean anything without you by my side to share it."

"I'll be right here, honey." *I want to share it with you, too.*

"But you won't be right *here*," C.J. emphasized, pulling Trystan into her side and putting an arm around her.

"I want to be by your side through it all, love," Trystan said, her voice husky, "but right now it's not in either of our best interests. I hate it, but that's the hard truth."

After a moment spent lost in each other's gazes, C.J. picked up Trystan's hand and kissed the palm. "I'll miss you."

"I'll miss you, too, but I'll be right here with you," Trystan touched C.J.'s heart. "I promise you."

"Will you be able to see the match today?"

Trystan mentally calculated. "I don't want to disappoint you, C.J. But if I promise you that and get waylaid, you'll be too distracted. It'll depend on how many treatments I have to do and what kinds of injuries present themselves."

"Oh," C.J. said, trying not to sound as let down as she felt.

Trystan squeezed her hand. "I'll do the best I can, okay?"

"Sure. I know you will."

"It'll be easier later in the tournament when there are fewer players around to deal with," Trystan said. "I hate feeling like I've upset you."

"Don't worry about it, honey. You've got a job to do—I understand that."

"I'll be rooting for you. I know you're going to kick ass." Trystan kissed C.J. on the temple.

"Thanks. I'm not planning on taking any prisoners."

"That's my girl."

The locker room was buzzing with activity as C.J. went through her pre-match ritual. She did her best to shut out the noise and concentrate on her breathing. Despite her best efforts, she found her mind wandering to Trystan and what she was doing. The training and treatment rooms were less than fifty feet away, and C.J. fought the urge to peek in and say hello. *Trystan is right—I've got to get my head in the game.*

C.J. checked her watch—ten minutes before she'd be called for the match. She glanced around her, looking for a private space in which to go through the tapping sequence Andrea had taught her. Short of locking herself in a bathroom stall, she couldn't think of a place where she could be alone. She closed her eyes and rubbed her temples.

"If you need a place to hide for a few minutes, try treatment room number two. I shut the door to reserve it for you."

C.J. opened her eyes, delighted to see Trystan standing there. "I didn't hear you come up."

"I only have a second." Trystan looked around to be sure no one was watching them. "I figured you'd need to take care of some pre-match things," she winked, "and this place is a zoo."

"Have I told you lately how much I love you?"

Trystan stepped back as two other players walked by. "I've got to get back. Good luck." She stared meaningfully at C.J. for a moment, trying to convey with her expression what she couldn't say.

"Thanks. I'll see you later," she said wistfully.

C.J. waited for Trystan to leave before heading for treatment room two. Alone in the blessed quiet, she began by using the "Cook's Hookup" for brain balancing. She crossed her left ankle over her right and put her left hand on her right knee. With her tongue behind her front teeth and her mouth closed, she breathed in through her nose and out through her mouth for a minute and a half.

She'd begun using the technique as soon as she'd resumed practicing in Sedona the week before. Although she'd been skeptical at first, she'd discovered that Andrea was right—the exercise really did help her get both sides of her brain working in sync—it made seeing the ball and concentrating that much easier.

When she felt balanced and relaxed, C.J. summoned up the rape and initiated the thought field therapy sequence, using her fingers to tap on the meridian points in her body as Andrea had shown her. She ran through the sequence twice, sitting and focusing on her body for a minute when she finished. She felt at peace, more so than she could ever remember being before a match. She smiled to herself, sending out a silent thank you to Andrea.

She'd just stood to leave when there was a light tap on the door. "Come in?"

Trystan slipped through the door and shut it behind her. "I couldn't let you go out there without this..." She leaned forward and captured C.J.'s lips in a kiss equal parts passion and tenderness. "I love you. You're going to be great."

"I will now," C.J. said, a dreamy expression on her face.

The match, as it turned out, wasn't much of a match at all. C.J. dispensed of Cynthia 6-0, 6-1 in less than an hour—she barely broke a sweat.

"Looking at C.J. Winslow today, it's hard to believe she's suffering from a back injury, Nancy." USA Network commentators Nancy Davidson and James LeRoy were broadcasting from a specially designed booth high atop Arthur Ashe stadium.

"She looks strong, confident, she's moving well, and if she continues to play like she did today, she'll be nearly unbeatable," Nancy said. "She's got a tough second-round match coming up, most likely against Roberta Ries-Mantonia. Ries is a very hard hitter but somewhat inconsistent. I can see C.J. getting clear through to the quarters without too much trouble, providing she stays healthy."

"Let's go down to Del Nordstrom, who's standing by with C.J."

"Thanks, James. C.J., that was an impressive performance. How's the back?"

"I feel good, thanks. I've spent two weeks recovering and getting myself ready for this tournament—I'm here to compete."

"I don't think anyone questions that after the way you came out today. Did you expect it to be so easy?"

"Cynthia is a very good player. I anticipate a tough match every time I step on the court with her."

"Rate your chances for going forward."

"This is the U.S. Open, Del. Every match is difficult—every opponent has the chance to win. I'm just planning to stick with my game plan, stay within myself, and play good, strong tennis."

"Sounds like a recipe for success to me. C.J. Winslow, thank you. We'll look forward to seeing you day after tomorrow."

C.J. walked through the tunnel and into the locker room. She stood for several moments at her locker, debating, before heading for the training room.

There were several players in various stages of treatment, and Trystan was nowhere in sight. As C.J. turned back around to leave, a cherubic blonde called to her, "Help you?"

"Hmm? Um, no. I was just…looking for some ice."

"I can help you with that. Come with me. I'm Nan, by the way, the assistant PT."

"I'm…"

"C.J. Winslow, I know. Come with me." She winked. Nan led C.J. down the hall. "I think what you're looking for is in here." Nan opened a door to an office, where Trystan was talking on the phone. When C.J. spun around to look at her, Nan simply smiled and arched an eyebrow.

"Thank you," C.J. said. "I can see why Trystan says she'd walk through fire for you."

"She's family to me—which means you are, too, now. Take good care of her."

"We'll take good care of each other." C.J. sighed dreamily.

Nan rolled her eyes. "Don't worry about me. I'll just be out there dealing with the masses. You two take all the time you need." Laughter trailed her down the corridor.

C.J. sat in the chair across from Trystan and watched her as she discussed treatment protocols over the phone.

"Sorry," Trystan mouthed.

C.J. waved the apology away. *I just want to be in the same space with you.*

When Trystan hung up the phone, she came around the desk. "You were brilliant out there, love."

C.J. stood so they were toe-to-toe. "You saw it?"

"Only on television, I'm afraid, but I'm so proud of you." She leaned forward and kissed C.J. tenderly. "Any problem with the back?"

"Not even a twinge."

"I'd still like you to ice it and take a whirlpool, just to be on the safe side."

"Okay. I've got practice scheduled for this afternoon, though."

"Ice and whirlpool now, then heat just before the practice, then ice again."

"Slave driver." C.J. smiled.

"It's all for you, babe." Trystan patted C.J. on the butt.

"You're probably going to be late, huh?"

"It's a little crazy out there right now. Hopefully, things will settle down a bit, but the night session doesn't start until 7:00, so I'd say you shouldn't expect to see me much before midnight." Trystan looked at C.J. apologetically. "I'm sorry."

"It's your job, don't be sorry."

"What're you going to do?"

"Practice, work out, then have dinner with Grant and Mitch. I'll probably watch some of the late matches on TV and go to bed early." C.J. waggled her eyebrows and flicked her forefinger over Trystan's nipple through the cotton of her shirt. "I'll be waiting for you."

Trystan closed her eyes as her nipple hardened. "What you do to me should be illegal."

"See you later, baby." C.J. winked as she exited the office.

As it turned out, later was *much* later. By the time Trystan finally stumbled into bed, it was 1:30 a.m. and she was beyond exhaustion.

"Mmm," C.J. murmured, rolling over and wrapping her arms around Trystan. "I tried to wait up for you," she slurred.

"Shh. It's okay, baby. Go back to sleep."

C.J. kissed Trystan's shoulder and snuggled closer. "See you in the morning. Love you."

The first week of the tournament passed in a blur as Trystan and C.J. fell into separate routines. C.J. spent her off days working out, practicing, and watching some of the matches. For her Wednesday, Friday, and Sunday matches, she followed the same schedule she'd used the first day of play, with pretty much the same results. She sailed into the second week having dropped only nine games total in eight sets of tennis. Everything would've been perfect, if it weren't for the fact that she caught only glimpses of Trystan here and there without any time to spend together.

Trystan, for her part, was running herself ragged. Her days started before 8:00 a.m. and ended well after midnight. There were players to treat, doctors to consult, and coaches to mollify. She wondered how she ever could've done it without having Nan on board. She'd yet to see one of C.J.'s matches in person, and it was making her testy. By the time she arrived home at night, she was too tired to do anything but sleep, and C.J. needed her rest.

In the mornings, they both had too many things to get done to do more than share a quick kiss, a hug, and a promise for something more soon. By Monday, another off day for her, C.J. was beside herself.

She was watching the night matches on television—the fourth-round match between Foster and Neurnden was just about to get under way. It was already 10:00 p.m., the match having started late because of a men's five-setter.

"The last match of the night has to be one of ours," C.J. complained to the empty living room. She'd been hoping for at least a little time with Trystan before she went to bed—her quarterfinal the next day wasn't until at least 8:00 p.m., so she could afford to stay up later. But Trystan wouldn't be able to leave the grounds until the last women's match of the day was completed.

C.J. sprang up from the sofa and began to pace agitatedly around the room. "All I wanted was a chance for one evening together." She glanced at the clock on the VCR. "Five more days of this? I'll go insane." She bit her lip. "The hell I will." She strode into the bedroom, changed her clothes, and called the doorman to get her a taxi.

Trystan was cleaning up the treatment area. After yet another full day of play, the place looked like a cyclone had come through. She could hear the cheering in the stadium and knew Sylvia Foster was most likely wiping the court with her opponent.

She ran tired fingers impatiently through her hair and checked her watch again—10:53 p.m. *I'm so sorry, C.J.—I really wanted to get home tonight. I miss you so much it hurts.* She sighed heavily and threw a towel against the wall. She gasped in frightened shock as a pair of strong arms wrapped around her waist from behind.

"Towel abuse merits a fine around here, you know. I happen to be friends with the head PT, and she wouldn't be happy at all." C.J. smiled into Trystan's hair, inhaling deeply as familiar scents enveloped her senses.

Trystan turned in the circle of C.J.'s arms to face her. "You scared me to death." She looked around guiltily.

"I couldn't take it anymore, honey. I had to see you, had to touch you—I miss you so much." C.J. moved in and took Trystan's mouth in a possessive kiss.

Trystan wanted to resist. In her rational mind, she knew there could be no logical explanation for C.J. being in the training room at 11:00 p.m. on an off day if they got caught. Still, the feel of C.J. pressed against her, the hunger in her belly, the seductive look of intent in her lover's eyes—all conspired to overwhelm her good judgment. She moaned into the kiss, turned on by C.J.'s aggression. Her hands found purchase in C.J.'s hair.

C.J. pushed Trystan up against the wall, her hands and mouth roaming feverishly. "God, I need to feel you." She insinuated her hand between them, sliding her fingers through silken folds drenched in passion. Trystan was helpless to do anything but surrender.

Anna DeWynter walked into the locker room from the stadium tunnel. She'd stuck around to see some of her best friend Sylvia's match, despite her own loss earlier in the evening. Cleaning out her locker was going to be a depressing task, so she had put it off as long as possible. With Sylvia's match almost over, it was time to stop procrastinating. As she rounded the corner, she heard a woman's guttural moan. Thinking someone might be in trouble, she followed the noise. She paused at the open door to the training room, her mouth agape at what she saw. She stood frozen to the spot for several long seconds before coming to her senses. She crept back through the locker room toward the tunnel as stealthily as she had arrived. *Oh, Sylvia, have I got the ultimate weapon for you.*

With great effort, Trystan managed to whisper, "C.J., we can't."

"There's nobody here, baby. You feel so good."

Trystan stilled C.J.'s hand by clamping down on her wrist. "I can't come again, honey."

"I bet I can make you," C.J. purred.

"C.J., the match will be over any second now. There's no way either one of us could explain away your being here. You've got to go." Trystan's heart hurt. She waited until C.J. opened her eyes and looked at her. "You've got to, love." Regret was written in every line of her face.

C.J. sighed heavily. "I know you're right. It's just..."

"I know, baby. I feel the same way. Soon, okay?" Trystan kissed C.J. one last time. "I promise."

"I'll hold you to that, Lightfoot."

"Cross my heart," Trystan said, disentangling herself and giving C.J. a push in the direction of the back exit. She leaned back against the wall and closed her eyes momentarily. *I love you, C.J.*

CHAPTER EIGHTEEN

C.J. sat in her chair on the sideline wiping a sheen of perspiration from her arms. The night air was cool and crisp, with a light breeze blowing. It was a perfect night for tennis. She felt great—the match with Randi Pace was well in hand. She looked to the tunnel again where Trystan had been standing for the entire match and smiled. *This is exactly the way it should be, Ceeg. It doesn't get any better than this.*

Within fifteen minutes, she had finished off the match and was gathering her things.

"Great match, C.J.," Del Nordstrom congratulated her as they stood in the middle of the court for the post-match television interview.

"Thank you."

"I think I speak for everyone in the stadium tonight when I say, *wow*. You've been virtually unstoppable this tournament."

The fans rose to their feet, cheering and stomping. The gesture and the noise sent a thrill through C.J. and gave her goose bumps. "The fans have been extraordinary—thank you all," she said, waving to the crowd on all sides. The cheering got even louder. "I feel your support and it's inspiring."

"Coming into this tournament, you were considered the underdog. Did that seem odd to you, and did it motivate you?"

C.J. smiled enigmatically. "Let's just say it didn't lessen my desire to win."

The crowd roared with laughter.

"If you face Natasha Meritsa in the semifinal on Thursday, it'll be a rematch of the Wimbledon quarterfinal you lost earlier this summer. How do you feel about that?"

"First, Natasha has a tough match tomorrow that I don't want to discount—I know she won't. If she wins, I'll be looking forward to seeing her on the other side of the net. She's a very smart, very strong player. I hope any match between the two of us would be entertaining for the fans and good for the game."

"Thank you, C.J. What do you say, folks? Looking forward to seeing this seven-time champion back day after tomorrow?"

The crowd, still on its feet, erupted in applause and whistles once again. C.J. felt a lump rise in her throat as she acknowledged the outpouring of affection. She walked off the court accompanied by the tour media director.

"Press conference in the media room in five minutes, C.J."

"Okay. Let me just freshen up. I'll be right there." She walked into the locker room, intent on finding Trystan. When C.J. spotted her, she was in conversation with a tournament official. Trystan sent her a helpless look. Although she was disappointed, C.J. nodded her understanding.

The media room was packed when C.J. appeared a few minutes later. Television cameras lined the back of the room, microcassette recorders dotted the podium, and every seat was filled. "Good evening. Isn't it past some of your bedtimes?"

The room erupted in laughter.

"C.J., you've been in the zone all tournament. Can you really sustain that for two more matches?"

"I think my record at the Open speaks for itself."

"The last Open you won was two years ago…"

"You're a student of the game, Stuart. I'm sure you're aware that I've dropped fewer games this tournament than I did in any of my previous seven championships. So in answer to your question, yes. I absolutely think I can continue to play at this level."

"If you win and Sylvia wins, it'll set up a rematch of last year's final where you lost badly, and it cost you the number one ranking…"

"Really?" C.J. asked, smiling to hide her irritation. "I'd forgotten about that."

There was tense laughter from the reporters and tournament officials who were standing around the sides of the room.

"Seriously, C.J., how do you feel about a chance to redeem yourself?"

"First, I would argue with your choice of words. There's nothing to redeem—Sylvia played a great match, and I didn't. Beyond that, I have a tough semifinal coming up day after tomorrow. I'm not looking at anything beyond that."

"Seems to me you're looking at *something* beyond that," the *Miami Herald's* Gwen Naderson mumbled loud enough for everyone to hear.

C.J. hadn't noticed her in the room until that moment. After their last contentious encounter at the press conference introducing Grant as her coach, C.J. had no desire to entertain Gwen's penchant for gossip. C.J. glanced at the media director, their usual signal that she wanted to end the press conference.

"Last question," the media director announced.

"All right," Gwen said, pushing off the wall against which she was leaning. "Might your success at this tournament have anything to do with the new love in your life?"

A buzz went through the crowd.

C.J. stood rooted to the spot, her fingers gripping the podium hard enough for her knuckles to turn white. She felt the room spin and hung on for dear life.

"Cat got your tongue, C.J.? Let me help you. My information from reliable sources is that *her* name is Trystan Lightfoot—*she* joined the tour back in San Diego as the new head physical therapist."

"Trystan?" Nan knew she was shouting—she couldn't help it. "Trystan, come here."

Hearing the alarm in Nan's voice, Trystan dropped the towel she was folding and ran to where Nan was standing in front of the closed-circuit television feed. "What is it? Are you all right?"

Nan pointed to the television screen, where C.J. was standing at the podium in the press room. Her face was pasty white and her eyes were wild. Trystan's stomach gave a jolt.

"Shall I repeat the question?" A voice off-camera asked. "Does your 'inspired' play at the Open have anything to do with the affair you're having with the *female* physical therapist for the tour?"

"No—there's no way…" Trystan's heart stopped beating; she covered her mouth with a shaky hand. "I have to get to her. Where's that?" she asked, pointing at the screen. She turned in a circle, as if a door to the media room would magically appear. "I've got to get to C.J." She was near hysteria, and her entire body was shaking violently. "Where is that?" she asked again, her eyes staring through Nan. She started to run.

Nan grabbed Trystan by the arms and pulled her tightly against her body. "You can't go in there," she whispered harshly into Trystan's ear. She'd never seen Trystan come unraveled.

"I have to…"

"No. Trystan, look at me," Nan said, holding her at arm's length. She waited for Trystan's eyes to focus. "If you go in there, it'll only make things worse. It's like confirming it. You'll be a target."

"I don't care about me," Trystan choked out. "C.J.'s in trouble."

"Yes, but C.J.'s a tough girl. Not only that, but she's been in the public eye a long time. Trust her—she can handle this."

"No." It was the cry of a wounded animal. Trystan sank against Nan.

There was complete silence in the media room and C.J.'s breathing sounded loud in her own ears. She moved her mouth, but no words came out. Clearing her throat, she tried again. "I-I've been training extraordinarily hard for this tournament, and it shows in my results." A million moments flashed through her mind —her first U.S. Open win, her last Wimbledon title, the first time she was named number one in the world. *None of it matters to these people—all they want is a juicy story.* C.J. swayed, grabbing on to the podium for support. She felt tears threaten and shook her head as if to will them away.

Out of the corner of her eye, she saw Trudy Skylar, who had just entered the room, stride past the befuddled media director and toward her. C.J.'s nostrils flared in anger at the imperious expression on Trudy's face. *This isn't about the tour's image, wench—it's about my life, and it's mine to answer or not.*

"Do you deny that you're involved with Trystan Lightfoot?" Gwen asked again. There was urgency in the question this time as the reporter also apparently spied Trudy approaching.

As Trudy reached the podium, C.J. held up a hand as if to ward her off. "No."

"No, what?" a reporter in the front row spoke up.

C.J.'s heart fluttered in her chest. *Last chance. Say nothing or deny it and you can go on exactly as you have been.* An eighth U.S. Open title was within her grasp, carrying with it a return to the top of the sport and scores of new endorsement deals. *You can maintain your legacy and secure a future for both of you, Ceeg.* She thought about Trystan, who had always lived her life honestly and openly. *You'd be asking her to stifle her own identity so that you can take the easy way out. How long do you think she could do that? Would she resent you in the end and leave?* Her stomach turned. *None of it means anything without her by my side.* C.J. squared her shoulders, took a deep breath, and lifted her chin. "No, I don't deny it."

Next to her, Trudy's shoulders slumped and her mouth hung half open. She looked at C.J. wide-eyed.

Thirty voices shouted all at once. The cacophony was such that C.J. couldn't distinguish one question from another.

"That's all," the media director said, rushing forward in an effort to salvage some semblance of control.

The reporters surged forward en masse as she shoved C.J. hard toward the side exit. There were howls of protests.

"You can't end it there. We have follow-up questions."

"C.J., did you know this woman before the WTF hired her?"

"How long have you been together?"

"Are you living together?"

"What do the other players think?"

"Is she treating your opponents?"

"Isn't this a conflict of interest?"

C.J. wanted to turn around and face the questioners—more than that, she wanted to defend Trystan—but Trudy and the media director had her surrounded from both sides. When they had cleared the doorway and were alone, Trudy whirled around to face her.

"What the hell was that?"

C.J.'s tone of voice turned icy. "I believe it was the press conference that's required by the WTF."

"You know what I mean. Do you have any idea what you've done?"

"Told the truth?" C.J. stood ramrod straight, her fisted hands held rigidly against her sides. She felt more raw and exposed than she ever had—all she wanted to do was find Trystan and fall into her arms. She fought with herself to remain civil.

"I warned you when you were in my office that there would be consequences. Your image, the tour's integrity—this is a nightmare."

C.J. narrowed her eyes dangerously. "I was asked a direct question and I answered honestly—I'm comfortable with my integrity."

"You didn't give any consideration to the predicament you put me in."

C.J.'s anger boiled over. "You? The spot I put *you* in? For nearly twenty years, I put up with being used as the poster girl for your fantasy image of the WTF. Never once did I complain or refuse to go along with your PR campaigns. Not only that, I've always respected the history of the game and the women who made it great. I've done nothing to dishonor that. I've dedicated my career to being a role model young girls could look up to."

"You've just blown that out of the water, haven't you?" Trudy's face was turning purple with rage. She began to pace.

"Quite the contrary—I've just shown that you can succeed at the highest levels of the game and not be afraid to be yourself at the same time." C.J.'s voice shook with emotion. "I've given hundreds of thousands of kids who felt isolated and alone someone to emulate."

"What you've done is overshadow the game and the tour," Trudy shouted. "You've done more damage in thirty seconds than all the good you might have done in twenty years."

The words struck C.J. harder than any punch could have. Although she was reeling, she stood her ground. *She's full of it, Ceeg. You've just brought chaos to her well-ordered world and you're a convenient whipping post. Blow her off.*

When C.J. didn't respond, Trudy turned her back dismissively and began to walk away. As she did so, her wild eyes locked on the media director, who was trying her best to blend into the scenery. "We have to get ahead of this thing. Maybe if we held a press conference…"

"You'd be bombarded with questions you don't want to answer. 'Was the tour aware of the situation?' 'Has she treated C.J.'s opponents?' 'Will Trystan Lightfoot be fired?'"

Trudy gnawed on the inside of her cheek. "If we fired Lightfoot, would the problem go away?"

"Some of the questions might, at least temporarily." The media director's eyes got big and round as she watched C.J., who was halfway down the hall, whip around and come charging back.

"You can't do that," C.J. said, pointing her finger at Trudy's chest. "Trystan hasn't done anything wrong. She's delegated treatment of my opponents to Nan as promised and kept to the agreement."

"Don't be naïve, C.J. This is business. It's your own fault—by choosing to answer the question, you made both of you fair game. I told you if this got messy, there would be consequences."

C.J. stepped closer to Trudy until she was towering over her. "You want to talk about consequences? Fine." C.J.'s voice was controlled fury. "I swear on everything I hold dear, if you make Trystan a scapegoat by firing her, I will keep this story alive indefinitely. I'll enlist every other lesbian on tour to come out in protest of the WTF's discriminatory practices. I'll organize a boycott that'll have so many big names pulling out you won't have enough players to field a tournament." C.J. had no idea where the words were coming from. She'd never been a poker player, and this was certainly the biggest bluff of her life.

"You couldn't. You wouldn't..." Trudy blustered.

"Wouldn't I, Trudy? After all, this is business," C.J. hissed. *No time to back down now, Ceeg. Hit her where it hurts.* "You have no idea the extent of what goes on in the locker room and how many lesbians there are in the WTF."

C.J. knew perfectly well what she said was true. Trudy was tolerated by the players on the tour but kept out of the loop and was universally disliked.

Trudy opened her mouth to speak, then closed it again. Without another word, she marched down the hallway, ripped open the door leading to the executive offices, and disappeared out of sight. The media director hesitated for only a fraction of a second before following suit.

C.J. slumped against the wall, closed her eyes, and slid down until she was sitting. Her whole body was shaking.

Trystan was frantic. The press conference had ended a half hour earlier and she'd looked everywhere for C.J. with no success. At her wit's end, she tried one last door leading to one last hallway.

"Oh, baby." Trystan broke into a run, skidding to a halt before C.J.'s shivering form. She dropped to the floor and gathered C.J. in her arms, pulling her into her lap and rocking them both gently.

C.J. grabbed onto Trystan's shoulders tightly and buried her face in her lover's neck. "I'm s-sorry, honey."

Trystan ran her fingers soothingly through C.J.'s hair. "You have nothing to apologize for, love. Everything's going to be fine."

"I w-wasn't expecting that. I d-didn't know what to do."

"I thought you handled it great, baby. I have no idea what I would've done in the same circumstance."

"You would've told Naderson to go to hell."

Trystan laughed. "I might have. But that's only because I'm not as good at handling the press as you."

"Yeah," C.J. scoffed, "because I did such a fine job of it tonight."

Trystan pulled back and lifted C.J.'s chin until their eyes met. "Yes, you did, love." When C.J. would've looked down, Trystan held her chin firmly. "I mean it. That was an impossible situation. I can't believe how courageous you were."

"I don't feel very courageous."

"Well, you should—because you are," Trystan said, kissing C.J. softly on the mouth.

C.J. took a shuddering breath. "I had a showdown with Trudy afterward."

Trystan stiffened. "What did she say?"

"It was all about her, of course. How I'd put her in a bad position, and what was she supposed to do now."

"And?" Trystan growled. "I know that's not all or you wouldn't be this upset."

C.J. shrugged. "I told her I'd been asked a direct question and I answered it honestly. She accused me of sabotaging the tour, yada, yada."

"And?" Trystan probed further.

"And what?"

"And what did she threaten?"

"What makes you think she threatened anything?"

"Because people like her are bullies, and that's what they do." Trystan gasped as a terrible thought occurred to her. "She didn't say she was going to suspend you, did she? She can't take the Open away from you, can she?"

C.J. smiled. "No, sweetheart. Can you see it now? The fans would go nuts. The media would be up in arms. The sponsors would have a cow." She leaned up and kissed Trystan warmly. "I love that your first thought was to be worried for me. She can't touch me, honey. I haven't done anything against the rules of the tour. If I hadn't done the press conference, she could've fined me or worse. Dealing with the media in a controlled setting after the match is required. So in a sense, it's her own doing, which I find deliciously ironic."

"Mmm," Trystan agreed. She was relieved to feel C.J. relax a little against her chest, but it didn't change the fact that she felt a burning need to know what had happened. "You've done a masterful job of changing the subject, but you're not off the hook."

"What?"

"Don't play innocent with me—what did Trudy say to make you so upset?"

"Honey, let's just go home. It's late, and I'm very tired."

Trystan slid away slightly, holding C.J. at arm's length and looking into her eyes. Watching her evade eye contact, the light finally dawned for Trystan. "It was about me, wasn't it?"

"I don't want to talk about it."

C.J. shifted as if to get up, but Trystan held her in place.

"What exactly did she say, C.J.?"

C.J. sighed heavily and surrendered. "She threatened to fire you."

"And she'd let me stay in exchange for what?" Trystan asked through gritted teeth. "For you retracting the statement? For you being a good girl and towing the party line?"

"Whoa. She didn't get that far," C.J. said, running her hand soothingly along Trystan's tight shoulder and neck.

"What do you mean?"

"I trumped her."

Trystan raised an eyebrow.

"I did. I used the old 'Hell hath no fury like a woman scorned' routine." When Trystan looked completely befuddled, C.J. said, "I told her if she messed with my woman, I'd make her life a permanent hell. I'd lead a boycott of the tour and marshal the lesbian nation on behalf of our righteous cause."

Trystan laughed. "For real?"

"Yep."

"What'd she do?"

"She turned tail and ran."

"No way."

"Way. Swear to God."

"The great and powerful C.J. has spoken," Trystan said, imitating a scene from the *Wizard of Oz*.

"You'd better watch out, honey. I've got game."

"Yes, you do," Trystan cooed seductively. She shifted again, meeting C.J.'s lips in a sweet, sensuous kiss.

A vibration between them made them both jump. "Wow, you're so powerful you make my body hum," Trystan joked, as she unclipped her cell phone from her hip and answered it. "Lightfoot."

"Trystan, it's Grant."

"Hey, what's up?"

"Mitch and I saw the press conference in the men's locker room. Are you and C.J. okay?"

Trystan could hardly hear him over the noise in the background. "Yeah, we're all right. Where are you?"

"The parking lot and the players' entrance are crawling with reporters. Your friend Nan spotted us before the pack did and hid us in her rental car. We're lying on the backseat."

"That sounds like fun."

"Very cute. Trystan, you can't come out—you'll be mobbed."

Trystan tipped the phone so that C.J. could hear, too. "Well, we can't stay here all night. What do you suggest?"

"Hold on, there's someone who wants to talk to you."

"Nice work, champ. Your girl's got backbone."

"Becca?"

"You were expecting Dirty Harry?"

"Very funny. Where are you?"

"Oh, just hanging around. Vacation got boring, you see and…"

"Knock it off."

"Spoilsport. I saw the press conference and was in the neighborhood."

"Uh-huh."

"Anyway, I figured you might need some reinforcements that the press couldn't recognize. Nan spotted me wandering around trying to talk my way into the locker room and rescued me. It's been so long since we've seen each other, we've been catching up."

"That's nice. I assume that while the two of you have been hanging around gossiping, you've come up with a plan?"

"Have we ever let you down?"

"Let's hear it."

"Since Grant is the only one of the four of us those media sycophants would recognize, he's going to provide the distraction. He'll make a big show of pulling Nan's car around to the players' exit."

"Lucky him," Trystan muttered.

"Meanwhile, Nan, Mitch, and I will meet you in my car at the front entrance. You jump right into the back, duck down, and off we go."

"As soon as it becomes clear we're not coming out to meet Grant, they'll get suspicious and make a beeline for us."

"That's the beauty of it. I brought along a friend of mine who looks similar enough to C.J. from the back to fool them. She'll jump in the car with Grant, and they'll head off in the opposite direction. I'm sure the media will love a tour of Queens."

"I'm sure," Trystan laughed. "I hope poor Grant and friend aren't stuck driving around all night."

"Nah," Becca said. "Once we've had enough time to get you two to my place, we'll call him and have him bring Betsy home, making sure everyone can see it's not C.J. when she gets out of the car."

Trystan smiled into the phone. "Have I told you lately how much I love you?"

Becca laughed. "You love me when I can bail your sorry ass out of trouble."

"Well, doesn't that count for anything?"

"I'll think about it. Sit tight. I'll call you as we round the corner to the front entrance."

"Thanks, girlfriend."

"The pleasure's all mine. You know I love a good challenge. I'd love to stay on the phone and chat, but I have a job to do."

Trystan could hear Becca open and close a car door.

"Ciao, baby."

CHAPTER NINETEEN

Becca maneuvered the car into a parking space in the underground garage adjacent to her building. "Well, that was fun," she said cheerfully. She noted C.J.'s pale complexion and the tense set of Trystan's jaw. "This way." She indicated a private elevator that would allow them to bypass the lobby. "You haven't told anybody where you're staying, have you?"

"No," C.J. said quietly. "Thank God," she added under her breath.

When they were settled in the living room, Trystan cornered Becca. "I thought you were on vacation. That was a pretty short one."

"I was. I never said I was leaving the city, however."

"You've been here the whole time?" C.J. asked. "Where have you been staying?"

"A girl likes to keep her secrets." Becca winked. "Do you want to watch this?" She nodded in the direction of ESPN's *SportsCenter*, which was just getting started.

C.J. groaned and leaned heavily against Trystan, who hadn't let go of her hand since they'd sat on the sofa.

"Turn it off," Trystan said, as the first picture of C.J. came up.

"No," C.J. said, her voice resolute. "I can't defend us if I don't know what they're saying."

"Baby, it's going to be ugly."

"I don't care. I can't pretend everyone's not talking about it, and I won't isolate myself." She leaned over and kissed Trystan on the mouth. "I'm not ashamed to be with the most beautiful woman in the world, and I won't stand by while the vultures rip us to shreds."

"Hear, hear," Nan said, as she grabbed the remote out of Becca's hand and turned up the volume.

The anchor was saying, "Tennis great C.J. Winslow served up a stunner this evening, but it wasn't on the court. In a post-match press conference following her easy victory at the U.S. Open, Winslow admitted to a lesbian affair with a staff member of the Women's Tennis Federation. For more on the story, we go to New York's Flushing Meadows and tennis analyst Polly Kent."

The scene on-screen shifted to the tournament grounds, where the reporter was standing with Arthur Ashe stadium in the background. "WTF officials are being tight-lipped at this hour about a scandal that has rocked one of the most venerated events on the professional tennis tour. C.J. Winslow, who has been setting the court on fire throughout this tournament, admitted in front of dozens of reporters tonight to a lesbian relationship with a physical therapist by the name of Trystan Lightfoot. So far, little is known about the mysterious Lightfoot except that she was hired by the WTF a little more than a month ago to travel with the tour and treat the players for their injuries."

"Polly," the anchor interrupted, "is there any truth to the rumor that the women were discovered in a compromising position in the women's locker room last night?"

"What?" C.J. yelled at the television. Her heart pounded furiously in her chest. "There wasn't anybody..." Her voice trailed off as she realized what she was about to say in front of their friends. Next to her on the sofa, Trystan sat stock-still.

"It's impossible to know," Polly was saying. "We can't get anyone to comment on the record about anything. I suspect we'll find out a lot more over the course of the next few days. C.J.'s next match is scheduled for day after tomorrow..."

"Shut it off," Trystan said, her voice deadly quiet. A muscle in her jaw jumped. The idea of the media crawling all over her and C.J. made her jittery and nauseated. She looked at her watch. "I'd better call my mother and tell her to expect company."

C.J.'s stomach roiled dangerously. "You're leaving?" There was a note of panic in her voice.

"What?" Trystan asked, distracted. "Leaving? Why would you think that?"

"You just said..."

Comprehension dawned on Trystan. "Oh, no. No, no, no, baby." She gathered C.J. in her arms and kissed the top of her head. "I just meant that I should warn my mother that reporters might come snooping around. I never meant... I would never... Shit." She felt C.J.'s body shake with tears against her torso. *That was sensitive, Trys. Damn it.* "Come here, love. Don't cry." Trystan looked first at Becca, then Nan, and finally at Mitch. They all wore identical sympathetic expressions. "C.J., I'm right here, and that's where I'm going to stay. We're in this together, you and me. I'm not leaving you, I promise."

"Speaking of leaving," Becca said, "I've got to get back to my vacation."

"I've got to go find poor Grant," Mitch chimed in, following Becca's lead.

"And if I don't get my beauty rest…well, let's just say it'll be ugly," Nan said. Becca and Mitch groaned.

Trystan gave a nod of thanks to each of them as she continued to rock C.J. in her arms.

"How about if we all meet back here for a late breakfast tomorrow morning? That way, we can strategize our next move," Becca offered.

"You don't need to do that," C.J. said, drying her eyes.

"No, we don't need to, but I want to—tonight was a bigger rush than I've gotten in years. You don't want to deny me that, do you?" Becca asked.

"I have to say, that was the most excitement I've had since I discovered that peanut butter came in super chunky," Nan added, standing up.

"You can't leave me out of the fun," Mitch said.

"You guys are too much, you know that?" C.J. shook her head. "I'm so very grateful for all of you right now."

"We're happy to help, C.J.," Becca said, as the others murmured their agreement. "And we're proud of you for the way you've handled a ridiculously difficult situation."

"I've never had friends like you," C.J. said with wonder. "I don't know what to say."

"Say you'll win the tournament, sweetheart," Mitch said, laughing. "I've already spent Grant's bonus."

When Becca, Nan, and Mitch had gone, Trystan led C.J. to the bedroom, where they quietly undressed. Trystan slid under the cool sheets first, opened her arms, and invited C.J. to snuggle. She nearly cried with relief at the feeling of their bodies sliding together. "I love you, C.J."

"I love you, too, Trystan. So very much."

They lay silently in the dark in each other's arms for several minutes, their steady breaths the only sounds audible in the stillness of the night.

"It was all my fault," C.J. finally whispered brokenly.

"What?"

"Somebody obviously was in the locker room the other night when I came to see you. That was so damn careless of me, but I couldn't stand it anymore—I had to see you. I missed you so much." C.J. rubbed the sore spot that had blossomed over her heart. "I didn't think…"

"Hey," Trystan said softly, sitting up and carrying C.J. with her. "You didn't do anything wrong and there's no blame, okay?"

"If I hadn't been so impulsive, nobody would've known."

"Stop, baby. It was a horrendous week, I missed you, you missed me. I don't ever want you to apologize for acting out of love."

"I ruined everything," C.J. continued miserably, as if she hadn't heard what Trystan said.

"No. No, honey. You followed your heart, and I love you for it." Trystan kissed C.J. on the forehead.

"Maybe I should've denied it…"

"Absolutely not." Trystan tightened her grip on C.J. "Do you have any idea how proud I was of you at that moment?"

"You were?"

"Hell, yeah. Honey, she painted you into a corner. Instead of backing down, you held your head high—you answered with dignity and class. Anybody else would've denied it. You didn't, and I think I loved you more in that moment than is humanly possible."

"You really don't mind that I outed us? It's going to turn our lives upside down."

"For a little while, yes. But in the long run, it's going to mean that we can live openly and honestly."

"What about Trudy?"

"What about her?"

"She could still come after you."

Trystan shrugged. "That's something we can't control. If she does, we'll…how did you say it?...'Marshal the lesbian nation to rise up in indignation.'"

C.J. smiled against Trystan's chest. "Have I told you in the last ten minutes how much I love you?"

Trystan pretended to think. "I can't remember, better say it again just to be sure."

"I love you, Trystan Lightfoot, more than anything in the world." She leaned up and kissed Trystan tenderly on the mouth. "How did I get so lucky?"

"I'm the lucky one," Trystan said, sliding them both back down in the bed.

At 9:30 the next morning Trystan's cell phone rang.

"Are you all right, Acheehen?"

"Amá? I wanted to call you last night, but it was too late. Are you okay?"

"I'm fine. I saw the news this morning. How's C.J. doing?"

"She's shaken, but strong. We had to scramble to outrun the media last night."

"I can imagine."

"They haven't found you yet, have they, Amá?"

"No. I haven't seen anyone."

"I'm afraid they'll bother you—they'll do anything to get a story."

"I suspect as much, too. Don't worry, Acheehen. I can take care of myself. I've informed the tribal elders that we may have some unwelcome visitors—it should be interesting. Besides, I have nothing to hide—I have two daughters now, and I'm extremely proud of both of them."

Trystan smiled into the phone. "I love you, Amá. Tell the council to be gentle."

"Take good care of yourself and C.J. Remember always that what you share is a sacred bond—together you're stronger than any outside force."

"Thanks," Trystan said, tears springing to her eyes. "I know you're right."

"Of course I am," Terri agreed. "I'm your mother. Goodbye, Acheehen."

As she hung up, Trystan heard a knock on the apartment door.

"Trys? It's just us."

Trystan opened the door to admit Becca, Nan, Mitch, and Grant.

"Why didn't you use your key?"

Becca quirked an eyebrow.

"Never mind," Trystan said, blushing. "C.J.'s in the shower."

"Did either one of you get any sleep?" Nan asked.

"Some. She's only worried that she somehow disappointed me. I assured her I'm proud of her, but I think it'll take time."

"Mmm-hmm," Becca agreed.

"Did you guys have any trouble this morning? Grant?"

"Nah, Becca hid me and Mitch, so it was all good."

"I think I love you," Trystan said to Becca.

"Careful there, you're already spoken for."

"Yes, she is," C.J. said, emerging from the bedroom. She wrapped her arms around Trystan from behind.

"Anybody hungry?" Mitch asked, as he juggled a large cardboard box.

"Mmm," C.J. sniffed appreciatively. "That smells great."

"We thought you might be hungry."

"Famished," C.J. answered, reaching into the box and snagging the stack of newspapers that rested on top of the food.

Grant put his hands on top of hers. "After breakfast, missy."

C.J. frowned but let go of the papers. "Have you been watching this morning?"

"Some," Grant said reluctantly.

"Bad?"

"Same stuff, different day."

"They don't have anything new yet?"

"Not yet. But the day is young."

"Right," C.J. said, squaring her shoulders. "Let's eat."

They'd barely dug in when Grant's cell phone rang. He looked at the number and scowled. "It's Dan. This is like the fifteenth time he's called since last night. What do you want me to do?"

"Who's Dan?" Trystan asked.

"C.J.'s business manager."

C.J. sighed and held her hand out for the phone. She closed her eyes and gathered her strength. "Hi, Dan. What's up?"

"What's up? What's up? Are you kidding me? I've been trying to reach you for ten hours."

C.J. held the phone away from her ear as the shouting continued.

"You don't answer my calls anymore? You turn everything I've done for you over the years on its ear, and you won't even take my damn phone call?"

Trystan rose abruptly, anger written in every line of her face. She put her hand out for the phone. "Nobody talks to you like that, I don't care if he's the pope."

"Shh, it's okay," C.J. mouthed. She ran a thumb soothingly over Trystan's hand. C.J. put the phone back to her ear. Out loud, she said, "Are you done yet, Dan?"

There was an audible whoosh of air on the other end of the line.

"I didn't have my cell phone on for obvious reasons. I apologize. It wasn't something I planned—the reporter asked a question." *This is hard enough, Dan—don't make it any worse.*

"So you decided on your own, without any input from an image expert or your manager, that you should answer it?"

C.J.'s eyes flashed dangerously. *Deep breath, Ceeg.* "What was I supposed to do, ask her to hold on while I consulted with my experts? Get real, Dan. It was a judgment call, I made it, I'll live with it."

"Or without it, as the case may be," he said.

"What's that supposed to mean?"

"I need to know where I can send you some new clothes."

"I don't need new clothes."

"I'm afraid you do," Dan said quietly. "All of your sponsors have dropped you, C.J. That happened in the first two hours after the press conference. You lost eight million dollars in endorsements with five words. Congratulations. I'm sending you new clothes, a new racquet bag that you'll have to use, and new sneakers. Oh, and any identifying features on your racquets have been painted over this morning. The stringer has them."

When Trystan stepped forward this time, it was because C.J. had turned deathly pale. The hand that held the phone was shaking. "What is it, baby?"

"I see," C.J. said into the phone. She fought a wave of dizziness as the world seemed to close in around her. "I don't know the address here. Hold on." C.J. covered the phone. "Becca? Can you tell my manager the address, please?"

"Sure, C.J." Becca took the proffered phone, gave Dan the information, and handed the phone back to C.J.

"Anything else, Dan? I have to go practice." She felt suddenly weary, tired, and years older.

"Listen, C.J. We're going to get through this. I'm already looking for new sponsors. I swear, I'll get you something before you step on the court for the finals."

"That's great, but I have to be on the court tomorrow for the semifinals."

"I'm doing everything I can. Just keep your head down and try to avoid the media."

"Sure, Dan." She laughed shortly. "Do you have any realistic advice?"

"Tell them you'll only talk about your game until the tournament is over. You'll address all their questions after that."

"They'll just find other sources willing to talk. It could get worse."

"You can't afford the distraction right now. The best thing you can do to salvage your image is to win the Open and get the ranking back. If you fall short of that…"

"Thanks for the vote of confidence."

"I'm not trying to give you a hard time. I'm simply telling it like it is."

"I see. Let me tell you something 'like it is,' Dan. You're fired." C.J. knew she shouldn't make a knee-jerk decision, but she couldn't stop herself. "I don't need or want someone in my camp who isn't behind me one hundred percent. As you said, after all—I need to focus." She shut the phone with a satisfying *snick*, then looked around the table at each of her friends. "Seems my sponsors aren't too happy today. They've all dumped me. And now I have no manager." Her lip started to quiver, her shoulders shook, and she collapsed into Trystan's open arms.

"It'll be okay, baby," Trystan murmured, stroking C.J.'s hair. "You'll show all of them. They're fools. When you win the Open and they come crawling back, we'll reject them and go with new sponsors—their loss."

"I wish it were that simple. I'm going to have all generic stuff when I walk on the court for tomorrow's match. Everyone's going to know I'm a pariah. I can't even have the logo on my racquet showing."

"If I might interject," Mitch said. "I spent most of my business life making deals. I can help if you want me to."

"Mitch is being modest," Grant said. "He was one of the top rainmakers at a major talent agency before I convinced him to give it up and travel with me."

"You never told me that," C.J. said, pointing a finger at Mitch accusingly.

"It never came up."

"I'll pay you…"

Mitch held up a hand. "Don't you even think about it. I want to do this. It's not every day lesbians the world over get the perfect role model."

"I won't let you do this for free, Mitch. It's not right." C.J. frowned.

"I tell you what. When I get you three or four sponsors, we'll talk."

C.J. reluctantly agreed. “You’re on.”

“I’ve got work to do,” Mitch said. “Do you have an office in this beautiful pad, Becca?”

“In the loft.”

“Right then. Later, folks.” He unclipped his cell phone from its holster and excused himself.

“We’ve got to get going—it’s practice time,” Grant said.

“You’re not going to Flushing Meadows, are you?” Nan asked. “They’ll be all over her.”

“Actually, I’d thought of that. I’ve booked us a private court in Westchester,” Grant said.

“No. I’m not going to change my routine—if I do, they win. I’m going to walk in there with my head held high and practice like I would under normal circumstances.”

“These aren’t normal circumstances, C.J.,” Trystan said.

“It’ll be okay, honey. We’ll get lots of security.”

“I don’t like it. Have you already forgotten the scene in the parking lot in San Diego after the newspaper photo of Grant kissing you? That was nothing compared to this.”

“I understand that, but I won’t hide—wouldn’t that defeat the purpose of coming out in the first place?”

“There won’t always be a media frenzy. Pick your battles,” Trystan said.

“This battle apparently picked me, and I’ve never backed down from a fight. I don’t intend to start now.”

Trystan chewed her lip. “What kinds of precautions are you going to take?”

“It’s in Trudy’s best interest to keep me away from the media. I’m going to demand that she assign me sufficient security to allow me to go about my business.”

“And if she doesn’t?”

C.J. took Trystan’s hand and kissed the palm. “I promise you I’ll hire my own if she doesn’t supply the muscle, but I know she will. I know her—the last thing she wants is me saying anything else to the press.”

C.J. narrowed her vision until all she could see was her racquet and the ball. She’d been assigned practice court eighteen since it was the most remote and Trudy’s security chief deemed it to be the easiest to protect. The security detail and the media had reached an uneasy truce after a tense trip from the locker room to the court in which one cameraman walking backward had lost his balance and inadvertently been stepped on by a security guard.

In the two hours they'd actually been practicing, cameramen and reporters had kept a respectful distance from the court, allowing C.J. to run through a relatively normal practice routine. She sent a crosscourt backhand long and Grant motioned her to meet him at the net.

"I know it's hard to concentrate, C.J." Grant intentionally pitched his voice low to keep his words from being recorded. "I would've thought there'd be something more important for all these media-types to focus on, like maybe Meritsa's match, for instance. But they're not going away, and we have work to do. Give me another good half hour and we'll move on to the Katamibar, okay?"

"Okay."

"If you're really good, I'll let you stop in and see Trystan for a minute since I'm pretty sure that's where your head's been these past few drills."

"I just want to know that nobody ambushed her before she got in the building."

"Trudy promised you no one would get within fifteen yards of her. She's stuck to her end of the bargain with you—there's no reason to believe she hasn't done the same with Trystan. I'm sure she's fine."

"I know you're probably right, but…"

"Come on," Grant said, playfully pushing C.J. back toward the baseline. "Thirty good minutes."

Once C.J. reached the safety of the players' lounge, which was off-limits to the media, the security detail faded into the background. The chief of security would wait for her to call him when she was ready to leave, and a detail would escort her to the parking lot and off the grounds.

C.J. made a beeline for the treatment room, where she spied Trystan watching the Meritsa match on closed-circuit television. She launched herself at Trystan, needing the comfort and safety of her arms.

"You okay, baby?" Trystan asked, stroking her back.

"I am now. I missed you."

"I missed you, too. How was the practice? Was it awful?"

"It was different, that's for sure—cameras whirring and clicking like it was the finals, television commentators reporting live from the scene—pretty wild stuff."

"Did security do its job?"

"Yep—no one even got close. One guy who tried got run over."

"Ouch."

"How about you? Did you get here okay?" After much debate, they had decided to arrive separately. Trudy had sent a car for C.J., and Becca had dropped Trystan and Nan off a few minutes later.

"No problem."

"I'm glad—I was worried." C.J. laced her hands behind Trystan's neck and pulled her in for a kiss.

When Natasha Meritsa walked in a few minutes later, they had barely broken apart.

"Well, isn't this quite cozy?" Meritsa commented. "You two make me sick. I wonder if Monica Duschene really got the best treatment on the court at the Acura. Or were you so anxious to help your girlfriend," she glared contemptuously at Trystan, "that you fudged it so Monica would withdraw?"

C.J. put her hand on Trystan's arm as she felt her body weight shift forward toward Natasha. "She's just trying to get you," C.J. murmured under her breath. "Ignore her."

"You know she'd have beaten you if she'd been able to finish," Meritsa said, turning her attention to C.J. "Just like I'm going to beat you tomorrow."

"We'll see about that," C.J. said to Meritsa's retreating back.

"Honey? Do me a favor?" Trystan asked when Meritsa was out of earshot.

"Yes?"

"Kick her ass."

C.J. laughed. "That's the plan."

CHAPTER TWENTY

When C.J. arrived in the training room three hours prior to her semifinal match with Meritsa, her nerves were already frayed. The media was hounding her relentlessly, even though security had thus far succeeded in keeping them at a distance. Everywhere she turned, it seemed, someone was talking about her.

The training room, which was usually her sanctuary, was no different. The television was tuned to ESPN, the volume turned down, but not so low that C.J. couldn't hear. As had been the case all morning, the commentators were talking about lesbianism in sports in general and her case in particular. The program was *Roundtable* and featured several sportswriters and broadcasters talking about the hot issues of the day in a moderated discussion format.

C.J. groaned, rotating her shoulders to relieve some of the tension in them.

"Is it surprising to you that she came out at this time, in the middle of a major tournament?" the moderator asked one of the panelists.

"Shocking, I think would be more like it. First of all, it's so out of character for C.J. Winslow."

"As if you would know," C.J. mumbled.

"She has always been a very low-profile champion—very workmanlike in her approach, respectful of the game and its traditions," another panelist agreed.

"Let's remember that she didn't come out willingly, folks. I don't believe she would've done so if it hadn't been for that reporter asking a direct question."

"But she did answer it. She could've avoided it—she could've left the podium without saying another word. So in a sense, coming out was her choice."

"In any event, what do you all think the impact will be on her chances for this Open? There's a number one ranking potentially at stake."

"She's got a very tough match today with an opponent who beat her badly last time they met, in the Wimbledon quarterfinal back in July. I say she's too distracted for that kind of challenge. Meritsa in straight sets."

"I have to agree that she's got to be considered a long shot at this point. She's been hounded by the media for two days, her practice session was a zoo, it's an emotional time for her—I just don't think she overcomes all that."

"The tennis challenge alone would've been nearly insurmountable for her. Let's face it—C.J. Winslow's best tennis is behind her. I agree with my colleagues here—C.J. won't even make it to the final on Saturday."

C.J. reached in her bag, grabbed her earphones, and turned on her iPod. She ignored the sadness that seeped into her chest, focusing instead on her indignation and anger. She selected a bike, adjusted the seat, and began pedaling—hard. *Washed up, am I? Hmph.* Nostrils flared, teeth clenched, eyes narrowed, she jabbed her finger at the controls, twice increasing the incline.

"Easy there, baby." Trystan powered down the bike several notches and spoke close enough to C.J.'s ear so she could hear.

"Wha?" C.J. pulled out one earpiece, startled by Trystan's sudden appearance at her side.

"You're pushing yourself too hard for a match day. Look at you," she pushed an errant lock of hair out of C.J.'s face. "You're sweating up a storm." Trystan peeked at the readout on the bike's computer. "Thirty-five minutes? Honey, that's too long."

"Sorry, I must've lost track of the time." C.J. was still breathing heavily.

"Is that all it was? What happened?"

"Nothing."

Trystan merely arched an eyebrow.

"Just more stupidity on ESPN, that's all, baby."

"Ah. You can't be thinking about that now, C.J. We'll have plenty of time to deal with all that later." Trystan cupped C.J.'s face in her hands. "For the next few hours, all that matters is the match, right?"

"Right." C.J. nodded tentatively.

"Say it with feeling."

"Right," C.J. said more definitively.

"That's my girl. You've got some serious ass to kick, and I know you can do it."

"Thanks—I needed to hear that."

"Any time. Are you going out to practice?"

"Just to loosen up and hit a few balls."

"Security?"

"Ready and waiting on my call."

"Good. We'll get through this together, okay?" Trystan searched C.J.'s face. There were black smudges under her normally clear eyes, stress lines that hadn't been there even two days prior, and a haunted expression that nearly broke Trystan's heart. "I promise."

"I know. I'd better get going. I don't feel like running into Natasha before the match today." She kissed Trystan softly. "Thank you for taking such good care of me."

"Always. I'll leave treatment room two closed for when you're ready." Trystan brushed her fingers along C.J.'s smooth skin. "You're going to be great today, baby. I can feel it."

"Mmm-hmm." C.J. threw herself into Trystan's arms, catching her off-guard.

"Oof. Hey, it's okay."

"Nobody thinks I can do this."

"That's not true. I know you can, and so does Grant. Becca, Nan, Mitch—we're all behind you, honey. There are always people out there who'll want to see you fail. You've got to prove them wrong. You always have—that's part of what makes you a champion. If anything, you're stronger than you've ever been, both physically and emotionally. You're better equipped to win. You have to believe it—you have to believe in yourself."

"I will."

"I'll be with you every step of the way."

"I'm counting on it." C.J. pulled away, feeling better than she had all morning.

Twenty minutes before the match, Trystan's cell phone rang. "Yes?"

"Trystan? It's Mitch. I'm still working on a few things, but it doesn't look like I'll be done in time for the match."

Trystan could hear the disappointment in his voice. "What should I tell C.J.?"

"I cashed in some chips with a lawyer buddy of mine. He tells me the clothing company can't do anything about her wearing an outfit that she bought, so I went on a little shopping spree. Except for the sponsor patches, no one will be able to tell anything."

"Thanks, Mitch. That was really sweet. She'll feel a lot more comfortable and a lot less self-conscious in her normal outfit."

"There wasn't anything I could do about the racquet and bag sponsor—so I bought her a really cool racquet bag and had it personalized. She'll be the sharpest dressed, best accessorized player on the tour. The racquet won't have any identifying marks, but I ordered a special paint job on it. I don't know the vendor, but he came highly recommended. I guess a lot of the other players use him."

Trystan laughed. "I can't tell you how much I appreciate the trouble you've gone to, and I know C.J. will be incredibly grateful, too."

"How's she doing? Did you see ESPN this morning? Grant said it was awful."

Trystan remembered the way C.J. looked on the bike. "No, I missed it, but C.J. saw it." The thought made her heart ache yet again for her lover.

"It was *Roundtable*, and they tore C.J. to pieces and threw her to the wolves. Bastards."

"Did you get the passes I left for you, Becca, and everyone else for the 'friends' box?"

"That's where we're sitting right now, girlfriend. Grant is waiting outside the locker room with all the goods. He's probably having a cow—you'd better go rescue him."

"Right. Thanks, Mitch—for everything."

"I haven't finished trying, you know. I've still got calls out and promising leads to follow. All we need to do is get her to the finals, and I'm sure I can close the deals."

"No worries then," Trystan said confidently. She hung up, walked to the locker room door leading to the tunnel, and found Grant pacing outside the door.

"How is she?"

"She's meditating at the moment. How was the practice?" Trystan asked. Although she'd caught a glimpse of C.J. going into the treatment room, she hadn't had a chance to talk to her.

"Not her finest hour. She's going to need to be a lot sharper than that to beat Meritsa. I don't know if she'll be able to focus—she was pretty scattered."

"I'll see what I can do to help." Trystan took the tennis bag Grant handed her and retreated back into the locker room. She knocked gently on the door of treatment room two.

"Yes?"

"It's me, baby."

"Come in," C.J. called.

"You okay?"

"Mmm. Having a little trouble settling down." C.J. sat on the plinth in her practice clothes. Normally, she would've been dressed for the match and ready to go with ten minutes until match time.

Trystan stepped forward, insinuating herself between C.J.'s legs. "If you're going to be unsettled, let it be in a really good way," she purred, running her hands under C.J.'s tank top, along her belly, and down under the waistband of her shorts.

C.J. gasped. "We don't have time…" She threw her head back involuntarily as Trystan's fingers found a particularly sensitive spot.

"I know. I just want you to remember how much I love you—no matter what happens out there today, C.J. The way I feel about you has nothing to do with tennis and everything to do with the incredible woman you are."

"Have I told you yet today how much I love you?"

"Hmm…" Trystan pretended to think. "I don't remember."

"I love you so very much."

"I'm the luckiest woman in the world." Trystan kissed C.J. once more before backing away.

"What's that?" C.J. pointed to the bag, which Trystan had kept intentionally obscured.

"Ah, this, my love, is the recipe for success." Trystan handed over the bag.

"If nothing else, I'll be the most fashionable player out there." She smiled thinly.

"You don't like it?"

"No, it's…great. It's just…"

"It's not what you're used to. I know, honey. The clothes are the same, and they're your racquets, just painted differently."

"I know." C.J. fought back tears. "It's never going to be the same, is it?"

Trystan sighed. "No. I'm afraid not. But I honestly believe it's going to be better. Mitch says he's very close to closing several deals for you—he just needs a little more time."

"Translation—he needs me to win today." She hopped down off the plinth. "I've got to get changed."

"Do I get to watch?" Trystan waggled her eyebrows playfully, hoping it would ease some of the tension.

"You wish. Out with you—no voyeurs allowed at this party." C.J. pushed Trystan toward the door. Before opening it and ushering Trystan out, C.J. indulged herself in a long, slow, sensuous kiss. "Thanks—for doing your best to make this bearable."

"I love you, C.J."

"I love you, too, Trystan."

C.J. waited in the tunnel for the player introductions. Everything seemed as though it should be the same, and yet it wasn't. Next to her, Natasha Meritsa hummed to herself and bounced on the balls of her feet. Neither woman looked at the other.

"A seven-time U.S. Open winner and great champion," the announcer intoned, "C.J. Winslow."

As C.J. appeared on the court, a cascade of boos mixed with the cheers. C.J.'s stomach lurched, bringing with it a wave of nausea. Never in her entire professional career had she been booed. *Keep walking—you have to shut them out.* She sat heavily in her courtside chair and unzipped her bag. As she unwrapped one of the racquets encased in plastic, a piece of paper fell out. Curious, she picked it up and examined it.

"You're a loser—no one will want to sponsor you now. Signed, Players for a Lesbian-free Federation."

C.J. dropped the note as if it was on fire. Her heart hammered in her chest, her vision tunneled, and a voice from the past echoed in her head.

"No one will want you now. You're lucky I took pity on you."

C.J. shook her head in an unsuccessful attempt to clear the memory. "No," she whispered on a broken sob.

C.J. jogged to the net where Jonas was waiting. She was feeling great after a particularly strong practice session.

"C.J., this is my new assistant, Terrance. He's going to help me out while I'm traveling. He'll be taking you to the clinic on Thursday, and I thought it'd be good for you to get to know each other a little better first. Terrance has offered to take you out for ice cream, then drop you at home."

There was something about Terrance's smile that made C.J. feel uneasy. Her earlier exuberance faded and the smile disappeared from her face. Still, she trusted Jonas and so went with Terrance.

"Oh, God." C.J. picked up a towel and buried her face in it. She wanted to curl up in a fetal ball; her whole body was shaking and she thought she might be sick. In her mind's eye, she saw him coming toward her again, his hulking body towering over her. She crossed her legs, the pain as real as it had been all those years ago. She gasped and sobbed into the towel.

"Ms. Winslow, warm-ups have commenced and the clock is ticking," the umpire said, leaning over and covering the microphone.

Without a word, C.J. rose shakily, grabbed the racquet, and walked automatically to the baseline. Her legs felt like lead, and her heart was still beating erratically. She took a deep breath in and let it out slowly, then another. The warm-up was little more than a blur, as her mind warred between disbelief and horror.

The first time she went to serve, C.J. knew she was in trouble. She felt the all-too-familiar panic grip her. She let the ball fall to the court and asked the ball boy for another. *Take your time, Ceeg. Remember what Andrea taught you.* She began the service motion again, this time connecting with the ball but sending the serve wide. She recited the alternative phrase Andrea had given her for moments when she was in public and couldn't stop to tap. "You can do it," she said, visualizing the tapping sequence. Although her next serve was in, Meritsa handled it easily for a winner. In less than thirty minutes, C.J. had lost the first set, 1-6.

The crowd was buzzing. C.J. was sure she could hear the commentators gloating over the slaughter. Disconsolately, she looked up in the stands to the "friends" box for the first time. A ripple of shock went through her, followed quickly by a smile. For as long as she could remember, her portion of the box had been empty with the exception of Jonas, then Grant. For this match, all but one of her designated seats was filled. C.J. gaped in wonder at Becca, Grant, Mitch, and most astonishingly, Terri and Andrea.

"How…" C.J. made a mental note to thank Trystan, who, she realized, must have arranged for Terri and Andrea to be there for support. She looked toward the tunnel and saw Trystan leaning against the wall, watching her. "I love you," C.J. mouthed.

"I love you, too," Trystan mouthed back. "Kick her ass."

Seeing Trystan standing in the tunnel exhorting her on along with all her friends in the stands filled C.J. with a mixture of pride and shame. *These people have put their lives on hold for you, Ceeg. If you can't do this for yourself, do it for them.* She rose and walked toward their end of the court to start serving the second set.

As she got close, Andrea leaned forward. "'Cook's Hookup' first," she shouted, "then you can do it." She gave C.J. a thumbs-up.

It took a moment for the words to register, then C.J. smiled, relieved. "Right, balance my brain first, then go to the phrase," she said to herself, nodding her understanding. Although C.J. knew it would be three games before she could sit down on a changeover and use the technique, the very fact that she had a plan made her feel much lighter.

She broke Meritsa for the first game, struggled with her serve in the second, eventually losing the game, and lost an opportunity for another break in the third game. She went to the changeover down 1-2 and knowing she would have to serve again when play resumed.

As soon as she sat and toweled off, she casually crossed her legs at the ankle, placed her hands in the proper position, and launched into the "Cook's Hookup" exercise. She didn't care if it looked odd—it was her only chance to salvage the match. "You can do it," she said, as she rose and headed back toward the "friends" end of the court.

This time when she looked up, her smile turned radiant. There was Trystan, making her way into the box to sit directly in front, right next to Grant.

Trystan pumped a fist and cupped her hands around her mouth as she yelled so that C.J. could hear her. "I'm right here by your side, C.J.—always. You can do it."

C.J.'s heart fluttered with a sudden surge of pure joy. "This one's for you, baby," she said, as she strode confidently to the baseline and served an ace. Three more convincing serves later and the game was hers. She smiled as she saw Trystan, Mitch, Andrea, Terri, and Becca on their feet cheering as the balls changed ends.

Within forty minutes, C.J. had fought back to even the match, capturing the second set 6-3. Finally, some of the boos turned to cheers as fans anticipated a climactic third set.

On the changeover, C.J. glanced at her opponent. Meritsa was muttering to herself about lost opportunities, upset, C.J. imagined, that she hadn't been able to put C.J. away when she had the chance.

C.J. recalled Meritsa's remarks of the day before. Then she thought about the note she'd found inside the protective plastic wrapping on her racquet when she'd opened it. Somehow, C.J.

thought, Meritsa's digs and the appearance of the note seemed a little too coincidental. A surge of adrenaline poured through her veins as C.J. connected the dots. *You slimeball.*

Abruptly, she stood and strode to the far baseline. *If you win, Ceeg, not only do you knock the bitch out of the tournament, but you get the sponsorships Mitch is working on. And you get a shot at number one. Here's your chance to send a message.* She bounced on the balls of her feet, prepared to play the set of her life.

Every time she thought she might falter, C.J. accessed her anger, played off the energy of the crowd, and stole a glance at her friends. All of them, even Grant, rose as one as she served for the match at 5-4, 40-30.

When she stepped to the baseline, C.J. summoned all her anger—anger at Jonas for not protecting her, anger at Terrance for raping her, anger at the adults in her life for not recognizing that something terrible had happened to her, anger at Natasha for the note. She felt the force of it coursing through her as she raised her arm to swing. She used its power—striking the ball as if wielding vengeance, releasing all her anger at the point of contact with a primordial scream.

For a long moment, suspended in time, C.J. held her breath and waited, watching as Meritsa lunged for the ball as it sizzled past her outstretched racquet.

C.J. stood stock-still, temporarily paralyzed by what she'd just accomplished. As reality set in, she dropped to her knees on the court, unapologetic as tears of relief flowed.

Her heart was pounding and her hands trembled. She let out the breath she was holding, exhaling powerfully as a feeling of freedom and euphoria seeped into her being.

She would have a chance to be a champion again—to get her life back. She had accessed the anger and harnessed it, conquering both it and Meritsa in the process.

She rose to her feet, letting out a yell of pure joy, a triumphant smile creasing her face. The crowd cheered even louder.

After the traditional handshakes with her opponent and the chair umpire, C.J. sat and covered her face with a towel. Her body shook with relief, her breathing was ragged, and her head was spinning. *You did it, Ceeg. You made it through.* She watched as Del Nordstrom, the USA Network commentator, readied himself for the required post-match interview in the center of the court.

She took one last deep breath and joined him.

"C.J. Winslow, that has to go down in history as one of the most amazing matches of our time."

The crowd whistled and stomped.

"I'm glad you all got your money's worth," C.J. quipped, surprised that her voice sounded as strong as it did. Before the commentator could ask another question, C.J. pushed on. "This hasn't been the easiest week for me…"

The fans chuckled nervously.

"…so it makes your support for the great level of tennis today that much more special. All I've ever wanted to do was play tennis and honor the sport. I hope I did that out here—I'd like to think I did. Trust me, I left everything I had on the court today. Thank you all for coming. I'll look forward to seeing you back here on Saturday."

C.J. waved to the crowd, returned to the sideline, gathered up her bag, and exited the stadium with her head held high. Trudy was waiting for her in the tunnel.

"That was smart—I have to give you credit. You have a good sense for dealing with the media. Still, I don't think we ought to tempt fate. I'm going to have you make a post-match statement, but you're not to take any questions."

"What is it you want me to say, Trudy?"

"I want you to tell them how you feel about winning this match and make a statement about being in Saturday's final. Then walk away—no matter what they ask," Trudy emphasized. "I've kept my end of the bargain—I expect you to keep yours and focus on the tennis for the good of the game."

"I'd say the *game* did quite well today," C.J. said, striding angrily away. She didn't stop walking until she reached Trystan's office. Without hesitation or preamble, she launched herself at her lover, who was standing next to the desk, obviously waiting for her.

"I'm so proud of you, sweetheart. You were fantastic," Trystan said, wrapping her arms tightly around C.J.

C.J. relaxed for the first time since she'd walked out on the court. All the stress and strain of the previous two days came pouring out in waves. Her body convulsed with tears as she stood within Trystan's protective embrace.

"I've got you, love. You're okay." Trystan merely held on, whispering soothing words, drying tears, and stroking C.J.'s back. Eventually, she said, "Hey, baby, look at me." She waited for C.J. to comply. "You did great out there. Really. Anybody else would've folded—you're a champion in the truest sense of the word."

"I can't believe you were right there in the stands watching."

"Of course I was," Trystan said hoarsely, her voice choked with pride. "You don't think I'd miss my girl's finest hour, do you?"

"Finest hour? Hardly," C.J. sniffed, her lips starting to tremble. "I had another memory," she whispered, tears starting to fall anew.

Trystan kissed C.J.'s eyelids, unsure she'd heard correctly. "Did you say you had another memory?"

C.J. nodded and took a shaky breath. She gazed at Trystan through watery eyes. "The tennis practice was the second time Terrance raped me, not the first." Her teeth chattered, and she began to sob harder. "I didn't know."

Trystan pulled her close, swallowing her own tears and outrage at C.J.'s pain, cradling her gently. "Oh, baby. I'm so, so sorry. He can't hurt you anymore." For several moments, they stood like that, Trystan rocking C.J. from side to side. "Andrea's standing by—she wanted you to know she's here to help."

C.J. smiled through her tears. "She saw it from the stands, you know. She helped me through it after the first set."

"I know, baby."

"I don't know if I could've won without…"

"You would've won regardless—you're the strongest person I know, C.J. Winslow, and I love you so very much."

"Thank you for arranging for Andrea and your mom to be here—that meant a lot to me."

"I couldn't keep them away." In truth, it had been Terri who suggested the trip, arguing that C.J. would need all the friendly faces she could find. Trystan had readily agreed and taken care of the details while C.J. was practicing the day before.

"I have to do a press conference. I'm supposed to be in there by now."

"Do you have to?"

"Yes, although Trudy's given me strict instructions that I'm not to take any questions."

"I'll bet. I don't suppose you'd let me be in the room?"

"Trudy would be apoplectic. Not only that, but you'd be attacked and chopped up into little bits."

"I want to be there with you," Trystan argued.

"You're always with me, love," C.J. said, kissing Trystan's palm and holding it to her chest.

CHAPTER TWENTY-ONE

C.J. could hear the steady heartbeat, feel the rise and fall of Trystan's chest as she slept, and it made her smile contentedly.

She felt the usual butterflies in her stomach that were always present on the day of a big match, and yet she was calmer than she had any right to be. She suspected the session with Andrea the day before had a lot to do with that. C.J. had been able to access the new memory and tap on it to take the power out of it. At the moment, she felt nothing but sublime peace.

"What are you thinking?" Trystan asked, stretching and pulling C.J. closer.

"Mmm. How much I love you and how happy I am. I can't imagine any place I'd rather be than right here in your arms."

"That's good because I wouldn't have it any other way." Trystan kissed the top of C.J.'s head. "How do you feel this morning?"

C.J. shifted so she could see Trystan's face. "I feel great—I slept well, the Broadway show was a great diversion yesterday, dinner with our 'family' of misfits was fun." C.J. sighed dreamily and stretched. "I'm relaxed and in love. It doesn't get any better than that."

"I'm glad."

"I never imagined I could have all this and play tennis successfully, too."

"You deserve to be happy, C.J."

"You make me happy." C.J. traced her fingers over Trystan's cheekbones, her jaw, her lips. "I still have trouble believing you're here…" Before she could finish the thought, her cell phone rang.

She flipped open the phone. "Yes?"

"Good morning—hope I'm not disturbing you two lovebirds. It's Mitch."

"You're up early and in an awfully good mood."

"Yep. Want to know why?"

"Okay, I'll bite. Why?"

"How do you feel about early morning press conferences?"

"You want me to face the press—today? Before the U.S. Open final? Have you lost your mind? Did you go overboard in some bar last night?"

Mitch laughed. "No, I went back to work after you left us, in fact. No dancing on the tables for me. I've got us a new major sponsor that wants to have the press conference, and your racquet and clothing companies are back on board."

"Wow. That's amazing. Details, please." C.J. said excitedly.

"The racquet and clothing companies came crawling back—said they'd overreacted."

"If I didn't like the racquet so much, I'd tell them what they could do with it. Likewise if the clothes weren't so comfortable."

Mitch laughed. "I figured that, so I made it a bit painful for them—I upped the ante and charged each of them another ten percent."

"You're evil—I love that."

"Are you familiar with Olivia?"

"As in Olivia, the travel company for lesbians?"

"Yeah, though I think they're branching out. In any event, they want to announce a major sponsorship deal with you this morning."

"That's the press conference?"

"Yes. They understood that you might not want to do an event on the morning of a match but asked that I bring it to you as a possibility."

C.J. chewed her lip. "I can't deal with the press this morning. Can we put out a joint statement, then I'll do something major with them to celebrate my win?"

"I like the sound of that. I'll propose it, finalize the deals if you're ready to sign off, and everything will be in place by the time you get to the locker room."

"You're the best, Mitch. I can't believe you pulled that off, and so quickly."

"Selling you is simple, C.J."

"You realize that was three, right?"

"Three what?"

"Three sponsors. Now I get to hire you as my manager and pay you."

"You don't have to..."

"Listen to me. If I hire you, nobody raises an eyebrow when you and Grant travel together until you're ready to come out."

"You're serious?"

"Very. In fact, I expect you to put together a statement making that announcement, too, if you agree."

"You're on. I've got work to do."

C.J. smiled as she hung up the phone.

Ten minutes before the match, Andrea emerged from treatment room two where she'd helped C.J. with some last-minute focusing exercises.

"Everything okay?" Trystan asked.

"Better than that, I think. Why don't you ask her yourself? She's waiting for you," Andrea said.

Trystan needed no further invitation. She knocked gently on the door.

"Come in."

"Hey, baby."

"Hi, beautiful."

"Am I going to interrupt your concentration if I tell you how much I love you and how proud I am of you?"

"Never. What kind of fool do you take me for?" C.J. crossed the room and took Trystan in her arms. "You make this time around so much richer for me, you know?" She captured Trystan's lips in a passionate kiss.

Trystan's voice trembled with emotion. "You're going to be great out there today. I can feel it."

"My heart's certainly pounding now, that's for sure."

"Best warm-up there is, right?"

"Right," C.J. agreed, kissing her again.

"I love you, C.J. I'll be right there with you."

"I know you will—I'm counting on it." She looked at the clock on the wall. "Show time."

When C.J. took the court this time, the cheers far outnumbered the boos. *Everybody loves an underdog.* She smiled. The noise was deafening—every seat in the stadium was filled. The familiar feel of her own bag, the look of her racquet—everything felt right.

She'd made a point of avoiding the news coverage all morning, having learned a lesson from the other day. This day, she preferred to focus within herself. She knew that every commentator would be rehashing her crushing loss to Sylvia Foster in the previous year's final and her subsequent freefall to number nine in the rankings before she'd gradually worked her way back up the ladder to within striking distance of the number one spot again. Then they'd go over her coming out and the additional pressure that must be putting on her, and make up their minds that C.J. couldn't possibly win against so many odds. She'd decided there was nothing to be gained by watching, reading, or listening to any of it.

She looked up to the "friends" box as she took the court for the warm-up. They were all there—Trystan, Grant, Mitch, Becca, Andrea, and Terri. It warmed her heart. Although Nan had wanted to sit in the stands, it would be her job to tend to either of the players if one of them got injured. C.J. spotted her standing at the mouth of the tunnel.

C.J. was loose and confident in the warm-up. Her strokes were easy, her serve on target, and her volleys crisp. She won the toss and elected to serve first.

Go for everything. Serve hard, play your heart out, leave everything on the court. Today is your day, Ceeg. This is your time.

C.J. bounced on the balls of her feet as she approached the baseline to start the match—a longtime habit she'd developed to ward off nerves. "Let's send a message." She hit a hard, flat serve deep to the center of the service box, forcing Sylvia to scramble to get out of the way. 15-love. Although outwardly C.J. showed no emotion, she was smiling on the inside. "That's for saying I don't have a dominating serve."

She'd seen Sylvia's post-match news conference following her semifinal win. When Sylvia had been asked to assess her chances against C.J., she'd blithely indicated that holding her serve would be the key to winning since breaking C.J. wouldn't be a problem. "We'll see about that," C.J. muttered, firing an ace, another service winner, and a high-kicking second serve that pulled Sylvia so far out of the court that C.J. was able to make it to the net for an easy put-away and a 1-love lead.

"They won't all be that easy, Ceeg—stay aggressive, press her, go to the net, make her run." C.J. repeated the game plan she and Grant had worked out while watching tapes of their match from the previous year's final and Sylvia's quarter- and semifinal matches from days earlier.

By the time the game score was 6-all in the first set, C.J.'s pulse was hammering in her temples. She'd followed the plan to the letter. The fact that she hadn't been able to pull away or get a lead scared her more than she wanted to admit. "Don't panic. Focus, Ceeg." She wiped sweat from her eyes.

C.J. breathed in slowly, held it, and let it go. She served the first point of the tie-breaker, a slice into Sylvia's body. Despite her nerves, C.J. pressed the point, following the serve into the net. A ball at her feet forced her to hit a half-volley and took her out of position. Sylvia responded with a forehand winner for a mini-break.

"You can do it, Ceeg. Break her right back." Anxiety was a living thing in C.J.'s chest. She bounced on the balls of her feet again. Because Sylvia's serve was so powerful, C.J. could do little more than guess in which direction she would hit it. If she guessed right, it would give her a shot at a winner. "If you're wrong, she'll eat you alive and the set will be over before you can blink, Ceeg."

On Sylvia's first serve of the tie-breaker, C.J. guessed correctly but sent the service return wide. "Love-2 in a tie-breaker is nothing. You can do it." C.J. continued to talk to herself as she readied for the next serve—a rocket down the middle that she parried back deep into the forehand corner, sending Sylvia scrambling. Taking advantage, C.J. hustled in to the net, leaving her in perfect position for an easy backhand put-away and getting her back on serve. She breathed a sigh of relief.

The remainder of the tie-breaker played out much the same way, with both players fighting for every shot. At 5-6, C.J. was down a set point. C.J.'s fingers trembled slightly on the grip. She backed away from the baseline and regripped the racquet. "It's not your day to lose, Ceeg. Today belongs to you. Now would be a great time for an ace." She stepped forward again, waiting while the crowd hushed. She bounced the ball several times, paused, and went into her service motion. She'd been planning to serve the ball wide, but just as she tossed the ball, she noticed Sylvia shift her weight in anticipation of that very play. C.J. adjusted in mid-swing, aiming down the middle instead. Caught off-balance, Sylvia barely reached the ball, knocking it far wide: 6-6. C.J. felt the knot at the base of her neck ease slightly.

On the next point, C.J. followed her serve to the net and put away a clean forehand volley winner.

At 7-6 and set point, she could feel the crowd getting behind her. For a brief moment, the butterflies receded. She looked up to the "friends" box, where even Grant was leaning forward. She winked at him, laughing to herself at his shocked expression. "That's it, Ceeg—stay loose and have fun." With a flourish, she sent a screaming forehand service return down the line for a winner, giving her the first set, 7-6. In her first outward show of emotion, C.J. pumped her fist as she walked off the court for the changeover.

Out of the corner of her eye, she saw Trystan standing, whistling with her fingers between her teeth. C.J. suddenly felt lighter than she had in years. "You're halfway there, Ceeg. One more set. You can do it."

Sylvia came out more determined than ever in the second set, going for more shots, sharpening the angles, playing more aggressively, and making C.J.'s game plan obsolete. C.J.'s heart began to race as the set spiraled quickly out of her control. "Don't panic, Ceeg. Work through it. You just need to buy some time to think."

The score was 1-4, and C.J. was down a service break before she found any answers to Sylvia's new tactics. Panic made her stomach contract sharply as she felt the title slipping away. Although C.J. managed to hold serve twice more, Sylvia ran out the set, 6-3.

When C.J. glanced up at the "friends" box after the set, she saw Trystan exhorting her on, while Grant simply looked concerned. It was her second three-set match in as many contests, and C.J. knew he was worried about her conditioning. His expression did nothing to ease her fears. Sylvia was significantly younger than her, and thus had the advantage. Adding to that the fact that momentum was also in Sylvia's favor, and the odds were definitely not in C.J.'s favor.

She buried her face in a towel. "One more set, Ceeg. Win one more set and you achieve something none of the 'experts' thinks you can. Figure it out, smart girl—this is what you're good at. Stop wigging and use your brain." She pondered what had changed in the second set. "She's more aggressive, Ceeg. She wants to go for more. Let her." C.J. felt her pulse slow and her world right itself as a new game plan took shape in her mind. If Sylvia wanted to push herself, C.J. would oblige, sending balls wide to both sides, forcing Sylvia to go for too much on her shots, to hit impossible angles—in short, to make more unforced errors.

The strategy worked like a charm—for the first three games, Sylvia sprayed balls all over the court, making some spectacular shots, but also committing a significant number of unforced errors.

On the changeover, C.J. was up 3-love. She could see Sylvia's frustration, could sense desperation creeping into her game—the same emotions she was sure had been written all over her face in the second set. "This is no time to gloat, Ceeg. You're a long way from the finish line." C.J.'s legs were starting to feel a little heavy—a sure sign of fatigue—and it worried her. She knew she needed to close the match out quickly if she could.

In the middle of the fourth game, Sylvia began to find a rhythm, and C.J.'s heart began racing with fear once again. Despite C.J.'s best efforts, over the course of the next few games, Sylvia put her on the defensive, hitting several well-placed winners and forcing C.J. into a couple of mistakes. Before C.J. knew it, Sylvia had evened the match at 3-all.

C.J. toweled off at the back of the court, using the time to regroup. She felt unsteady on her feet and weak. "You have to work through this, Ceeg. Don't panic." She glanced up at the "friends" box.

Trystan rocked forward, cupped her hands around her mouth and screamed, "You can do it, C.J. I believe in you. Three more games."

C.J. wasn't sure if it was the fire in Trystan's eyes or the power of her words, but the nerves that had been plaguing her melted into the background. She felt a renewed sense of purpose.

She nodded for a ball, walked to the baseline, and unleashed a killer serve to the backhand corner. Her pulse slowed to its normal rhythm. She followed that with a serve and volley that surprised Sylvia, who wasn't expecting that kind of energy so late in the match. C.J. felt an adrenaline rush. Two more aggressive plays gave her the game and a 4-3 lead.

As she walked to the sideline, C.J. heard Trystan whistle again. "Almost there, baby."

"Stay focused, Ceeg. You can do this. Keep thinking." C.J. sipped water and evaluated her options. Focusing on the strategy eased the tension in her shoulders. Sylvia appeared to be tiring, too, and she had played the last game looking somewhat tentative. "She's scared, Ceeg—more scared than you. Capitalize on it."

C.J. walked to the far baseline with one thing on her mind—to break Sylvia's serve. Concentrating on that one objective helped settle C.J.'s nerves even more. She felt a calm steal over her.

On the first point, C.J. guessed correctly that Sylvia would aim at her body. By moving just before the ball was struck, C.J. put herself in position to hit a sharp-angled return for a clean winner.

Sylvia won the next point back with an ace that evened the score at 15-all.

"She likes the wide kick to your backhand, Ceeg. Guard the line." Sure enough, Sylvia hit a high topspin serve to the backhand corner. C.J. returned it with more topspin of her own and deep in the court. She followed the shot to the net, a move that again caught Sylvia off-guard. 15-30.

"Two more points here, Ceeg, and you can serve for the match. You can do it." She looked across the net. Sylvia was showing signs of nerves—pacing back and forth, bouncing the ball, and talking to herself. C.J. smiled.

Sylvia netted the first serve and sent the second serve long, committing an uncharacteristic double fault. 15-40, double break point. C.J. backed away, pretending to fix her strings. She fought to clamp down on a surge of euphoria. She wanted to give Sylvia time to think about it—double break point and if C.J. won the game, she'd be serving for the match.

The serve, when it came, was a full fifteen miles per hour slower than Sylvia's normal pace. C.J. moved in, taking the ball on the rise and attacking. She sent a bullet of a forehand screaming crosscourt. Sylvia barely managed to send back a weak reply. C.J. moved in closer yet, slamming a volley hard at Sylvia's feet. Game, C.J., 5-3.

"Just serve it out, Ceeg. Serve it out and be done with it." She finished toweling off. Standing at the baseline, she swallowed hard, ignoring the tightness in her chest at the thought of closing out the match. As soon as she tossed the ball, C.J. felt that familiar panic seep in. She hesitated minutely at the top of her swing and watched helplessly as the ball sailed long. She took the next ball and bounced it several times. Again her movements were tight—she let the ball drop without hitting it.

She said the tapping phrase. "You can do it, Ceeg." She settled once more at the baseline and prepared to serve. "You can do it." She tossed the ball, arched high, and put everything she had into the serve. Sylvia, who had been expecting a typical second serve, swiped ineffectually at the ball as it whizzed past her racquet. 15-love.

"You." She bounced the ball. "Will." She bounced it again. "Not." She bounced it a third time. "Beat." She bounced it a fourth time.

"Me." She gritted her teeth, tossed the ball and launched a perfect serve down the center "T" for an ace. 30-love.

She took a deep breath after she missed her next first serve. "You can do it." The second serve, while in, wasn't what she hoped, and Sylvia ran around her backhand to slam a forehand winner crosscourt. 30-15.

C.J. searched for Trystan. She was sitting on the edge of her seat, leaning over the railing, rooting C.J. on. The sight gave C.J. a sense of peacefulness. "This is my time. No more ghosts." She cranked a one hundred sixteen-mile-per-hour serve at Sylvia's body, following the serve in for another easy put-away volley. 40-15, double match and championship point.

The entire stadium rose to its feet, clapping and cheering. C.J. had never seen anything like it—not in any of her previous U.S. Open wins. For a moment, all she could do was stand there. Across the net, Sylvia was pacing like a caged tiger, fiddling with her strings nervously.

C.J. took a ball from the ball boy. "This is what a champion looks like." She listened as the crowd noise reached a crescendo, soaking up the energy. Then she stepped to the line, paused for a second to gather all her strength, and unleashed her best serve of the night, a one hundred seventeen-mile-per-hour stunner that Sylvia likely never even saw. Game, set, match, and championship to C.J., 7-6, 3-6, 6-3.

The applause was like thunder, but C.J. barely registered it. Her only thought was that she needed to be with Trystan—to share this moment with her. She ran to the net and completed the obligatory handshakes, even as her eyes were glued to one spot in the stands. She dropped her racquet and sprinted to the far side of the court, jumping up to grab the railing separating the stands from the court. Several sets of hands helped her as she climbed up and into the "friends" box. Without a word, she gathered Trystan in her arms and kissed her hard on the mouth.

She pulled back and framed Trystan's face with her hands, staring deeply into her eyes. "I love you, Trystan. I couldn't have done that without you."

Trystan leaned forward so that their foreheads were touching. "I love you, too, C.J. I'm so, so proud of you. You did it."

"We did it," C.J. answered, wiping tears from her eyes. She smiled. "You do know every camera in the place, including the live television broadcast, just recorded that, right?"

"I hope they got my good side," Trystan said, laughing.

C.J. felt a hand on her shoulder and turned to find herself whisked into a bear hug by Grant.

"You were magnificent."

"We make a great team, don't we?"

"We sure do."

"I had to win—after all, Mitch has already spent your bonus." C.J. winked. She hugged Andrea, Terri, Becca, and Mitch, then looked around sheepishly, trying to figure out how to get back down to the court for the trophy presentation.

"How about if you try the stairs this time, Ms. Winslow?" The advice came from a beefy security guard who had finally made his way to her side.

C.J. kissed Trystan one more time before following the guard back down to the court, where she would once more take her place as the world's top female tennis player and eight-time champion of the U.S. Open.

EPILOGUE

C.J. and Trystan strolled arm in arm down Park Avenue in Manhattan looking in the shop windows. Terri and Andrea had caught morning flights out of the city, Grant and Mitch were headed to Fire Island, and Nan had taken Becca up on an offer to show her the sights.

At the Borders bookstore on Park and 58th Street, Trystan stopped dead in front of a window display. Her heart stuttered once, then resumed its normal rhythm. She took a deep breath, amazed that the pain was gone.

"What is it…" C.J.'s voice trailed off as she saw the life-sized standup of author Jamison Parker announcing that she'd be doing a book signing that day from noon to 2:00 p.m. C.J. looked at her watch—1:20 p.m. "We've got time if you want to go in," she said quietly, her chest suddenly tight.

Trystan stared at the sign for a moment, then turned and faced C.J., her heart overflowing. "I don't need to, thanks."

"No?" C.J. whispered.

"No," Trystan answered. "You're all I need and all I'll ever want. I love you, C.J." Taking C.J. in her arms in the middle of the sidewalk, with people passing by them and a line around the block for the book signing, Trystan kissed C.J. softly. "Let's go home."

"You are my home. I love you, Trystan."

The End

Visual Epilogue™

Trystan and C.J. are two strong, beautiful, and sensuous women from very different worlds, both determined, both guarding their hearts, until they meet each other and discover the power of love to heal all wounds.

Follow their journey not just in words, but in photographs, courtesy of phenomenal photographer Judy Francesconi. We invite you to study the progression from the woman on the front cover, to the women on this page, and, finally, the affirmation of togetherness and love on the back cover.

Judy paints stories with images the way I try to paint images with words.

We hope you enjoy.

Lynn Ames

JUDY FRANCESCONI

You can purchase other Phoenix Rising Press books online at www.phoenixrisingpress.com or at your local bookstore.

Published by
Phoenix Rising Press
Phoenix, AZ

Visit us on the Web: **www.phoenixrisingpress.com**

LaVergne, TN USA
11 January 2011
212026LV00007B/189/P

9 780984 052127